Lara Temple was three y
her mother to take the dic
story. Since then she has l
day she is a high-tech inv
who has lived and worked
when darkness falls she loses herself in history and romance…at least on the page. Luckily her husband and two beautiful and very energetic children help her weave it all together.

Also by Lara Temple

Lord Crayle's Secret World
The Reluctant Viscount
The Duke's Unexpected Bride

Wild Lords and Innocent Ladies miniseries

Lord Hunter's Cinderella Heiress
Lord Ravenscar's Inconvenient Betrothal
Lord Stanton's Last Mistress

Discover more at millsandboon.co.uk.

LORD STANTON'S LAST MISTRESS

Lara Temple

MILLS & BOON

All rights reserved including the right of reproduction in whole or in part in any form. This edition is published by arrangement with Harlequin Books S.A.

This is a work of fiction. Names, characters, places, locations and incidents are purely fictional and bear no relationship to any real life individuals, living or dead, or to any actual places, business establishments, locations, events or incidents. Any resemblance is entirely coincidental.

This book is sold subject to the condition that it shall not, by way of trade or otherwise, be lent, resold, hired out or otherwise circulated without the prior consent of the publisher in any form of binding or cover other than that in which it is published and without a similar condition including this condition being imposed on the subsequent purchaser.

® and TM are trademarks owned and used by the trademark owner and/or its licensee. Trademarks marked with ® are registered with the United Kingdom Patent Office and/or the Office for Harmonisation in the Internal Market and in other countries.

First Published in Great Britain 2018
by Mills & Boon, an imprint of HarperCollins*Publishers*
1 London Bridge Street, London, SE1 9GF

© 2018 Ilana Treston

ISBN: 978-0-263-93291-1

MIX
Paper from responsible sources
FSC C007454

This book is produced from independently certified FSC™ paper to ensure responsible forest management.
For more information visit www.harpercollins.co.uk/green.

Printed and bound in Spain
by CPI, Barcelona

To Omer and Maya,
I am so lucky you are part of my home and my heart.

Prologue

Island kingdom of Illiakos, the Mediterranean —1817

'Fools! Shooting into the fog like that. Two more minutes and they would have seen the Maltese colours! And if they must actually shoot someone, why not a Maltese? Why an Englishman? Now that Napoleon is finished the English navy rules the sea, which means it would be very inconvenient for me if he died.'

'I am sorry for that, your Majesty,' Christina said as she continued sorting through the herbs she and little Princess Ariadne had collected from the Palace Gardens.

'Is he going to die, Papa?' Ari asked, her hand sneaking into Christina's.

From the first night the King had sent Christina to the royal nursery, the four-year-old Princess had struggled into her bed and curled into her heat, her soft plump cheek resting on Christina's palm. That moment Christina had fallen in love, as thirsty for affection as the little girl had been. Each time Ari still reached for her hand, Christina's heart would squeeze at this remnant of their shared childhood. She stroked Ari's curls and handed her another bundle of herbs to sort.

'I don't know.' The King gave a huff of frustration. 'I don't trust that fool of a doctor. He says the bullet is out, but he doesn't think the man will survive the fever. The poltroon sent for a priest. I want you to see to him, Athena.'

'See to him?'

'Yes. You always helped your father with patients. Use those herbs the women come to you for. I don't like this. I've seen the man—everything about him says wealth and privilege and yet he carries nothing on him but gold, not even a letter. The Maltese captain says he paid above the asking price to be taken from Venice and that he saw him in the company of one of the Khedive's top men in Alexandria. Someone like that, the English will come looking for. If he must die I would rather he does so elsewhere, so make him well enough to travel, Athena.'

The note of worry in the King's voice distracted Christina from the enormity of the task and the knowledge she was wholly inadequate. She would do anything in her power for the King and Ari. She owed them more than her gratitude; she owed them her loyalty and her love.

'You know I will do anything I can to help, your Majesty.'

'I know that. You can be as stubborn as the Cliffs of Illiakos when you set your mind to something. So go and set it to getting this Englishman on his feet. Off with you now.'

'Can I go and swoon over him, too, Papa?' Ariadne said hopefully.

'What in the name of Zeus do you mean by *swoon*, Ari?' Usually people quaked when confronted head-on with the King's anger, but twelve-year-old Ari clearly knew as well as Christina that her father's bark was worse than his bite.

'I heard the maids say he is as handsome as a god and they take peeks and swoon over him. So may I?'

'No, you may not. There will be no swooning. But you have a good point. When your father died, Athena, I swore on Zeus's head I would protect you just as I would my own daughter and that applies as much to your modesty as to your life. You will don veils while you attend to him and I will have Yannis stand guard. We know nothing of him, after all.'

'But, King Darius, tending to a patient in veils is not very—'

'And take some of my English newspapers to read to him.'

'If he is unconscious, reading to him is hardly likely to—'

'Must you argue with me over everything, Athena?' the King interrupted, throwing his hands to the sky. 'Perhaps hearing his mother tongue will remind him of his duties and revive him. Now go and see what is to be done, do you hear me?'

'Half the castle can hear you, your Majesty,' Christina replied as she brushed the remains of the herbs from her hands. 'I will return soon, Ari.'

'And tell me if he is really beautiful?'

Christina smiled at the King's growl as she pushed back the tumble of dark curls from Ari's forehead.

'It isn't a man's beauty that matters, Ari, but his heart,' she said, a little pedantically, and added for good measure as she went towards the door, 'Not to mention his good nature and even temper.'

She didn't wait to hear the King's response

to her mild impudence, but went directly to the prisoner's room. She had no real expectation of being able to oblige the King by reviving the Englishman. She might share the King's disdain for the doctor who took her father's place, but she didn't presume she could do better.

'Hello, Yannis, the King sent me to see if there is anything that can be done for the Englishman.'

Yannis, one of the King's most trusted guards, raised his brows.

'Kyrie Sofianopoulos says he won't survive the fever.'

'Then I am not likely to do any harm, am I?'

'Not much good, either. But if the King told you then of course he knows best.'

Christina smiled at the blind acceptance of the King's infallibility and entered the room, preparing for the worst. As she approached the sickbed her mind did something it had never done before—it split in two. Sensible Christina assessed the hectic colour in the Englishman's cheeks and all along the left side of his bare chest. The wound was just below the ribcage and was covered with a linen bandage stained orange and brown with dried blood. But even as she set to work removing bandages and cleaning the wound, a part of her that was utterly foreign raised its head and offered an opinion.

The maids were right. He might be dying, but he was the handsomest man she had ever seen.

She had sometimes watched the fishermen in the port stripped to the waist and though they, too, might possess impressive musculature, this man was on a different scale. Tall and lean, but with shoulders and arms that looked fit to topple a temple, and a whole landscape of hard planes and slopes, marred here and there by scars, several of which looked suspiciously like old knife wounds, including two rather deep gashes to his forearm. Aside from these imperfections he looked like a northern version of Apollo, with silky, light brown hair, like a field of wheat seen from afar. Even in his fever there was a tightness of action in his expression—his features were chiselled into spare lines, with no excess of flesh on the strong angles of his cheekbones and chin and the carved lines of his lips. His mouth was bracketed by two deep lines that put the final touch on a face that was more that of a statue of what Apollo might look like on a rather aggravating day of dragging the sun across the sky than an actual person.

But it wasn't his looks that held her immobile. For a moment, as she stood over him, his eyes opened and latched on to hers. They were an ominous deep grey, shot with silver like clouds poised the moment before succumbing to a storm. His voice was rough thunder, a warning ending on a plea.

'The snow…it's freezing… Morrow shouldn't have left her. Too late.'

He was looking through her, but she grasped his hand to answer that plea.

'It's not too late.'

'Too late,' he repeated, and this time his eyes did fix on hers and she smiled reassuringly because even if he was dying, he shouldn't do so without hope.

'No, it isn't too late, I promise. Trust me.'

His gaze became clearer for a moment, moving over her, his pupils contracting until she could see the sharp edge of silver about them. But then his lids sank again and his restlessness returned, his hand pulling at the bandage, and she dragged her attention away from his face and focused on her duty.

A look at the ragged and inflamed state of the wound and the sickly tint of his skin under the heat of his fever told her the doctor was not unjustified in his gloom. It would take more than a newspaper to revive this man.

'He's in bad shape, isn't he?' Yannis asked conversationally over her shoulder. 'Told you.

I told the King to put him on the next boat to Athens. Let him die there. We don't need trouble with the English.'

She unlocked her jaw. There was no point in being angry at Yannis.

'And what did King Darius say?'

'Nothing I can repeat to you, little nurse.' Yannis grinned. 'My punishment is to stand guard and help you see he doesn't die. So. What do we do first?'

'First you send for a large pot of water while I fetch my father's bag and those foolish veils.' There was no point in hoping the King would forget his stipulation.

'Veils?'

'The King said I must wear veils while I see to the Englishman.'

'Good idea,' Yannis approved. 'Can't trust a man without a name. Who knows what he's running from?'

She didn't answer. Not because it was foolish to see ghosts where there were none, but because there was something in the Englishman's eyes and voice that gave too much credence to Yannis's half-joking words. It didn't matter—all that mattered was that a man might be dying and perhaps she could save him and thereby repay some of the debt she owed to her adoptive family.

* * *

Thus began of one of the strangest weeks of Christina's life. She came several times a day to tend to the Englishman while Yannis helped ensure he drank the broths she prepared. She even, though she felt rather foolish, did the King's bidding and read the English newspapers to him every day. Within two days what she had thought would be an irksome task took on an almost superstitious weight. It was imperative he survive, not just for the King, but because it just was. She fought for his life with the same fervour as she would for Ari or the King had they been ill, which made no sense at all.

The veils were a nuisance, but soon she found they had a peculiar freeing effect. Like a toddler who is convinced they can't be seen when covering their eyes, Christina found herself free to truly watch the Englishman without worrying about being pierced again by his icy gaze. In the darkness imposed by the cloth, she didn't have to avert her eyes from his face or magnificent physique, despite the shame of finding herself doing covertly what the female servants did overtly every time they brought provisions or tidied the room.

'Isn't he as handsome as Apollo? And look at those shoulders...' they would sigh in Greek as Christina tried hard to ignore their raptures and her own internal upheaval.

After a week, his pulse steadied and she noticed his expression change when she read the newspapers, his sharply carved mouth shifting as if in internal conversation with the topic. Politics would be accompanied by a frown and news of London society with a faint curl of his thin upper lip. But his face became most expressive when she indulged in her own fascination—the advertisements in the agony columns. She had never read these before, but when she exhausted the more respectable pages of the two newspapers she became completely enthralled in reading them. There was something so touching and perplexing about them—little snippets of drama and romance that would remain unexplained for ever. Without even noticing it she began discussing them with her unconscious patient.

'Here, listen to this,' she informed him. 'This is a very passionate fellow. "*To M-A*"—which I presume is Maria, or could it be Margarita? That would add an exotic touch. Anyway, he writes: "*Do I deserve this?*" In capital letters, too. I wonder if that costs more? Then he continues: "*Is it generous? Is it equitable? If I hear not from you by Wednesday hence I will strike thy graven memory from my heart and endeavour to efface thy sweet smile from my soul. Orlando.*" This was three weeks ago, so Wednesday has come and gone and I shall never know if Orlando has been blessed by his Maria or whether she has chosen someone rather more sensible. I think living life in capital letters might be a little tiring. Oh, no—here, this one is even worse! "*To P. If you could conceive of the sorrow and despair into which I am plunged, you would not raise your head. With you I could suffer every privation. Alone I am all misery. A hint of kindness could obliterate all pain. S.B.*" Goodness. Well, I think it is very brave to put such pain on paper, but I cannot imagine ever writing something so…'

'Maudlin.'

The paper scrunched between her hands. The word was faint but decisive and for a moment she searched the room for its source until she realised it came from the Englishman. He was awake, not the brief surfacing of the past few days, but truly awake and inspecting her. Lucid, his eyes were even more dramatic—as sharp and steely as a sword.

'Where the devil am I?' he asked as she remained tongue-tied, her pulse as fast as his had been at the height of his fever.

'Illiakos.'

'Illi… Hell. I remember. The storm. They shot at us.'

'They thought you were pirates.' She tried to be conciliating, thinking of the King.

'We were flying Maltese colours. Clear as day.'

'Yes, well, it wasn't. A clear day, that is.'

He groaned as he tried to shift on the bed.

'I remember. The blasted fog. We rode up on the shoals. Why are you reading the agony columns? Out loud, too, for pity's sake.'

'King Darius requested that I read the English newspapers to you. He thought it would help you recover.'

'That mawkish pap is more likely to send me into a decline. I had no idea people wrote such drivel.'

'It is not drivel to them. Anyone willing to bare his or her soul like that deserves some sympathy, whether you approve or not.'

His mouth relaxed slightly in what might have been the beginning of a smile. It was the first time she had seen that expression on his face and her pulse, which had begun to calm, went into another gallop.

'You didn't sound very approving yourself

just now, so I don't think you can claim the moral high ground.'

Christina flushed, wondering how on earth they had reached the middle of an argument when she should really be summoning the doctor or doing something sensible, but the taunting glimmer of amusement in his eyes kept her in her seat and she groped for something to say.

'For your information, I have already read you the political pages from end to end. Twice. And those are equally as depressing. More so.'

He frowned.

'I remember now—you were reading something about the Tsar and the Sultan. But that news was well over a month old.'

'The mail takes a while to reach us. The pirates have made trade difficult so the ships travel in convoys. Hopefully next week we will receive new newspapers from Athens.'

'We… Who are you and why are you wearing a tent? You sound like you're underwater.'

'It is a bridal veil,' she replied, with as much dignity as possible. 'Brides on Illiakos wear them in public for the first month of marriage. It symbolises the period during which the married couple is dedicated wholly to one another.'

'Good God, more sentimental drivel. I don't envy you or your groom your wedding night.'

His laugh ended in a gasp of pain as he tried to sit up and she dropped the newspaper.

'Please lie down, the doctor removed the bullet, but you lost a great deal of blood.'

She sat on the side of the bed and pressed him back gently as she had during the throes of his fever. Except it was different now. His skin was no longer burning, but hers was. The moment her palms flattened on his shoulders she froze. She tried to reason that he was merely a sick man she was tending, but that wasn't what it felt like. Her fingers were trying to curve over the velvet surface that covered the rock-hard ridges of his shoulders. Sitting like that, if she just leaned towards him a little, raised her head… Took off her veils…

She removed her hands, but couldn't gather any more resolution to rise. So she sat there with her hands clutched in her lap, waiting.

He froze, too, and there was a confused frown in his ice-grey eyes now, as if he was struggling to remember a word.

'You were here before, weren't you? I remember…'

He reached for the veils and she surged to her feet, which was a mistake because she tripped on the awkward yards of cloth and stumbled backwards.

'Careful!' His arm shot out to right her and with a groan of pain he turned chalk white and fell back.

'Don't move.' Christina's concern overcame her confusion and she gently pressed back the bandages, sighing with relief at the unbroken scab beneath. 'That was foolish.'

'I wasn't the one leaping like a scalded cat,' he muttered through gritted teeth. 'You made your point; I won't touch the veils. That blasted doctor may have extracted the bullet, but I think he left a sheave of knives inside me instead.'

Despite her discomfort, her mouth curved upwards at his quintessential Englishness.

'Not a sheave, just one. It is considered good luck.'

'You are jesting, right?' His eyes widened and she smiled at the apprehension in his voice.

'Of course I am. He is merely terrified of the King which makes him a little clumsy. Please lean back while I apply some salve, it will soothe the inflammation and the pain.'

'I don't need any more ministering. That fool of a doctor did enough damage already by the look of it, and I'm damned if I will let you smear some noxious folk remedies on an open wound. What I need is to get off this island.'

'It is merely some boiled herbs, including

witch hazel and vinegar which are excellent for preventing putridity in wounds. I promise there are no bat wings and ears of newts. If you wish to recover swiftly, I suggest you let me apply the salve.'

His mouth held firm for a moment at her scold, and then with a curse worthy of a sailor he leaned back and closed his eyes.

His skin was hot and velvety beneath her fingers as she spread the salve. She worked slowly, smoothing it as gently as possible over the reddened area around the wound, her fingers just a butterfly's flutter on the wound itself. He didn't wince, but she could feel the tension in his muscles and see it in the way his hands fisted by his sides. She had an almost overwhelming urge to bend down and press a kiss to his bare chest, to ease that control, to reassure, explore… She knew she should draw back, but her fingers kept up their soothing strokes, until she exhausted her excuse and had no choice but to stop.

For several heartbeats the room was utterly silent. His chest rose and fell slowly and his eyes opened, pinning her.

'You have dangerous hands, little nurse.'

She curled her fingers into fists and looked down.

'I don't think they qualify as dangerous. Not

next to whoever did these to you.' She indicated the scars on his arm and shoulder, but tried not to look further. He raised his arm, inspecting the scars as if surprised to see them.

'These are just useful reminders not to wander around the bazaars of Constantinople after a night of heavy drinking when you are not welcome in that town.'

'Someone tried to kill you?'

'Not everyone finds me charming.'

'I can understand that, but it is hardly a reason to try to kill you.'

'Thank you. Foolish of me to expect a disavowal.'

'Besides, not all these scars are from the same event or weapon,' she added, ignoring his unconvincing attempt to look offended.

He glanced down at his torso with a frown.

'No. I'm afraid I carry a diary of my follies on my person. This new one will be a particularly inglorious chapter; I didn't even do anything to merit it but be in the wrong place at the wrong time. How demeaning.'

'The others *were* merited?'

'Except for this one.' He turned over his left hand to show a white patch along the root of his palm. 'This was from trying to save a friend from his folly when he climbed back into our room at school in the middle of the night during a storm and almost ended up an ornament on the bushes below.'

'Folly appears to be contagious. Are your friends as foolish as you?'

He smiled.

'No, Raven was like that before I met him. I was still deep in my obedient phase and very determined not to succumb to the family curse of depravity. I held out quite a while, too.'

She frowned at his tone. 'I don't believe in curses.'

'Of course not, nurses must be sensible, right? I'm not fond of the notion myself. Too Greek. I accept full responsibility for choosing which side of my family tree I emulate. I made every effort to behave like the proper half of that tree for almost two decades and found it not only stultifying, but also unappreciated. So for the past five years I have been enjoying a grand tour of the other half. Aside from these…' he indicated the scarred topography of his body '…I am finding it suits me very well.'

'I am glad, because I would hate to think you derived no pleasure from trying to kill yourself.'

She hadn't meant to speak quite that sharply. He smiled, a slow wolfish smile, and her legs pressed together, readying herself to move.

'I'm deriving a great deal of pleasure at the moment from being resurrected. I'd derive even greater pleasure from seeing what my little saviour looks like under those veils, but don't worry, I don't need to be slapped more than once to learn not to steal cakes from cook's table. I will just have to exert my imagination; it is very creative. Shall I tell you what it is weaving?'

'No, thank you. I have little doubt it is an improvement on the reality. Now, you might be accustomed to injury, but you are still very weak and what you need most is rest. If you need help, call for Yannis. He is outside. The King is a good man and has every interest in seeing you in good health so I suggest you not try anything foolish.'

'You are a fiery little thing, aren't you? You don't sound as terrified of this King as the doctor appears to be.'

'I have no reason to fear him. I owe him everything and he has always been kind to me. However, he does have a temper and I suggest you don't provoke it if you wish to have your way.'

He smiled, his eyes lightening with laughter.

'That is excellent advice, darling. I promise not to provoke him, but I don't know if I can promise the same to you, as it is too much of a pleasure to watch, or rather listen, to you rise to the fly. I do promise to keep my hands to myself, but for your information, the best way to put a man's fantasies to rest is to confront him with reality. Perhaps these veils have more merit for newlyweds than I gave them credit. Marriage is a tedious business and anything that introduces a touch of mystery is welcome.'

'Are you married then?' The words were out before she could stop them, her skin still tingling from his casual endearment.

'No, thank God. I've watched too many disasters on that front. When I do marry, in the very, very distant future, it will be to someone whose expectations can be measured in worldly goods and who knows her limits and mine.'

It had nothing to do with her, but it hurt like a personal rejection.

'I will return later with a tisane for the pain, but you should rest now. If you need anything, summon Yannis and he can send for me if there is a need.'

'And pull you from your husband's arms? Tempting but not very chivalrous, my dear. I shall make do with this Yannis.'

The lingering falsity of her marriage stuck in her throat. It wasn't like her to lie. Not that she had actually said she was married, but she had certainly not corrected him and that was bad enough, wasn't it? All she had to do was tell him—*I'm not married; the veils were the King's idea*. Then he would laugh and tell her to take them off, that she stood in no danger from him.

And that would be a lie, too. Even if *he* meant it. He might poke fun at her, but somehow she knew the moment he knew she was unmarried even that taunting freedom in her presence would cease. She might not know him, but she knew that. Still, the next time he said anything about her married state she promised she would tell the truth. However uncomfortable.

She glanced back—he looked weary, but his smile lingered as he watched her, part warmth and part mockery. She was so tempted to stay so she left.

If she had an ounce of sense she would have stayed away from that point forward, but she didn't. The first week of his illness was unsettling, but the second exhausted all her reserves of self-control. She found all forms of excuses to visit the Englishman, though any servant could have delivered the tisanes she prepared and she was gaining no favours with the doctor by insisting on applying her salves to the wound. She drank in every moment in his company like the

Illiakan plains drank in rainwater after the long dry summer. He never demanded she remove the veils again, and thankfully he never again referred to her marriage, so she could at least continue to shove away her guilt at perpetuating the lie and enjoy the pleasures of his company, from the unsettling effect of touching him as she nursed him to the more innocent pleasure of reading to him. She loved lingering over the agony columns just so he would tease her and then she could berate him for his insensitivity and watch the laughter light up his austere face.

'Enough. That one was by far the most pathetic,' he stated after she found a particularly tearful advertisement. 'What is wrong with people? One would think with all of human history at our fingertips we would have realised this love nonsense is a waste of energy. Imagine how much could be achieved if only we applied all that energy to something productive.'

'I think love can be a great force for good, perhaps the greatest. I do know that love changed my life. My parents didn't really know how to love me, they were too busy with their concerns, but when I came to live with the Princess when I was ten and she four, I discovered what it was to love and be loved and my life changed utterly.

I can't imagine who I might be today if I hadn't been so lucky.'

'I'm glad for you, but that kind of love is different.'

'How? Love is just love. It is caring for another person, sometimes more than you do for yourself. It is wanting that person to be happy, feeling their pain, wanting to understand them and wanting them to understand you. How is it different?'

'Because what you are describing is not what people mistake for love between men and women, but affection between siblings or a mother's love for her child. At least I presume it is. My own parents were sadly deficient on that front, though to give my father credit he meant well—he was just so sanctimonious. But I think I can understand a little of what you described—when I was ten my father remarried a lovely woman who did her best to make up for both my parents' deficiencies.'

'Did she succeed?'

He smiled and warmth spilled through her. Love. Perhaps this was an answer, too. It *was* different.

'Up to a point. From that point she did something even better, she gave birth to my sisters. I was also ten when this happened and it changed my life, so I think I can understand what you mean. What was wrong with your parents?'

'Perhaps there was nothing wrong with them. Perhaps the fault was in me.'

'Good God, no. Trust me on that. What were they like?'

'My father was a doctor and my mother was very ill and couldn't tend to me. So I was sent to stay with my uncle and aunt against their will until my mother died and my father came to work at the castle. Coming here saved me. Are your sisters like you?'

His mouth quirked at her change of subject and for a moment she thought he would persist, but then the mocking smile returned.

'That sounds suspicious. What is *like me*?'

'Are they also convinced they are cursed or are they more sensible?'

'Oh, much more sensible. And since my mother's side is the bearer of the curse, they don't have to carry that particular burden. They aren't like me in the least; they both take after their mother, thank goodness.'

'Do they share your belief that *you* are cursed?'

He hesitated.

'For the moment they are too young and sheltered to think I am anything but their big brother. Hopefully they won't despise me too much when the scales fall from their eyes. I admit I resolved to despise them when they were born, but I held out for about three minutes from the moment I set eyes on them. I would certainly do anything for them. On most matters I am distinctly on the sinful side of my joint family tree, but my sisters and my two best friends still manage to bring to the surface whatever of my finer principles remain intact.'

She sighed.

'I'm envious. I always wished for an older brother. My cousins were brutes so they don't count and the King is more like an uncle.'

His eyes narrowed.

'I'd volunteer for the post, but that wouldn't be quite honest since brotherly feelings aren't what you evoke in me. Which brings me back to the distinction between the love you described for the Princess and what you might think exists between men and women. Those two are very different in both quantity and quality, believe me.'

Under the veils, the now familiar heat gathered, like steam in a tent. She wanted to rip everything off and bare herself, lies, dreams and everything. She prayed he wouldn't say the words that would force her to honour her promise to tell the truth. She didn't want this to end yet, not yet.

The sting of her need made her voice hard. 'You may be as cynical as you wish, but you don't know everything.'

'Hardly, but I have a little more experience on that front than you and your young love.' His eyes had become stormy grey again, a transformation which always marked the point she felt she was trespassing on something personal.

'How can you have more experience in something you don't believe exists?' she countered and his mouth curved into a reluctant smile.

'In its fallacy I do. Certainly in the varied shades of relations between men and women. On the strength of that advantage may I give you some advice?'

'I don't think I will appreciate it, will I?'

He laughed and the storm grey turned warm and inviting again, sinking her further.

'Good point. I have had reams of advice flung at me by my father and appreciated none of it. Still, you can do what I do and ignore it. For what it is worth I suggest you never depend on your husband to fulfil all, or even most, of your needs. That is a recipe for disaster. Men are rather useless fellows and tend to buckle under pressure, especially when that pressure is applied by women. Especially by someone like you who is far too strong for their own good and as argumentative as one of those philosophers who lived in a cave or a barrel or wherever. Learn to row your own boat. There, if only you listen to my advice I'd consider my debt paid in full.'

She took a deep breath. She had made a promise after all.

'I am not married.'

'Excuse me?'

'I'm not married. You assumed I was because of the veils.'

'I assumed… But you said…'

'I said the veils are bridal veils and they are. The King ordered me to wear them while I tend to you, for my protection. After all, we did not know anything about you. Well, we still don't since you won't even tell us your name, but… But I am not married.'

Her hands were clenched so tightly together they hurt. She unclenched and flexed them. There was no need to feel so horrid and guilty and…exposed.

The silence stretched and stretched and stretched and she leapt into that yawning pit.

'I didn't mean to lie. Well, I didn't *lie.* I just… It seemed easier. Safer. Men respect married women. I can see that on the island. I mean, they wouldn't go into someone else's house without being invited and it is just that way with women, right? We are considered property, aren't we? So even with Yannis outside it seemed safer to allow you to think…'

'I see. And for some reason you now think it is safe to tell me the truth?'

Her heartbeat thundered like a horse down a mountain, far too fast and stumbling over rocks. She didn't feel safe. She felt terrified. But not of him.

'I don't know, but I promised myself if you mentioned marriage again I would tell the truth. I don't enjoy lying, not even by omission.'

'For someone who doesn't enjoy lying you are very adept at it. Are you quite certain the only reason you didn't share this minor little detail is because you wished to remain…safe?'

His anger was as cold and hard as a steel rapier being shoved slowly through her lungs.

'What other reason could there be?'

'Precisely what I am asking myself. Athena. Is that your name or is that a lie as well?'

'That is what the King calls me. The Princess calls me Tina for short.'

'I see how this works. Not a lie, but not quite the truth—rather you offer with one hand while you hide something with the other. You would make a fine cardsharp, or perhaps I should introduce you to Oswald, he would appreciate your skill.'

'Who is Oswald?'

'Leading me off the trail again, Athena? If you wish. Oswald is my uncle and the man who sends me on the errands which have left the trail of scars you were admiring.'

'Was he why you were in Alexandria and why you won't tell us your name?'

'If you wished to know my name you only had to ask. My name is Alexander, but my friends call me Alex.'

She knew he was doing precisely what he had accused her of doing—distracting her from her quarry and with an offer empty of any real value, but it worked. Her mind wrapped itself about the sound and colour of his name, her mind filling with its fire. Alex.

'Alex.'

He breathed in, deep and sharp, and for a moment she surfaced from her internal fog, worrying something had jogged his wound, but as she reached forward instinctively he caught her hand and they froze.

She waited for him to release her wrist, but his hand slid under hers, raising it. A lock of his hair, touched with gold from the afternoon sun streaming in the narrow castle windows, fell over his brow as he leaned forward. It was like a picture from a book—the gallant knight bowing over a maiden's hand. Until his lips skimmed over the back of her hand and came to rest just above her knuckles. She had once scalded her hand boiling herbs and it had also taken her a shocked second to realise she was in agony and snatch her hand away. She tried to do so now, but he just tightened his clasp.

'What are you doing?' Her voice wavered a little and he looked up and she saw danger in his eyes, an intent concentration, like a hawk hovering over a field mouse, wondering whether it was worth the plunge. But his words were almost casual.

'Thanking you. Is showing gratitude not acceptable on Illiakos?'

'Not like that.'

'That's a pity. Perhaps you should have let the lie lie. You were right your married status was an effective barrier to flirtation. Now there is nothing to stop me from telling you I find myself fantasising about what you look like under that curtain, is there?'

'You would only be disappointed. I am not in the least remarkable.'

'I have had a little experience with women, my dear, and though I don't know what you look like, believe me when I say that you underestimate yourself. And if I *were* your brother I wouldn't make do with that lug Yannis napping on a bench outside the room.'

The humour that did so much damage to her resolve transformed his eyes from ice to the colour of thunderclouds, but even though his hold softened, she was no longer trying to escape it. His hand encompassed her wrist, his fingers marking her thudding pulse. She knew he couldn't see her, but she felt he saw right through her, not merely through the veils, but through her skin, to the flow of blood in her veins, to her very thoughts, chaotic and forbidden.

She tried desperately to regain her advantage as his nurse.

'I will have you know I do not need Yannis to see to my welfare. I can see to it myself, so you had best tread carefully.'

A glint of mischief sparked in his eyes and his hand tucked hers into his as if it was the most natural thing in the world to sit there, hands clasped.

'Or what?'

'Or...'

She couldn't think of anything. Not just a

reasonable punishment, but of anything but the surprisingly sweet mischief in his eyes and that sense of rightness in sitting there with him, his fingers caressing the core of her palm and sending shivers of heat up her arm, her body aligning, readying to be his.

'I don't think I would mind any retribution you could deliver, you know.' His voice rasped over nerves that were already dancing. The mere thought that he might feel the same attraction was as intoxicating as his touch. He was probably just playing with her as he no doubt played with all the women he claimed to have experienced. But in her mind a common bond of need had snared them both, inescapable.

'I would never wish to hurt you,' she replied, her own voice just as hoarse at the depth of that truth. The mischief in his eyes doused immediately, the shadows under his cheekbones becoming even more pronounced. When he spoke now his voice scared her, it was deep and raw, as compelling as an edict from the gods.

'Take off the veil. I need to see you.'

She shook her head—it wasn't just that he would see plump and drab Christina James, the daughter of an English doctor, but that he would see her thoughts in her eyes as clear as spring water. This was a game to him, but it wasn't for her. He was clever and watchful and she would not be able to hide her feelings and then she would see not just disappointment but pity.

'No.'

'Damn it, take them off. I won't do anything, I promise. I just want to see you.'

'I can't.'

'Of course you can. This is madness. Someone like you shouldn't even be here, locked into a servant's life. Look, I am almost well enough to leave. Come with me.'

'What?'

'There is a whole world outside these walls and those veils. It's obvious in everything you say that you are fascinated by it. I'm asking you to come discover it with me.'

'You're mad.'

'Probably. A little. Well, more than a little. But I mean it. I know some of the things I do are dangerous, but I would arrange it so that you are never at risk and if anything happened to me you would have everything you need; you would never have to depend on anyone ever again. If anyone is unsuited to be at someone else's beck and call all their lives, it is you. All that passion in you will bubble over one day and burn everything in sight. I can show you how to set it free. Take off your veils, Athena.'

She dragged her hands away and stood, stumbling backwards. Waves of heat and ice rolled through her and her lungs felt as tight as if a boulder was pinning her down.

'Stop it. This is my home! My family!'

He struggled to his feet, his hand braced against his side, and she felt tears burning on her cheeks at the clashing currents of fear and concern and need.

'You would rather remain a servant here?' he demanded and she clasped her hands together.

'I am not merely a servant. I would never leave the King and Ari; they are all that matter in my life.'

He looked away, the heat disappearing in a flash from his mouth and eyes as if it had never been. Like this he looked more than ever like a statue and it was hard to reconcile this stony façade with the appealing charm and that almost boyish need of just a moment ago. One of them had to be a lie, didn't it?

'It hardly matters,' he said after a moment. 'Fantasy is so much more rewarding than reality, anyway. But if you wish men to respect your boundaries, I suggest you refrain from flirting with them.'

'I don't flirt.'

'More fantasy, darling. A dangerous one, too.

Someone with your temper would do better to face your flaws or one day that meek little handmaiden act will go up in a ball of fire and then all hell will break loose.'

'You don't know me!'

His mouth flattened.

'I know your kind.'

'My kind?'

'Yes. Clever, quiet, with everything tucked in tight until it explodes and takes everyone with it without thought of the consequences.'

The maelstrom of unfamiliar emotions gathered round a single core of fury and she clung to it with savage relief.

'You are arrogant and presumptuous and annoying, and I am tired of sitting here in these horrible veils while you taunt me. I will tell the King you are perfectly able to travel and I hope he puts you on the very first ship off the island.' She switched to Greek, stalking towards the door. 'Yannis, open the door, I am coming out!'

'Wait!'

But she was already through the door, shoving a surprised Yannis aside. She stripped off the veils and left them in a heap in the corridor.

It took two more days for Alex to be dispatched. She knew the King had visited him, a chessboard under his arm, and once he even took Princess Ariadne, who came back bouncing with delight at how funny Apollo was.

Though she held firm in her resolve not to see him again, she couldn't prevent her disappointment that he never sent for her. His offer, offhand though it had been, burned like a lanced boil on her soul, but whether she hoped for it to be repeated or not, there was nothing but silence. Clearly he had had his fun, but now that he was to be on his way she was no longer instrumental. It was all for the better, she told herself, but it took every ounce of her resolve not to go and tell him precisely what she thought of his ingratitude and his stupidity and his insensitivity, just so she could see him one last time.

The day he was escorted down to the King's own frigate to be transported to Venice, she and Ariadne watched the procession from the Princess's rooms. The dismal winter weather had burst into a benediction of sunshine in a transition typical of the Mediterranean, transforming the bay into a crystalline sparkle of sapphires and emeralds. Even leaning on a cane he stood almost a head taller than the men around him, the sun striking his hair with silver and gold as he boarded the white-sailed vessel.

'Apollo is taking the sun with him.' Ariadne sighed, her chin propped on her arms.

Christina's heart squeezed and shrivelled. Ariadne's words were soppily sentimental, but that was precisely what it felt like. Ridiculous, she told herself. Just like the agony columns—absurd, mawkish, silly, stupid. Pathetic. Perhaps if she threw enough insults at this pain it would shrivel as well.

The next day the rainclouds returned and life went on.

Chapter One

London—1822

'You cannot be serious!' Alex, Lord Stanton, paused with his glass halfway to his lips.

'I am always serious,' Sir Oswald Sinclair replied.

'That is the gospel truth.' Lord Hunter raised his own glass with a complicit grin at Alex and Lord Ravenscar, but Alex was in no mood to appreciate his friend's sense of humour.

'Hell, Uncle. The man had me shot and imprisoned. I still have a nasty scar to show for it. I have no intention whatsoever of inviting them to Stanton Hall, negotiations or no negotiations.'

Sir Oswald's expression rarely changed. Rather he used his quizzing glass as a way to communicate human emotion. It went up now, a faint but definite rebuke.

'While you are indeed heir to the Marquessate and the Stanton estate, your father is still Marquess of Wentworth and as such he decides who is welcome at Stanton Hall and he and your delightful stepmother have expressed their willingness to allow me to bring guests to the hall for a few weeks while they are away.'

'Don't split hairs with me, Uncle. Why the devil can't the discussions be held in London? And if not in London, why at Stanton?'

'Because he asked. You might have put aside your past as agent for the War Office these five years for a more respectable post in the Foreign Office, but surely you are still aware how important it is that we secure Illiakos as a naval base in the Mediterranean.'

'I am fully aware of its importance. The last thing we need is another bone of contention between the Turks and Greeks setting off the squabbling between Russia and Austria. I just spent a week with Razumov and Von Haas convincing them it is in everyone's best interests to allow the English to take this particular piece off the board—for a price, of course. Just because I no longer run dubious errands for you around the world doesn't mean I have become witless, Uncle.'

'I am well aware of that, Alexander. But it

might interest you to hear that Lucas sent word from Russia that though Count Nesselrode is on board and has convinced the Tsar of its wisdom, not all the powers in Russia are happy with this move since it might weaken the Greek position should they proceed with their resistance to Turkish rule. I prefer to have the King and his daughter where I…where *we* can control their surroundings and ensure they remain focused on the prize. We all want the same thing in the end.'

'Not quite in the same way. So, my delightful Sinclair cousins still work for you?'

Oswald's mouth almost bowed into a smile. 'They haven't yet wearied of me as you did.'

'I don't think "wearied" is the right choice of word. Grew up might be closer to the mark.'

'Ah, but that had nothing to do with me,' Oswald replied and Alex's lungs constricted with remembered shame and self-contempt. Trust his uncle to go for the jugular without the slightest effort.

'No. That had nothing to do with you,' he admitted and his uncle had the grace to show a glimmer of remorse, but before he could speak, Lord Ravenscar intervened.

'His daughter? There's a princess in there, too?'

Hunter's brow rose. 'Shall I tell Lily you were asking?'

Ravenscar grinned and raised his glass. 'I'd back Lily against any princess, or a queen for that matter. I was thinking of our stubbornly unwed friend here and his annoying tendency to look down upon us married mortals. It's about time he fell off his high horse. Maybe a princess will do it. Have you met her, Sir Oswald? Is she pretty?'

'I met her yesterday at their hotel. She is very pretty.'

'There. It's as good as done. Damned if I start calling you your Majesty, though.'

'To Prince Alexander.' Hunter raised a toast. 'You will make a fine despot.'

Alex shook his head at his friends' nonsense, but their attempt to dispel the tension Oswald's comment introduced was welcome. There was no point in arguing, after all.

'Why don't you just tell me what is expected of me since it is apparently already arranged?'

'Good. I will travel down with them from London to Berkshire tomorrow and see them settled. We will expect you the next day.'

'Will you?'

'Don't scowl, Alexander. I am impervious to shows of temper. I am well aware you are otherwise occupied with Canning on the business of the Congress over the next couple of days, so I offered to escort the King and Princess to Stanton myself until you can join us. It will be an opportunity to keep our Russian and Austrian friends under my eye.'

The same eye was currently grotesquely magnified by the quizzing glass and Alex knew he had lost. It was damnable, but his uncle could always get his way without the slightest show of effort or emotion.

'Lucky them. Very well, I will come as soon as Canning is done with me. But I draw the line at courting princesses.'

'A pity. The island is most strategically located for our navy and a marriage would be more effective than a treaty. Never mind. I will bid you gentlemen good evening.'

Alex cursed and sat down in his armchair as the door closed.

'One day I will walk out of a battle of wills with him the victor.'

'I doubt it,' Hunter said. 'He's a true cold fish, that man. You just act like one. Or at least you have for the past five years.'

'Better a cold fish than a landed one like you two old married men.'

Ravenscar propped his boots on the grate and sighed.

'Here we go again. Another smug lecture from the bachelor. We had best see him hitched soon, Hunter. Either that or take him round back and show him a thing or two.'

'You could probably use the exercise, Raven,' Alex taunted. 'When was the last time you went to Jackson's?'

'Oh, we get plenty of exercise, Alex.' Hunter grinned. 'And not merely at Jackson's.'

Ravenscar laughed. 'Careful, Hunter, you're embarrassing him.'

'It's a pity neither Nell nor Lily have sisters.'

'Damn it, Hunter. If you dare take up matchmaking...'

Hunter raised his hands in surrender.

'I'm not such a fool. Besides, I would rather watch you fail on your own. Perhaps we should put a wager on it, Raven? Think the Princess will do the trick?'

'Don't waste your blunt, Raven. When I do marry it will be to a biddable female who understands the rules just so I can finally put a stop to your crowing and my father's unveiled hints. Until then I intend to continue to enjoy being the only one in the Wild Hunt Club who hasn't been leg shackled and domesticated.'

'Just you wait. When you fall from those icy heights, you'll fall hard, King Alexander.'

'You forget, I met the Princess some six years ago and though she was just a child, I hardly think she has grown into anything that might tempt me to change my state of unwedded bliss.'

Raven frowned.

'I remember now. When you came back to London with that hole in your side, you mentioned a veiled nurse who brought you back from the dead. I always liked that touch of mystery. What was her name? Athena, right? Very romantic.'

'Hardly romantic,' he answered Ravenscar's comment as lightly as possible. 'If wearing those curtains is part of the wedding ceremony on Illiakos that is another incentive to stay away from the Princess. That poor nurse was about as unsuited to be a biddable bride as any I've come across.'

'You are hardly an authority on who is suited to be a wife, my friend. You probably think you should marry someone like your stepmother.'

'And why not? Sylvia is sweet, practical and undemanding. What more could one want in a wife? After almost ten years with my mother my father deserved someone who didn't push him to the edge of insanity. I know you two have become disgustingly smug since you wed, but not everyone wants to be dangled over a ravine on a daily basis.'

'I rather like the sensation,' Ravenscar mused. 'Lily is magnificent at both dangling and catching me before I hit the ground. An excellent combination.'

'For you. When I have to finally account for the title I think I will choose someone a little more docile than your Lily and someone rather less subversive than Nell.'

Hunter laughed. 'That is assuming the choice is yours, Alex.'

'One always has a choice. That is what distinguishes us from animals. We might have urges, sometimes even powerful ones, I grant you, but in the end we choose how to act upon them. It is as simple as that.'

Ravenscar considered him over the rim of his glass.

'Simple is never that simple. You might have thoroughly reformed yourself these past five years since what happened with Countess Vidanich, Alex, but you might be surprised to find there are areas outside even your control. Life has a way of turning us down new roads and we only realise we are there when it is too late to turn back.'

'You make it sound like something mystical, Raven.'

'Sometimes if feels like that. For example, I remember thinking at the time that you were rather unusually taken with that little nurse when you described your forced stay on Illiakos. Perhaps that Athena was a priestess in disguise and she cast a spell on you.'

'Very creative, Ravenscar,' Hunter approved. 'I'm beginning to hope your veiled temptress will be accompanying the little Princess so you can thank her yourself. In person. That might be even more enjoyable than losing you to a kingdom. You could finally put that little mystery to bed. Literally.'

Alex shrugged. 'It is hardly likely the nurse will accompany the King and Princess on a state visit. She is probably married now and with a full brood of children so I will have to remain with my fantasy of what lay beneath those voluminous veils. Now are we going to Cribb's or are you two under curfew?'

Ravenscar stood and stretched.

'Careful, Alex, your romantic petticoats are showing. Next you'll be saying you don't want to marry because you left your heart under some faceless chit's veils.'

'My what?' Alex enquired politely and Hunter laughed.

'You do have one, you know. One day you'll stumble over it and fall flat on your face.'

Chapter Two

Berkshire

Christina leaned her forehead on the window and watched as the sun speared itself on the trees at the edge of the lawn. Like Ari, she was a little disappointed to leave London for Stanton Hall so soon after their arrival in England, but with each mile into the rolling green hills of Berkshire she had felt the rise of an unfamiliar mix of peace and homesickness. She had never expected to discover she actually missed the green and grey of England. No doubt after a couple of weeks of English autumn she would be pining for the sun, but for now she and Ari could enjoy the quiet of the countryside while the King was engaged in his negotiations.

She looked around their shared parlour. It was both large and cosy, a difficult combination but one a clever hand had succeeded in throughout Stanton Hall. Perhaps it was the choice of colours: deep-forest and light-grass greens with muted gold and a great deal of wood. It was like being in an ancient, dignified forest, dappled in sunlight. Most peculiarly it was a forest populated by a series of exquisite wooden figurines, mostly of people and animals. Ari had exclaimed over them with delight when they had arrived and, though Christina hadn't been quite so vocal, she felt her eyes drawn to them again and again, almost expecting them to begin moving about the room or join the conversation.

'What shall I wear for our dinner with the political emissaries?' Ariadne looked up from inspecting the fashion plates in a copy of *La Belle Assemblée*. 'I think the white-and-silver gauze Papa brought from Athens and the white peacock feathers with the gold clasp? What will you wear, Tina?'

Christina picked up the figurine on the windowsill, her favourite thus far. It was of a kneeling girl staring into the distance and though it did not show the exquisite skill of the others it continued to draw her, like a child begging to be picked up.

'I shall wear my nightdress and be tucked into bed with a book and very thankful for it. I doubt I shall be invited to any of the formal dinners, Ari. We are no longer in Illiakos. Here in England companions aren't treated as guests.'

Ariadne sighed.

'England is much less enjoyable than I thought. First we leave London after only a few days and Lord Stanton and Papa will likely be all about politics and war and now you say they won't even let me be with you which means I shall have to sit with Lady Albinia, who is interested in nothing but gardens. Well, if you remain in your room then I shall, too, and so I shall tell Papa!'

As if conjured by his daughter the King walked into the parlour.

'Ready to come and see the gardens, little star?'

'Papa! Tina said she will not be invited to dine with us, is this true?'

The King turned to Christina.

'What nonsense is this, Athena? I have more important matters to see to here than your English pride. You might not be family by birth or law, but in all other respects that is precisely what you are and you will attend all events Ari does. There are bonds that transcend the accidents of nature. On Illiakos we understand this even if you English are slow to recognise what truly matters. Is Ari not dear as a sister to you?'

'Papa,' Ari protested, but Christina met his gaze and replied more fiercely than usual.

'You know she is. You know I would do anything for her.'

'Except come to dinner, apparently.'

She couldn't help laughing.

'If I must, I shall even do that.'

'Good. Now, what is this, Ari? Hurry and change your dress. But not the blue dress I brought you from Athens, I want you to wear it when Lord Stanton arrives tomorrow.'

'Oh, must I waste that lovely dress on a stuffy politician, Papa?'

'You didn't think him stuffy six years ago, little star. I seem to remember you called him Apollo at the time.'

The figurine fumbled from Christina's hands, but she grabbed it before it bounced to the floor, her shocked gasp overshadowed by Ari's squeal.

'No! Apollo is our host? Why didn't you tell me, Papa! How exciting. I wonder if he remembers me.'

'I am certain he does, though at the time you were hardly the lovely young woman you are today. Now go and change, Sir Oswald and Lady Albinia are waiting.'

Ari rushed to her room and Christina sank into a chair. Alex. This made no sense.

'But…that is the man your guards almost killed!'

'Nonsense. A misunderstanding. He is a diplomat, he understands that, and Minister Canning assures me he bears no grudge. It was a long time ago, after all.'

'*It* was only five years ago.'

'Almost six. And much has happened since. Now I am squeezed like a nut between the fists of Russia and Austria as they play the Turks against the Greeks. I prefer to test my fate with the English and their navy. I like the English. My years as a student at Oxford were some of my finest.'

'But he can't possibly want you to stay here… in his home. You all but kidnapped him and held him prisoner.'

'Only at first. Then when he was better, I treated him well, didn't I? We played chess. He is one of the best opponents I have met, and his given name is Alexander, apparently. A fine name for a future King of Illiakos. King Alexander, it has a nice sound to it, yes? I think I wouldn't mind if he married Ariadne.'

'You wouldn't mind…'

Christina waited out the sensation of still

being on board the ship that had carried them to England. She should be used to the King by now, but sometimes he still took her breath away. Or perhaps that was the realisation of where they were. Or rather, whom they would see tomorrow. Oh, no, she couldn't do it. Not again. She should insist on leaving to visit her cousins. They might not want her to come, but surely they wouldn't turn her away?

'Perhaps while you are occupied here I should visit my family for a few days.'

'Nonsense. It is not at all convenient that you leave when Ari needs you most, Athena. This behaviour is not like you. Are you unwell?'

The combination of solicitude and the reminder of her duty crumbled her resistance.

'I am well, your Majesty, but...'

'Good.' He clapped his hands together in satisfaction. 'We are done here. Go and make certain my little star is in a good mood. She must make an excellent impression. My enquiries tell me Lord Stanton has had the most exquisite of women and his palate is no doubt jaded, so Ariadne must be polished to the finest shine if she is to capture and hold his attention. She is beautiful, yes, but she is still a little rough despite all your efforts to make her the perfect English girl. You should have tried harder.'

'I…' She almost let loose her frustration when she saw the expectant mischief in his eyes. He might be fifty, but sometimes he was no better than a little boy.

'I shall endeavour to do so, your Majesty.'

He sighed.

'One day you will lose your temper with me, Athena.'

'I shall endeavour not to do so, your Majesty.'

'A pity. I think it would do you a world of good. Meanwhile you are looking a little off colour. Why don't you find yourself a book in that monstrous library you were admiring earlier? Reading always cheers you and you heard what Lady Albinia said, once Lord Stanton arrives, the library and the state room will be in use for the negotiations so take advantage of it being empty while you can. Ari and I will make your excuses. But now go and tell her if she isn't downstairs in twenty minutes I will…well, do something or other.'

He strode out but Christina didn't immediately go to do his bidding; she needed time to recover from his unwitting blow.

Lord Stanton. Alexander.

Alex.

What a fool she was. Almost six years had passed. One would think that was enough time for a foolish infatuation to fade, but her thudding pulse was proof the memory of those weeks was still alive inside her.

She couldn't face him…

Of course you can, you silly girl. He won't even recognise you. Why should he? He was delirious half the time and the rest of it those ridiculous veils covered you like a tent. Besides, you were just a girl and he was as handsome as a god and as charming as a devil. Of course you thought you were in love with him. But you are older now and quite a bit wiser.

Perhaps this will even do you good, you will see an Englishman all starched and trapped in cravats and waistcoats and bowing and scraping to the King like all the other officials come to pay court. It would be different now.

It had to be different. She didn't want to have to nurse her way through another bruised heart in silence.

Chapter Three

Alex held his bay purebloods steady as he turned his curricle through the gates of Stanton Hall. It was usually at this point in the drive from London that his conflicted emotions reached their peak. He loved London and the excitement of his work at the Foreign Office, but there was something about coming to Berkshire and to his own wing at the Hall that calmed him, in particular when his father wasn't in residence. It wasn't that he disliked his sire and he certainly cared for Sylvia, his stepmother, and had a real and deep love for his two half-sisters, Anne and Olivia, but when they were away he revelled in having the Hall to himself. Then he could lower his guard and forget about duties and policies, Stantons and Sinclairs. Almost.

This particular return, however, was overshadowed by the unwelcome guests awaiting him.

'Have my uncle and guests arrived yet, Watkins?' he asked his butler as he came downstairs after changing out of his driving clothes.

'Yes, my lord. You were not expected until tomorrow and Count Razumov and Graf Von Haas and their entourages recently arrived and are resting in their rooms, but I believe his Majesty and the Princess and her companion, Miss James, have gone with Sir Oswald and Lady Albinia to inspect the gardens. Apparently his Majesty also has an interest in horticulture.'

'Oh, God help me.'

'Indeed, my lord. I presume you will join them outside?'

'Not for the prospect of world peace, Watkins. I have work to do. They will manage without me until dinner.'

He entered the library, a generously proportioned room overlooking the lawns and lake. He had his own study on the other side of the house, but he liked the combination of space and leather-bound warmth the library offered, with its deep, cushioned and curtained window seats overlooking the lake.

Halfway to his desk he noticed a pair of pale yellow kid shoes on the carpeted floor by the curtains drawn over the far window seat. There was nothing peculiar about them except their very presence in the library when his sisters were away. He moved towards them but stopped when the curtains twitched and two stockinged feet peeped out below, moving slowly towards the discarded footwear, like a cat trying to escape detection. He remained silent, watching with appreciation the elegant line of foot and ankle, the slim calf, and with regret the appearance of the hem of a muslin skirt as the feet finally encountered the shoes and slid into them, sneaking back just as stealthily behind the curtains.

'I'm afraid it is a bit late for concealment,' he said, trying not to laugh. He had no wish to embarrass anyone, especially not if this was the Princess. 'I am Lord Stanton. Will you please come out so we may introduce ourselves?'

There was a moment's silence and then the curtain was pushed aside. A young woman stood up, shaking out her skirts, her finger still held between the pages of a book.

She was clearly embarrassed, her cheeks hot with colour, but she was just as clearly not the Princess. The Princess had been a child with black hair and brown eyes, not hair the shade of dark mahogany and eyes of a peculiar teal blue. His uncle had also claimed the Princess was exceedingly pretty and he was a stickler for accuracy. The woman facing him didn't evoke the overused epithet 'pretty', but her features had a compelling harmony and her large, wide-set eyes were like staring into the distant shadowing of the ocean, the kind that fuelled travellers' anticipation and fear. Then reality returned and he recalled Watkins's words—this must be the Princess's English companion.

'I am sorry,' she said, her voice low. 'When I am reading, I forget myself. I hadn't even realised I had taken off my shoes until I heard someone moving in the room.'

The silence stretched as he tried to focus on her words, but they faded away from him, like a vaguely familiar foreign language. All that reminiscing with Hunter and Raven was clearly having some ill effects on him—for a moment he had been dragged back in time to a very different room. He struggled to regain his footing.

'There is no need to apologise. You are more than welcome to use the library, Miss…' He groped for the memory of the name Watkins had mentioned. 'Miss James?'

She smiled and her face transformed for a moment, solemnity disappearing under the weight of embarrassed amusement, quickly checked. It was a powerful transformation, like sun breaking through clouds above a stormy sea. He might have to reassess his initial impression—she might not be a beauty, but there was something about her features that went beyond classical features and made it difficult to look away.

'I apologise, Lord Stanton. We were told you weren't expected until tomorrow. I wouldn't have come to the library if I had known you were arriving sooner.'

'And why is that?' he asked, moving closer. Surely if this was the girl who had nursed him she would say something, show some sign of recognition. But her eyes showed only embarrassment as she hugged the book to her.

'Lady Albinia said the library is your domain when you are at the Hall. I meant to take a book upstairs with me, but then I saw the window seat and forgot. I don't think I could have conjured a more perfect place.'

He glanced at the window seat, at the cushions arranged into a little nest in the corner, still bearing the outline of her body. She turned and began arranging the cushions, plumping them back into shape, her skirts falling forward to accentuate the soft curves of her hips and behind. There was nothing intentionally provocative about her actions, any more than the surreptitious manoeuvre with her shoes had been calculated, but his body wasn't in the least concerned with intentions. It was focused on actions and on curves and was heading deep into unrealisable potential when she finally finished and turned, her cheeks flushed and the apology still in her eyes.

'There, now you won't even know I was here.'

He searched for an answer, something polite and non-committal and removed from the impressions his mind was struggling to master and the messages his suddenly rebellious body was sending.

The silence began to sag in the middle and then, thankfully, there was a movement in the window and he forced his gaze to the sight of his uncle and aunt coming up the path from the gardens with the King and Princess. He grasped at the opening they offered as he would at a rope in a stormy sea. It made no difference whether this was the veiled girl or not. She was the Princess's companion and a guest. His guest. Everything else must be put aside to be dealt with later, if at all.

'Your solitude is about to be interrupted anyway. Why didn't you join them? Don't you like gardens?' he asked, more bluntly than he might have intended, but Miss James didn't appear to find anything strange with his question. She answered it as given, glancing down guiltily at the book she held.

'I do, but I love books more. Please don't tell Lady Albinia, I know how she adores her gardens and I would hate to offend her.'

'Of course not. You are more than welcome to use the window seat when you wish, whether I am at the Hall or not. The only time I am afraid the library is out of bounds is when we will be busy with the negotiations in the stateroom, which is through those doors. Other than that you are welcome here.'

He wondered what on earth he was doing, trying to make her comfortable when the last thing he wanted was to have his privacy invaded any more than absolutely necessary. As they watched, the group in the garden turned on to the lake path.

'Well, you have just earned another half hour. My aunt is probably taking them to see what remains of the water lilies on the lake. So, what are you reading? Won't you sit down?'

Embarrassment was often very useful. Now that he was overcoming his initial discomfort he resolved to make the most of hers. People revealed more when off balance and he wanted to know what he was dealing with here. He indicated the window seat again, using his superior height to press her back. She sat down but her eyes narrowed at the manoeuvre. She was a peculiar combination—her expression was cool and calm, but something in the blue depths contradicted that assessment. He stepped back and pulled over a chair, suddenly noticing she held Bruce's *Travels to Discover the Source of the Nile*. The veiled nurse had had a preference for agony columns, he remembered.

'This is a rather unusual choice of reading material. There are shelves of novels in my sisters' parlour next to the conservatory, you know.'

'I love novels, sometimes I think they are the anchors of my sanity. But I love tales by people who have seen the world and been stretched to their limits. I hadn't even realised how much time had gone by.'

Her face had descended into a serious look, but then another smile dispelled it almost immediately. It was like light reflecting off conflicting currents in a lake, confusing hints of forces at work beneath the surface, shifting as soon as the eyes settled on them. Once again his concentration shattered, but the certainty that had struck him when she had first spoken was fading. Her voice was already her own and he couldn't for the life of him remember if it resembled that young woman of six years ago or whether it had been a trick of his own memory. Perhaps he should just ask her...what? *Were you the girl who saved my life? Remember? I'm the idiot who made a fool of himself and asked you to run off with me?*

'That has effectively stifled all conversational gambits, hasn't it?' she said into the silence, the amused self-mockery in her deep voice rousing him from another round of uncharacteristic stupor. He shook his head, trying to keep to the surface of the conversation. It should have been easy, but he felt himself struggling to find the anchor of polite patter that was second nature to him and usually took up no more than a tenth of his mental effort while the rest of his mind was engaged on more momentous matters.

'Does the Princess share your interest in tales of adventure?'

'No, she is much saner than I. We are currently reading Mrs Carmichael's *Hidden Heart*. But you wouldn't like her.'

'Why wouldn't I?' he asked. But his hope that the conviction in her statement might indicate an admission of familiarity faded with her next words.

'Most men despise novels, don't they?'

'Just as most women love them? Isn't that simplistic? I have very little time for fiction, unfortunately, but with two sisters I have been exposed to more novels than I can remember and I certainly don't despise them. Hers haven't come my way, though. Are they any good?'

'I like them; they are almost as good as my dreams.' Her words ended on a little surprised sound as if she had remembered something or merely realised that she was being a tad too honest. She stood up abruptly and handed him the book.

'Thank you for the use of the library and your book.'

He stood up as well, taking the book automatically. Between his bulk and the chair he knew he was impeding her exit, but he wasn't quite ready to conclude this conversation.

'Formally it is my father's library. Why are you convinced it is not his book as well?'

She had to look up at him, her head tilted back, accentuating a very stubborn chin. Then she smiled again.

'I guessed,' she said simply and slid past him in the manner of a child slipping past a strict parent and he found himself turning as if he could capture her scent as she passed.

This time it was his memory that took precedence, just a flash, a moment from when he had still been caught in the fever of the wound, perhaps the first time he had really been conscious of her, or of her scent. He hadn't thought of it since, but the memory had somehow remained—like a soap bubble that had formed years ago about the girl's essence and had only now burst. Wildflowers deep in the woods. At his desk he placed the book on the blotting pad and smoothed unseen wrinkles on the leather binding. It was warm and supple, as leather is after being handled, not surprising if she had been curled up with it in that sunny corner.

Almost as good as my dreams... What a strange thing to say, whether she was that veiled nurse or not. What on earth would she have done if he had asked her to describe those dreams? She might be peculiar, but that would probably have stymied even her. Possibly. Maybe not.

He pushed the book to the edge of the desk. He had work to do before he had to play host to his problematic guests. Whatever she was made no odds. He had a task to complete and that was the sum of his interest in the King's affairs or employees.

Damn Oswald.

Chapter Four

'Mint and valerian.' Lady Albinia smiled, patting the empty spot on the sofa as Christina entered the drawing room in the wake of the King and Princess. Christina sat down with relief, happy to escape another direct encounter with Lord Stanton as he came forward to greet the King. It took her a moment to register Lady Albinia's strange comment.

'I beg your pardon?'

'Earlier today you asked if I happen to grow horsetail and hyssop, but then we were distracted by his Majesty's interest in impatiens and periwinkles for the castle gardens. If you need horsetail for stomach ailments, mint and valerian might do, as well. I am not familiar with hyssop's qualities.'

Christina smiled.

'Thank you, both will do very well. It is actually for a tisane I sometimes prepare for the King when he has trouble sleeping. I saw you have cowslip and chamomile and woodruff which are wonderful. On Illiakos I grow bird's foot and pennyroyal, as well.'

'My mints are mostly down by the lake,' Lady Albinia replied, leaning forward as if to guard a secret. 'They are thirsty things, the dears. My pennyroyal never took, but I shall bring you some spearmint if you like. Very soothing.'

Lady Albinia's faded face was lit from within and Christina almost regretted the topic had ever been broached. Herbs had been her father's passion and she continued to tend the herb gardens he had planted, but for her they were instrumental, not the passionate occupation they appeared to be for Lady Albinia. By her vague expression Christina guessed the current Marquess's sister was very used to spending hours propping up walls whenever events at the Hall required her attendance in the absence of Lady Wentworth herself. In thirty or forty years Christina might become much the same at the Castle. Once Ari married perhaps her herb garden would be all that was left to comfort her on Illiakos. The thought terrified her, but she stifled it.

'That would be very kind, Lady Albinia.'

'It would be my pleasure. So few people appreciate herbs. Flowers are always popular, but most people find herbs rather dull,' she said wistfully and Christina smiled.

'Herbs are often more potent beneath the surface, but even the most beautiful flowers can have hidden depths, like foxgloves, for example. I believe we should judge each plant on its own merits.' She cringed a little at her pedantic response, but Lady Albinia's smile warmed.

'I cannot decide which you are.'

'Which what?'

'A flower or an herb. Usually I can tell right away. You have elements of both. I shall reserve judgement.'

She sounded so serious, Christina restrained her urge to laugh and looked around the room, forcing her gaze to skim past Lord Stanton as swiftly as possible. Even a brief glance told her he was magnificent in evening wear, the contrast of black and white accentuating the austere perfection of his features. But it also confirmed that although she had been too shocked by his sudden appearance that afternoon to assess their encounter calmly, she had been right about one thing—he had changed. Or perhaps *she* had. If she didn't know better she might have assumed this was that man's older brother. Incredibly like him in looks, more virile, but less swashbuckling. Just…different. The alternating sardonic charm, flirtatiousness and irritability were gone, replaced by watchful politeness. For a moment in the library he had even appeared a little confused. He had probably been thinking about something else and her presence had been unwelcome, but his manners had prevailed.

He was still the most attractive man she had met, but at least she hadn't made as much of a fool of herself as she might, especially after being discovered huddled in that corner in her stockings. She flushed again at the memory and pushed it away. She had survived that meeting quite well, certainly better than anticipated. It was a relief that he made no connection between Miss James and his newspaper-reading nurse. And really, why should he? She had been negligible then and was negligible now.

She glanced again in his direction. He stood with the King and Princess, his head bowed slightly towards Ari's who was laughing at something he said, her silver-and-white fan clutched in her hands in a gesture Christina knew betokened excitement. They looked beautiful together, a perfect melding of north and south and at least outwardly it appeared the King might realise his ambition, but Christina couldn't help being worried, and not merely because of the lingering damage to her own heart. Lord Stanton might be leagues beyond any of the men who came to pay court to Ari at Illiakos, but she didn't know if he could make Ari happy. He might have changed, but she remembered bitterness and anger under the flirtatious charm five years ago that she doubted would have just disappeared. None of that was in evidence now, but there was something distant about him despite the charm of his smile and the appealing curiosity he had exhibited while talking with her in the library and which he was clearly exerting on Ari even now. Beyond that something else lay, but she had no idea what it was and it scared her a little.

She drew herself up at that wholly ridiculous thought. He was merely an English diplomat whose only agenda was to secure a treaty with Illiakos. Fear had no place here.

Lady Albinia gave a slight sigh and patted Christina's arm as the butler entered to announce dinner.

'Come along, child, we have a long evening ahead of us.'

Christina followed her into the adjoining room. She was accustomed to splendour after years of the King insisting she accompany Ari to all state dinners, so when she entered the

Stanton dining hall she was impressed, but not cowed. It could clearly accommodate several dozen people, but the central table had been shortened to fit their modest number and the elaborate silver epergne shaped like an eastern temple had been moved to a side table and replaced by a China bowl bursting with flowers. It was a peculiar touch amidst the sparkle of crystal and silver and gold-embossed dinnerware, both modest and lively. Christina thought the arrangement was not only tasteful but clever. It tied the group together in a warm intimacy and masked their antagonistic agendas.

Lord Stanton was seated at one end of the table and the King at the other, flanked by the Austrian and Russian envoys. Christina noted this concession to the weaker parties as she took her seat between Ari, seated to Lord Stanton's right, and the Russian Tsar's envoy, Count Razumov.

Again Christina felt her kinship with Lady Albinia. The older woman sat on Lord Stanton's left, and as he listened to Ari's happy chatter, she occupied herself with her food and a calm oversight of the servants who moved about, placing and removing covers with silent efficiency. Had Lady Albinia ever dreamt of being anything else but what she was? Of a family and home of her own? She had a pleasant face and she was not unintelligent. Had life just slipped past her while she tended her herbs and her brother's family? She didn't appear unhappy, but was that just resignation or true contentment?

'… Miss James? Miss James!'

Christina turned at the King's peremptory use of her name. He was frowning and the envoys were staring at her in surprise and for one mad moment Christina wondered if she had committed some horrid social solecism, but could not for the life of her think of anything she had been doing other than meandering through her own less-than-optimistic thoughts.

'The trade treaty with Naples, you remember, what year did we sign it?'

Christina's shoulders eased. The only social solecism was the King's. Not that he cared it wasn't acceptable to address anyone at the dinner table other than those directly seated by his sides.

'Two years ago in May, your Majesty.'

'Yes, that is right. Was that before or after I went to Rome?'

'A month after your return, your Majesty.'

'That's right. That fellow came, the one with the big ears, what was his name, di Vicenti or something, yes?'

'Signor di Vicenza, your Majesty.' She angled her voice lower, but he merely grinned at her unspoken rebuke.

'What have I said? He was very proud of his big ears, said they got that way from all those years keeping them to the ground.'

Razumov and Von Haas laughed, and without thinking she turned towards Lord Stanton. He was smiling, but there was the same watchful look she noticed in the library and it struck her suddenly that by placing these three men side by side he was not making a gesture of goodwill but setting the stage to gauge their reactions to each other. He appeared relaxed, but she could see the echoes of the tension and intensity that had been so clear in the wounded man of six years ago.

She looked down, her eyes snagging on his long fingers which were idly caressed the stem of his wine glass. With a spurt of alarm she realised she remembered his hands, even the feel of them on hers. They stopped suddenly and she raised her eyes, meeting his gaze. His eyes narrowed, the candlelight throwing gold shards in with the silver, but raising no warmth in them. Convention demanded she look away modestly and if she had been able to think she would have done so, but under his gaze she remembered just how *seen* she had felt, even under those veils. Seen by someone like her, vulnerable and in need, but holding his own need at bay with a ferocity she could never match. She remembered it perfectly—the knife-sharp intensity of his eyes, stripping away everything that kept her safe, forcing her to acknowledge that she had only one regret in her life and that it was that she had not grasped with both hands his impetuous offer that she join him six years ago. He would have regretted it—she was certain of that, and therefore so would she, but at least she would have had more to regret. It was too late, far too late, but it was still there, a slash in the very material of her life—deep and still bleeding.

'You have spent many years on Illiakos, Miss James?' The heavily accented question from the Russian envoy on her right startled her and she struggled to regain her composure.

'I… Yes, your Excellency.'

'Did the lovely Princess speak English before your arrival or does she owe her superb diction to you?'

'She has a natural ear for music, which is useful for acquiring languages. Her French is just as flawless.'

'Not only a lovely but talented young woman. King Darius is to be commended.'

'Indeed. Your own English is flawless, your Excellency. Are you perhaps musical as well?'

He smiled.

'I was sent to an English school at a young age. As a younger son I was marked for a diplomatic life at birth.'

'Ah.'

'Yes, "ah"! I know the English quite well, which has proven useful over the years. They remind me of the Baltic Sea in winter—this perfect cover of ice, sparkling when the sun shines on it, that is your peoples' dry wit, and underneath a chaos of currents that is the real moving force of everything. My father would take me fishing on the ice—the servants chop a hole through the deep cover and we cast our lines into the depths. I remember thinking as a boy that the water beneath looked like the twisting of souls in hell, viscous and luminescent.'

Christina smiled at the descent into the darkly poetic, so typical of the Russians she had met in the King's court. She could not determine if he was merely making conversation or in search of something. Whatever the case, she was grateful for the distraction.

'That is a wondrous image, your Excellency,

but I am not certain I find it complimentary to have my people compared to an ice-bound hellish chaos whose only redeeming feature is their dry wit.'

His smile widened.

'I say this with the greatest admiration, Miss James. The English capacity for self-restraint is legend. Take our friend here…' He lowered his voice and glanced down the table at Alex. 'You would not guess from seeing him today he was the same man I knew five years ago. That was when he was still engaged in the dubious activities many of us were forced to entertain both before and after Napoleon dragged the Continent into such chaos. Those were very different times. Now we have all become sadly respectable. And older.' He sighed and patted his receding hairline. 'But then we were young and rash and a challenge was a challenge.'

'A challenge?'

He focused back on her, a touch of malice in his dark eyes. 'Women do love the scent of a *duello*, don't they? Hard to believe it of our respectable Lord Stanton, but as I said we were all rather more fiery in those days, him more than most. But he is precisely an example of what I spoke of. The moment the balance between chaos and ice was upset, ice won and chaos was banished and the result is our very esteemed Lord Stanton, rising star of the Foreign Office. Had you told me of this development six or seven years ago I would have toasted your fertile imagination. As it is it reinforces my conviction that we Russians could use a little more ice and a little less chaos. As for wit, we have our own brand, but mostly we have our poetry. And our vodka.' He glanced mournfully at his wine glass.

'Don't worry, you will have your vodka, Dimitri Dimitrovich; though you don't appear to need its aid to sink into maudlin reminiscences.'

They both turned to Alex and Christina hoped the candlelight disguised her flush. Razumov didn't appear to share her embarrassment at being caught gossiping about their host, nor did Alex appear bothered about continuing the King's breach of form by addressing them across Princess Ariadne.

'Ah, but vodka makes them so much more palatable, for me at least.' Razumov replied. 'I am afraid Miss James's charm is just as effective to that end as the finest vodka.'

Alex's mouth quirked up at one end, but the same faint question was in his eyes as they settled back on Christina.

'Slowly. Miss James isn't familiar with your particular style of…diplomacy.'

'I presume it is like most diplomacy, a shiny veneer with an agenda beneath it,' Christina replied. It was a little too honest a reply and she smiled at Razumov to take the sting out of it.

'You have a low opinion of diplomats, then, Miss James?' Alex asked.

'Not at all. It requires talent to keep veneer and agenda untangled; I am all admiration for those who do it well. We meet a great many diplomats at court, don't we, Princess Ariadne?'

'Oh, yes,' Ari said. 'There are always statesmen coming to see Papa and he insists we be present for most important meetings. After all, I shall be Queen one day and it is important I understand how to be a good ruler.'

'I am convinced you will be, your Highness.'

Ari returned Alex's smile and Christina's heart stuttered. Her mind was still stumbling over Razumov's words and what they revealed about Alex and she did not need to add jealousy to the mix, especially not of Ari.

'I will certainly try. Father said one key is finding people you trust and listening especially hard when they disagree with you.' Ari's expression sank from seriousness into a grin. 'Which means I listen especially hard to Tina.'

'Unfair. I rarely disagree with you.'

'But when you do, goodness!'

'Miss James has a temper, then?' Razumov asked, a little too hopefully.

'Well, not like Papa. He can make the windows rattle. Tina merely has this *look*. Her eyebrows go up, just a little. It is terrifying. There, you see?'

Christina shook her head and picked up her wineglass, trying not to smile. It was impossible to be annoyed with Ari when she was so clearly enjoying herself, even at her expense.

'Formidable.'

She met Alex's gaze and again felt her stomach clench around a sensation she had not felt for many years.

Ari nodded. 'Yes, that's a better word. Formidable. I sometimes practise that look for when I shall be Queen. Shall I show you?'

Alex transferred his gaze to Ari and smiled. 'Do. Let us see the formidable Queen Ariadne.'

'Well?'

'Well what? I'm waiting,' he said, his eyes softening. Christina tried not to look because this was probably what it felt like to be kicked down a very long flight of stairs, one by one.

'But that was it! See?'

'Are you certain that was it? I must have blinked and missed it.'

Ari giggled. 'Is he making game of me, Tina?'

'I'm afraid he is, your Majesty. Not very diplomatic at all.'

'Well, as Count Razumov pointed out, I am somewhat new to the diplomatic game, Miss James, so you must excuse my deficiencies. Perhaps if you demonstrate your formidable look I shall know what to look for. Or does it only appear when one transgresses? Shall I?'

'It would have to be something big for Tina to lose her temper,' Ari said doubtfully. 'Like the time I ran away and went down to the beach below the castle on my own; do you remember, Tina?'

'I do. You were only seven. You fell asleep behind some rocks and it took us hours to find you. I don't remember being angry, though, merely frightened. I believe your father was doing all the shouting.'

'Yes, but I remember how you looked and I remember being afraid you would leave me. I didn't know you were scared, too.' Ari laughed, clearly embarrassed. 'But this is a silly topic for the dinner table. Not at all the impression a formidable queen should make.'

'I disagree.' Alex said. 'If more people with

power over others' lives experienced fear and need, we might have fewer wars and more compassion for those who had to endure them. I think you do have the makings of a truly formidable queen, Princess Ariadne.'

'Indeed,' Razumov agreed. 'I would toast you, but I am saving myself for this vodka you promised, Stanton. Is it chilled?'

'Of course. It is in the icehouse and will only be brought in when we are ready for it. You and Count Nesselrode trained me well.'

'May the saints and their icons bless your soul, Stanton.'

'What is this?' the King interrupted his discussion with Von Haas and Sir Oswald. 'What are we blessing?'

'Vodka. Chilled. That demands a benediction,' Razumov announced.

'There is ouzo as well, your Majesty,' Alex said before the King unleashed his opinion of the Russian beverage, and the King's lowering brows rose again.

'Excellent. Everything is always clearer with a glass of ouzo in one's hand.'

'Once the ladies retire, of course,' Alex continued, smiling at Ari who pouted charmingly, her discomfort flown. Lady Albinia proved she had been listening closely enough to meet her cue to announce the withdrawal of the ladies while the men lingered over their port and more exotic libations and Christina rose with relief. She might have her share of English restraint, but there was a limit and she had exhausted hers for the day.

Chapter Five

'Yesterday set the stage quite well, don't you think? The vodka was a clever move. I think our Russian friend is feeling a tad less beleaguered.' Sir Oswald polished his quizzing glass as the King and Princess strolled ahead with Lady Albinia and the two foreign dignitaries.

Alex nodded, pausing at the head of the path towards the lake. King Darius and his daughter would be fine without their presence. Whatever the King's hopes for a more personal alliance between England and his daughter, Alex wasn't interested and the very last thing he wanted was to excite unwarranted expectations. He had learned his lesson well. Where he couldn't avoid susceptible young women he made certain they regarded him just as his sisters did.

'With any luck we can have a decent agreement signed in a week.'

'A little longer, I believe,' Sir Oswald replied as they turned back towards the house. 'The general line is clear, but we must pace this. This is the most monumental decision in King Darius's political life, Alexander. He will not wish to be perceived as rushing into anything.'

'I know that.'

'I know you do, hence my surprise at the pace you are setting. Razumov and Von Haas are also still hoping for some more decisive concessions and we must dress the scraps so they can make them look succulent to their superiors. It has been many years since I have had to caution you to patience. Is there something the matter?'

Alex shook his head, resisting the urge to rub at the scar below his ribs; it was humming with discomfort, something that hadn't happened in quite a while. Also for the first time in many years he had dreamt of being back on Illiakos, a veiled woman standing over him as he tried to disentangle himself from a blanket of seaweed while the sea flooded the room.

There was no point in sharing his unease about Miss James with his uncle. He was still both convinced this was the girl and convinced it wasn't. Not that it made any difference either way, did it? Except perhaps to his vanity.

'Did anything strike you as strange about yesterday's dinner?' his uncle asked.

Alex shrugged, wishing his uncle had stayed in London; he was far too perceptive. When he didn't answer, Sir Oswald continued.

'I found the King's choice of appealing to Miss James as an authority on his diplomatic affairs rather telling. I was already a little surprised when Albinia informed me the King insisted on including his daughter's companion-cum-governess in the social events, but now I wonder if perhaps she is a little more than that despite the disparity in their ages. There was an assumption of intimacy even in the way she scolded him. Perhaps you should make an effort to charm the young woman and discover the nature of her hold on the King. I know you no longer like to employ those methods, though it is a sad shame as you were so very good at it, but perhaps judiciously applied… She doesn't strike me as particularly susceptible, though. There is more beneath the surface than above it there.'

Alex looked out over the familiar, orderly beauty of the garden. It was possible Miss James was the King's mistress. He would not have thought it from his meeting with her in the library or from her cool elegance at the dinner, but he had to agree with his uncle that a great deal more was happening beneath her surface than above it. There was nothing about her to draw attention and yet for some unfathomable reason she did. Everything else that had occurred at dinner had been almost tediously predictable, but every time he had looked down the table, his attention had stumbled over her, his mind worrying over the question as it would over a stubborn code.

At the first possible opportunity he would just ask her outright and get this over with. He was allowing the puzzle to become entangled in wholly unnecessary observations, like lingering over the way she drank her wine, of all things, almost feeling the impression of her glass pressing down on her lush lower lip—cool, rounded, smooth. He had found himself raising his own glass, as if he could feel her through that mirrored action. He had put it down and forced himself to return his attention to the Princess and the business at hand, but for the rest of that meal he had remained unnaturally aware of Miss James, as if she constituted a threat to the proceedings, which was ridiculous. It had certainly coloured his response to Razumov's flirtatious nonsense. That final discussion had been far too personal on all fronts. Not something he would normally encourage unless he had a specific objective in mind, but in this case he had none, just this cursed curiosity.

'I'm going for a walk. I need some air.'

Sir Oswald nodded in approval.

'Good. Clear your head. I need you focused to keep all these balls in the air.'

Alex raised a brow.

'I hadn't realised I had dropped any.'

'You haven't. Let us ensure you don't.'

Alex mouthed a curse that almost made his uncle's thin lips stretch into a smile, then he turned in the other direction. He didn't have time to go riding or sink into any new project in his workshop, but he needed a moment of quiet and the herb gardens should be empty.

Except they weren't. He entered through the gate in the moss-covered stone wall enclosing Albinia's extensive herb gardens and stopped. First his library window seat and now Alby's garden. There was surely something wrong about this young woman's tendency to infiltrate places not meant for guests.

She was even kneeling on Lady Albinia's cushioned gardening board by a rambling dark-green plant with spiky leaves and humming to herself, her mouth bowed in a smile. The same sense of discomfort that had beset him last night during dinner returned—she seemed far too present for someone who should be utterly negligible in the scheme of things. She didn't even have the grace to notice him standing there as he inspected her, trying to untangle the problem. She didn't look threatening in the least—at the moment she looked like a painting titled *Young Woman in Herb Garden*. Her bonnet lay on its side by her skirts, its ribbons like outflung arms on the grass. The sun struck through the chestnut tree behind the garden wall in hazy streaks, adding strawberry lights to her mahogany hair. It was gathered in a simple knot, but by its weight he could tell it was thick and heavy, made to be set loose down her back.

Then she would belong in a different kind of painting altogether.

He pushed that thought aside and focused on the problem. She looked different than she had at dinner. The watchful control was gone, as if the warmth and scents of the garden had shed years and barriers, leaving only a young English girl, ready to embrace life wholeheartedly. He had been wrong about her looks, too. She might not be a beauty like the Princess, but under the cool mask was a very feminine invitation she was probably not even aware of since she made no use of it—in fact, so far she had done everything to school it into non-existence. But with her smile, and her hair only loosely gathered it was as evident as the sun warming her contrasting colours.

He breathed in and moved forward as resolutely as if he were cresting a hill with full expectation of meeting a hostile army on the other side. He watched her fingers move through the plant, seeking the paler leaves and putting her clippings into the wicker basket by her side. Time to pull this particular thorn.

'What is that?'

She gasped and dropped the shears, swivelling towards him. He crouched down and fished the delicate scissors from the tangle of greenery. A lemony tang wafted up from it, but underneath was another scent, cooler and deeper, and he had to hold himself back from leaning in to capture it. He handed her the scissors and looked down at the plant, trying to redirect his thoughts.

'Here. I apologise for startling you. What is this plant? It smells of lemons.'

'It is called pelargonium and it is good for all manner of needs, including chasing away mosquitos, though that isn't quite as relevant here as it is back on Illiakos.'

He raised the edge of the linen napkin draped over the wicker basket and a swirl of scents rose, heightened by the sun that warmed the fabric of his coat against his back. It all contributed to a distinct sinking feeling in his stomach—a proficiency in the healing powers of herbs was definitely weighing in on the wrong side of the scales.

'What else have you purloined from Cousin Alby's garden?'

Her smile was as bright and as sudden as lightning and just as potent, but her answer was restrained.

'I have full permission to take what I need, my lord.'

'I am not here in the guise of magistrate, Miss James. My cousin is not in the least possessive about her herbs, but she usually doesn't invite just anyone into her gardens. This is a serious compliment.'

The smile returned and this time it lingered.

'I am not just anyone. Apparently I am neither herb nor flower, or was it that I am both? Whatever the case I think she is studying me and perhaps allowing me into the garden is in the manner of a test. Does she categorise everyone?'

'Usually only those who don't bore her. She won't tell me what I am, which bodes ill for me. People can be a vegetable or fruit as well, you know. Since she told my father he was a turnip, I am rather relieved to be excluded.'

'A turnip? Then I hope I remain a mystery as well. All my expectations will be dashed if I discover I am merely a cabbage, or worse, fennel. I hate fennel.' She laughed, a warm joyous sound that reflected in the warming teal of her eyes. The scales sank further. He remembered that laugh from when he had teased her about her agony columns, inventing nonsensical sequels just so he could hear it. He had forgotten doing that.

Oh, hell.

At least it explained his immediate discomfort upon meeting her in the library. Her voice and her scent must have triggered his memory even if it had not fully broken surface immediately. So Miss James was his little nurse after all.

Well, not his. The realisation was no excuse for his body to transform one form of curiosity for another. Except that he couldn't deny she looked so very right here, her eyes brimming with laughter and her plain muslin skirts rumpled against the grass, but clearly outlining the rounded curves of her thighs and hips and then over that backside she had so innocently exhibited while plumping the window-seat pillows. She was not in the least like the women who he usually made arrangements with, but he couldn't deny he would have been very willing to explore new avenues of femininity if only she had been more experienced and available for discreet liaisons. Though if his uncle's insinuations had any merit and she was the King's mistress she might be quite experienced, though not available.

He dragged himself back into the conversation. Whether true or not it wasn't his concern. Fennel.

'Not my favourite either. I hate liquorice.'

Her nose wrinkled in distaste and he actively resisted the urge to run his finger down that pert line and settle on the still-smiling lips. Damn, he wanted to do something about this. He wouldn't, but it was a sad shame he couldn't.

He lowered one knee to the ground, shifting against the unwelcome rise of pressure in his buckskins.

'What *do* you like, then?' he asked, unwilling to end the conversation quite yet. Even now that he knew who she was, the puzzle remained. Alby and Oswald were right, there was something unclear about her, too much tucked away, but still resonating. 'Perhaps you could offer Alby... Lady Albinia some guidance in her conundrum.'

She tilted her head and gazed at the far wall where Alby's border garden was weaving and bobbing in the breeze like a rainbow tossed about on the waves. A thick wave of mahogany hair was beginning to slip its pins and was resting in a loop against her nape. He wanted to see it shake free and slip down her back. How long would it be? Long…

'I don't think I would like to be narrowed down to just one plant. I wish I could be something different every day. Being named would be like having only one book. I can't imagine that. I need a whole world of books. It's different for someone like you.'

'I think I can understand that sentiment very well. Why do you think it is different for me?'

'Because that is already how you live, isn't it? Perhaps that is why Lady Albinia won't categorise you.'

'You think that is how I live my life? Doing as I will, when I will? It is true I have more freedom than you, than most people, in fact, but a great deal of that is in appearance only. In the end we are all tied down by our duties. There are well over two hundred people dependent on these estates and quite a few more dependent on the Foreign Office's attempts to keep people from succumbing to the often comprehensible urge to kill each other. I might not be a big cog in that particular clockwork, but I take my role there seriously. In the end I do not have a great deal more freedom than most.'

Her eyes moved over his face as he spoke, as if searching for something, and instead of his resentment sparking hers, her expression softened in degrees so that by the time he finished she was smiling again. The breeze picked up, just sifting through his hair and cooling the flush of heat on his temples, but it felt as if she had touched him. Once again it took an effort to focus on her answer.

'They say envy is petty and it is. I had no right to drag you down simply because I wish to climb. I didn't mean to imply you are volatile. It is clear that you are a consummate diplomat and that you take your duty very seriously. But from what we have heard you have certainly had many adventures in your life and you at least have the privilege of choice, even if you don't always exercise it. I do hope you and King Darius can find a solution that will keep Illiakos safe for many, many years.'

The wistful note in her voice weakened his resentment, but he couldn't prevent it colouring his response.

'Are you so worried for him?'

She bent to arrange her clippings in the basket. 'Of course. Especially for Ari…for Princess

Ariadne. I want her to live a long, happy and safe life. I know that may depend on what is agreed here. And Illiakos is my home, too.'

'You weren't born there, surely?'

'No, I was born in England, but Illiakos is my home nonetheless. Home is where one is wanted and needed.'

'If that is your criterion, then a great many people are homeless.'

'Yes, I think they are. I was for many years so I know the difference. For the first ten years of my life I was neither wanted nor necessary to anyone, unless one considers taking the blame for my cousins when they broke something being necessary.'

'I can understand that. I doubt I would have been missed during my first ten years either, except by Alby. What happened then? Is that when you went to Illiakos?'

'Yes, with my father. Ari and the King might be my employers, but quite soon after we arrived at the castle they made me feel wanted, even necessary. That is why I care what happens. Lady Albinia says you have two younger sisters. What would you do if someone threatened their well-being?'

'Remove the threat.'

Her eyes widened slightly at his tones and the

fierceness was replaced with a rueful smile as she returned her attention to the herbs.

'I dare say you would. Well, there you have it. Ari may not be my blood, but she is my family. I know the King is doing this to safeguard her future. He doesn't want her caught in a battle between the Greeks and the Turks any more than you do.'

Alex watched her hands move among the clippings as she spoke, separating them into little bundles. Her fingers were long and elegant, but they were not ladylike—they were too strong to merely clasp a fan or teacup. Hands with a purpose. He remembered those hands touching him… He reached towards them, only diverting at the last minute from the impulse to test the absurd need to feel them against his skin and see… Instead he extracted a twig from her clippings, a long branch with sharp lanced leaves and tiny white flowers furring the tip.

'What is this?'

'Spearmint from down by the lake. Here.'

She took a leaf and crushed it between her fingers and handed it to him and even before he reached out the scent of mint engulfed them, making his mouth water. He grasped her hand, raising it, the leaf still caught between her fingers, breathing her in.

'What is spearmint for?' he asked, not because he was interested but because he wanted to draw out the moment before he put an end to the charade.

'For…for many things. Stomach ailments, irritability, nervous disorders.'

'Is it sweet?'

'Sweet?'

'Spearmint.'

He was so tempted to answer the question himself, taste the green tint of moisture on her fingertips.

'No. Not like the smell until you infuse it and add sugar. I use it to prepare tisanes.'

Her words were sensible, but her voice shook. Her hand as well. He was making her nervous which wasn't surprising. This was not how one acted with virtuous young women. Any properly bred young woman of his acquaintance would have either swooned by now or be planning their bridals. He should let her go, stand up and leave, but he didn't. He didn't even let go of her hand. Instead he pressed his fingers over hers, further crushing the fragile leaf into a dark pulp, raising her hand to capture the scent. Her scent. He had been right—under the effusion of lemon and mint he caught the contrasting currents of wildflowers and something cool, distant.

'Why do you need a tisane? Are you unwell?'

She shook her head, her gaze still on the fingers pressed between his, but he didn't respond yet to the unspoken demand to release her.

'For the King. He often has trouble sleeping.'

'Such dedication. What else do you provide for the King's well-being?'

She tried to pull her hand away, but he tightened his hold. What would she do if he asked her outright if she was the King's mistress? Probably stab him with those scissors. Whatever her external façade, he had heard anger and frustration flash too often in her voice six years ago to believe her truly meek and obedient. She was cool surface and fiery core. He could feel it now, in the tension in the hand he held, the taut-bowstring quiver along her arm, waiting to strike. This was no meek servant. This was a woman with the power to play an ambitious role—insinuating herself into the royal family's good graces, making herself indispensable. The perfect handmaiden draped over a will of steel. She had laid her ambition bare in her own words—she wanted to climb.

He dropped her hand and pushed to his feet. She looked up, the sun striking sapphire contrasts in her eyes. On her knees, with her face raised, she looked both innocent and utterly knowing, Eve caught in the moment of transition after eating from the fruit of the tree of knowledge. He had an impulse to reach out, capture her head in his hands, unravel her hair and lay her down on the grass amidst the tangle of herbs. But he would do nothing of the sort.

'I dare say I should thank you for your nursing skills six years ago, shouldn't I, Athena?'

Caught in the act of rising, she almost dropped her basket, her face suffusing with a very English blush, her eyes widening in shock. Her surprise was so vivid it was clear she had never expected him to recognise her.

'How did you know? Did Ari tell you?'

'No. I don't know which of us should be more insulted by your assumption I wouldn't recognise your voice and mannerisms. Whatever the case, I seem to remember I didn't thank you properly at the time. So at least this is an opportunity to right that wrong.'

She wobbled, as if considering a curtsy and thinking better of it.

'You are welcome, my lord. Now I had better take these inside, they must be prepared while still fresh.'

'Of course they must. Heaven forbid you would fall short in your handmaiden's duties and the King's slumber be disturbed.'

It wasn't in his character to snipe, but her dismissive coolness was aggravating. At least his comment shook her calm, her eyes narrowing.

'I had forgotten how…outspoken you can be. Not what one usually expects from a diplomat.'

He clenched his jaw at the truth of her words and forced himself to smile.

'You are right. I am being churlish. Politicians like to believe they are awake on every suit and I am feeling rather foolish I did not recognise you immediately. I shouldn't punish you for the blow to my vanity.'

'That is foolish. How could you recognise me? I was completely invisible and it was many years ago.'

'So it was. So is your real name Miss Tina James? Or is it really Athena?'

'No, it is Christina James, but Ari… Princess Ariadne was just a baby when I came to Illiakos and she called me Tina and I think that is why the King began calling me Athena.'

'Which do you prefer?'

'I beg your pardon?'

'Which name do you prefer? Or do you just accept whatever name happens to suit your interlocutor?'

'What I *prefer* isn't a currency in the lives of women like myself,' she replied, sudden anger making her voice shake. 'There is what I must, what I cannot bear and, in the privacy of my mind, what I would like. The first two are my boundaries in what is utterly *your* world. The third is the only space where I can exercise any freedom. People like you…men like you have no idea… The very fact that you can speak to me this way, ask me such questions and think you know the answers says nothing about me, but is just another sign of how…how ignorant and arrogant and…and spoilt you are!'

He hadn't needed her stumbling fury to tell him he was being an ass. Whether she was the King's mistress or merely what she appeared made no difference whatsoever. He bent and picked up her bonnet from the grass as he searched for some way to re-establish polite equilibrium, but somehow the words escaped him anyway.

'Your bonnet, Miss James. Perhaps you are not aware, but in England it is improper for a young lady to go outside uncovered.'

She snatched the bonnet and stalked off without a word, the basket swinging precariously, and he watched her until she disappeared.

'I believe I suggested you charm the young woman, not send her scurrying. What was that in aid of?'

Alex cursed under his breath and turned to face his uncle.

'Are you following me, Uncle? Do common notions of respecting other people's privacy not apply to you?'

'I would not be where I am today if they did, though I usually no longer have to listen at keyholes, thank goodness. But I admit to being curious when I heard that particular tone in your voice, Alexander.'

'What tone?'

'An unfamiliar one and one that is out of place in our delicate negotiations. If that young woman is the King's mistress, you have just alienated a potential ally. I am wondering why.'

'I am not accountable to you, Uncle.'

Sir Oswald fingered the ribbon of his quizzing glass, but did not raise it. Instead he smiled.

'Assuredly you are not. You are accountable to Canning and Canning is accountable to the King and the English people. I do not come in to the equation. Come along, I need a glass of wine to fortify me before we return to our discussions.'

'Blast!'

Christina shook her fingers as boiling water spattered out of the kettle she removed from the hob along the edge of the fireplace. It was all her fault. She had been misled by Alex's veneer of politeness and charm before he had shown his true colours. She should not let him upset her—again. He wasn't worth it.

She breathed in the scents of spearmint and chamomile, but their usual calming effects weren't forthcoming. She could still feel the angry flush tingling in her cheeks and up her neck. It had been a long time since she had lost her temper. Years. Six long years. It felt strange, like someone else had entered her and shaken her cage.

She only wished she hadn't stormed off like an outraged debutante. Now that it was too late, she could think of half a dozen worthy retorts to his taunting comments. Not that he showed to greater advantage in that encounter—after his initial charm he had behaved like a cad. It was very clear what he thought of her. Even years ago she remembered he had made some very cutting comments, but she had been so foolishly infatuated she had forgiven and forgotten anything that didn't fit her starry-eyed image of that beautiful young man. And just now, instead of snatching her hand from his, or better yet, administering the slap that any well-born young woman would administer at the liberties he had taken, she had allowed him to hold it and she had even felt an absurd dizziness at the expectation he was about to raise it to his lips. No wonder he thought he had a right to make assumptions about her relationship with King Darius. She had not behaved at all like a proper young Englishwoman.

No, she corrected herself as she brutally crushed dried chamomile flowers and tossed them into the kettle, he had *no* right. Merely because she was to all intents and purposes a servant did not mean he could address her with such disrespect and so she should have told him.

At least the charade was over.

She truly hadn't expected him to recognise her. And if she had hoped he might, her fantasy had usually proceeded along very different lines. He would be amazed, grateful, appreciative, would want to know all about her and how she had found herself in such a position.

Instead he was not just a cad, but an ungrateful one at that.

Well, she was glad. If she hadn't been a fool back then she probably would have seen him for what he was—a spoilt little…well, not so little…pretty boy accustomed to everyone fawning over him. He had probably had countless women falling over themselves to secure the favours of the wealthy, titled, handsome Lord Stanton, heir to a Marquessate. She was glad to discover that he was so very shallow and ill tempered. It would make it easier to bear the next week and then return to her life knowing she had nothing to regret, nothing to pine for. Her girlish infatuation would finally have the ground pulled out from under it and she could pack it away like all first infatuations should be.

She set the kettle to cool and sat back on her heels, scrubbing at the steam that scalded her eyes. Soon she would have to go downstairs again and face him. Not that he was likely to pay her any more attention than he had during yesterday's meal. He had made his point.

He would likely flirt with Ari again and she would sit there and do as she was told, precisely as he had said, because she had no choice. Well, she would do so with her head held high. She had nothing to be ashamed of and she would not allow him to belittle her. Handmaiden, indeed!

She was done with Lord Stanton.

Chapter Six

'Lady Albinia? Lord Stanton requested that the ladies join the gentlemen in the music room.'

Lady Albinia glanced up from her stitching as the butler entered the ladies' parlour where she and Ari sat listening to Christina read Mrs Carmichael's latest novel.

'Dear me, did he?' Lady Albinia sighed. 'I thought they would enjoy a working dinner today. The Russian envoy smokes those dreadful cheroots that quite ruin one's appetite.'

Watkins's narrow face shifted into the faintest hint of a smile.

'I believe I overheard his Majesty mention he wished for some distraction before resuming their discussions, Lady Albinia. Shall I inform them you will be down in half an hour?'

'No, we shall all do fine as we are. Unless you

wish to send word you are resting, my dear?' Lady Albinia asked Ariadne, a touch hopefully.

'This is so typical of Papa to send for us when we are about to discover the hero's true identity!' Ari objected. 'What do you say, Tina?'

Christina laid down the book, schooling her nerves. Lord Stanton had to be faced eventually.

'I think we should go if your father needs help, don't you, Ari? We can return to our hero later.'

Ari sighed, but bounced to her feet. 'Very well. Am I presentable?'

'You are lovely, as always. Just let me straighten your fichu. There. Now we are ready.'

At least outwardly, she added, as they approached the door to the music room, wishing she had taken the excuse Ari had offered after all. Luckily she was given no chance to be cowed. The moment they entered the room the King strode forward.

'Ah, good. Ari, Miss James!'

'Yes, your Majesty?'

'Sir Oswald is curious about Illiakan culture. Ariadne will sing some of our ballads and you will accompany her.'

'Oh, Papa, no!' Ariadne murmured, blushing to the roots of her hair and looking charmingly flustered.

'No false modesty, child. You sing beautifully. Come, Athena.'

Christina stood, turning towards Ariadne on the pretext of arranging her shawl. At least she was not alone in this predicament—there was some comfort in sharing misfortune.

'Best we do it. He's nervous,' she whispered encouragingly for Ari's sake and the Princess's dark eyes widened and then crinkled in a smile.

Sir Oswald, at a glance from his nephew, moved to accompany the Princess while Alex himself moved to the pianoforte, opening the wooden panels painted in elaborate scrolls of blue, cream and gold.

'Can you play without music, Miss James? Shall I send someone to your rooms to fetch it?' he asked quietly. There was the slightest hesitation in his voice and she could almost imagine there was an apology there, but when she looked up she could detect nothing in his gaze that would support her wishful thinking. His grey eyes were watchful and his face expressionless. She forced herself to look away.

'No, thank you, Lord Stanton. Her Highness knows the words.'

'That wasn't what I asked,' he replied, but moved away, leaving her feeling she had somehow misstepped. Again.

'Demeter?' Ari asked as she leaned her hand on the pianoforte and Christina nodded. She kept her eyes on Ari as the Princess sang of Demeter's grief at the abduction of her daughter Persephone. The guests might not understand the words, but she was certain they could hear the pain in Ari's clear voice. It always made Christina's heart ache though she hardly knew for what. She had no reason to be homesick; her only home was Illiakos and she would soon be returning to it.

'Píra tin agápi mou kai me áfise keno.'

You took my love and left me empty.

She knew why the King had insisted. The picture Ari presented as she stood by the pianoforte, her dark eyes glistening with emotion, her slim figure weaving with the words, was all the King could have desired to showcase his daughter and attract the discerning attention of someone as experienced as Lord Stanton.

She glanced over at him and experienced the same sense of dismay at the change in him from the young man of six years ago. Unlike in the garden, his face showed no emotion at all, it might as well have been the bust of a Roman general, looking out into the distance but giving nothing away. He certainly didn't appear to be caught in rapt admiration of the Princess's beauty. But in the split second her eyes didn't do as they ought and look away, he met her gaze and she saw past the blank mask to a shifting scenery—there was anger, confusion and something tucked behind them that reminded her of the pain she had heard in his fevered mutterings. The memories were so sharp that instead of the coolness of the ivory keys beneath her fingers she felt the heat of his skin as she had tended him. It was so sudden and clear she almost lost her place in the music before she lowered her eyes to her hands and remembered where she was. The applause was just a rumble, muting her thudding heartbeat, and the ivory keys thrummed in memory of the last notes of the goddess's lament.

The King rose, embracing his daughter with pride.

'But she can sing as well in English and Italian, can you not, my star? Athena, Mozart. That pretty aria you were practising before we sailed.'

Christina nodded. This time she would not look up. When the aria was done, she stood before the King could command another performance, but there was no need. Alex was already signalling the removal of the men back to the library to continue their discussions and he moved to lower the cover on the pianoforte. She resisted the urge to flee, waiting for him to withdraw, watching his hands on the lacquered wood.

His hands were more expressive than he was. She had noticed that back on Illiakos. They showed tension more faithfully than his features, but they were also unusually gentle for a man. Like that moment in the garden when he had taken her hand in his—it hadn't been a rough grasp in keeping with his hands' size and strength, but more an embrace, enveloping her with warmth, firm without exerting any pressure. Her skin had found its own shape against his, moulding to it like an animal burrowing into the inviting warmth of another's fur. For a moment she had even felt the most natural thing would be if she leant forward and…

Thankfully she had done nothing so foolish, and thankfully he had shown his true colours. But watching them now as they secured the cover and rested for a moment on its polished surface, she found it hard to cling to her disdain. What would happen if she placed her hand on his? Would the planets stop spinning on their axes and the world come crashing down? Perhaps that would be a relief.

'That was lovely,' he said after a moment, and though his words were complimentary his tone was still clipped, bringing her back to reality.

'The Princess has a beautiful voice,' she replied.

'Yes, she does. No wonder the King is so proud of her. She is a charming young woman—beautiful, intelligent, well-mannered and talented. Why has she not yet married? Surely at nearly eighteen there have been offers?'

Christina ignored the snake of jealousy writhing at his fulsome praise.

'There have, but King Darius is an affectionate father. He prefers her to find someone she cares for rather than force her into an alliance of pure convenience.'

'Commendable for a parent, rather difficult for a sovereign. I seem to remember he mentioned his own marriage was arranged with a woman he had never met before the wedding. Is that why he is so determined to indulge his daughter?'

'I believe you should ask him these questions yourself, Lord Stanton.'

His eyes narrowed.

'That is rather what I am doing, isn't it? Since the two of you seem so much in accord.'

'Are you insinuating I have no independent thoughts of my own, Lord Stanton?'

'Not in the least. I am of the opinion that you have a great many independent thoughts, Miss

James, but you also have the enviable skill of putting them aside when they don't serve your will. Or your purpose.'

'And you appear to have a great many opinions, Lord Stanton, not all of them well founded.'

He surprised her again, the coldness melting away in a sudden smile.

'Aren't they? What a blow to my vanity. I always considered myself a skilled reader of the human psyche. I am developing a habit of offending you, aren't I? Which is bad form when I am very grateful for your nursing skills all those years ago. The doctor who saw me on my return to London said I was luckier than I deserved. I told him luck didn't come in to it, or rather that luck had some assistance from a very methodical and stubborn nurse.'

'I was only doing my duty.' It was an ungracious reply to his attempt to placate her and she made an effort to match his lighter tone. 'But I am very glad you suffered no lasting damage. We were quite worried at the beginning.'

He moved to lean his hip against the corner of the pianoforte, his bulk forming a barrier between her and the room.

'Were you?'

'It would have been very inconvenient if you had died.'

His smile widened at her prim tones.

'I remember you saying something of the sort at the time. I am glad I could oblige. It would have been rather unfortunate if my demise had sparked an international incident—not the kind of exit a diplomat would wish for.'

'But you weren't a diplomat then, were you?'

He smoothed his hand over the top of the piano.

'Why do you think that?'

'I don't, I didn't… It merely occurred to me that if you had been a diplomat then surely you would have told us your name at the outset. Count Razumov also said…'

'Razumov said?' he prompted and she plunged forward, too curious to be careful.

'He mentioned he knew you in Russia, five years ago, and that was after you were on Illiakos and that you were not yet part of the Foreign Office.'

'I thought Dimitri had a hard head, but clearly he needs to watch his intake of wine.'

'He did say those were different times, but he was merely making conversation. I apologise, I should not have said anything. I do not wish to cause trouble.'

'You may not wish to, but you have a knack for it, Miss James. I wonder what it is about you that pries open doors and mouths best left closed. A very useful talent in my calling. Razumov had best beware of you; I certainly shall.'

'You make it sound as if I deliberately encouraged indiscretions.'

'Everyone wants to feel they are meaningful and curiosity is a powerful form of flattery. Just as you were curious about those sad souls from the agony columns. I am convinced they would have loved to have you listen to their tales of woes.'

'You remember that?'

'It may have failed me a little on our reunion, but in general my memory is particularly retentive, Christina James.'

The rumble of his voice over her name worked its way under her skin and she moved away from the pianoforte, but he placed his hands on his hips and she stopped, eyeing the now tiny gap left between his elbow and the wall. To push by would be not only undignified but would involve precisely the kind of contact she didn't want… or did, which was worse. Her face was already tingling in embarrassment and her body in anticipation. Would he move away if she walked right at him? Something in his eyes told her not to test him.

'Why didn't you tell me who you were the

first day in the library?' His tones were clipped, making it more a demand than a question.

'It honestly never occurred to me you might recognise me.'

'That still doesn't answer my question. Why not just say, "Hello, we were never formally introduced, but my name is Christina James and I saved your life six years ago"?'

'I didn't save your life. In any case, I am here merely as companion to Ari…to Princess Ariadne. It wouldn't be proper for me to presume upon our previous acquaintance.'

'So it is a matter of propriety? That is rather a peculiar position to take given you had no problem tending to me when I was half-naked.'

If he had grabbed her by the hair and plunged her whole into the hot springs of Mistras the instant rush of heat could not have been more potent.

'Lord Stanton!'

He smiled at her outrage.

'Yes, there's the fire I remember. I was beginning to wonder whether my memory was at fault or whether those veils had smothered it completely.'

'I only wore those veils while tending you.'

'I wasn't talking about those veils and you

know it. Something about you doesn't make sense.'

'Simply because you aren't intelligent enough to understand something doesn't necessarily imply it doesn't make sense.'

He laughed, shifting from foot to foot and even more definitely sealing her into her corner.

'Do you know what my friends tell me my worst quality is?'

'How easily you are offended when you discover you don't know everything?'

'No, but you are close. My friends have often warned me of the pitfalls of curiosity. It tends to spark when I notice something is off the true.'

'Off the true?'

'When something is incongruous, not quite in line even though it should be. When she was young my sister Olivia used to hide her books under cushions all around the house. You could always tell where they were by that suspicious bulge.'

'And I have suspicious bulges?'

His gaze mapped her, slowly, and his smile shifted, his lips just parting. 'Not a suspicious bulge amongst them. But perhaps I should check more thoroughly.'

'Perhaps you haven't changed *that* much,' she

muttered and took a step forward, hoping he might cede some ground. He didn't.

'That doesn't sound like a compliment.'

'It wasn't, it was an observation. You don't strike me as someone in need of compliments. May I pass?'

'What are you running from this time, Miss James? I can hardly pose a threat here in this civilised setting.'

'This time?'

'You've run before. On the island. In the library. In the garden. It's quite a blow to my vanity. Usually women are heading in the other direction. There, that's better, I knew if I tried hard enough I could make you smile.'

'Why would you want to? More vanity?'

'Precisely. And curiosity again.'

'Well, there is nothing to be curious about—I am not running from you.'

'From yourself then.'

She had forgotten what this particular brand of anger felt like. The last time she had felt it had been six years ago.

'Of course *you* would know all about running from oneself.'

Her instinctive counter-attack hit its mark and the speculative humour faded.

'Yes, I would. The difference between us is

that I don't deny it, I embrace it. Enjoy your stay at Stanton Hall, Miss James, and thank you for your charming recital. You are clearly a very talented performer.'

He bowed and turned before she could think of anything intelligent to say, or think of anything intelligent at all.

Chapter Seven

'You keep fondling them, you know.'

'What?' Christina dragged herself out of her reverie and turned to Ari. With her curls tumbling over her shoulders and her feet tucked under her on the sofa, she looked more like a girl than a grown woman.

'Those statuettes,' Ari explained and Christina frowned at the row of figurines she had gathered from around the room and placed on the windowsill. It looked like a peculiar woodland classroom, with animals all gathered, each poised on the verge of action, but frozen in the act of listening to a rotund woman seated on a bench, her legs planted wide with a basket between them and a babe's head peeking out from the woven surface. It was an extraordinary achievement in such a small figure, both touching and slightly comical.

'Especially that one.' Ari added, pointing to the roughly hewn kneeling woman Christina was holding. 'You used to do that with Emma, the doll with the blue dress, remember? The one with the curls and the little bow that kept slipping.'

'Of course I remember. You gave it to me the week after I arrived on Illiakós. It was the first gift I had ever received and I remember being terrified your father would be angry at me for accepting it, but I loved it. I don't remember fondling it, though. I hope no one but you saw me do it. People already thought I was odd.'

'Not odd, I just don't think they ever knew what to make of you. But you were always different when it was just us in the nursery. When other people came you were very Miss James. But when no one else was there, you used to hold Emma tucked against you even when you were doing something else like reading me a story or helping me with my lessons. That's why I remembered when I saw you with those statuettes, it was like being back all those years ago.' Ari touched her fingertips to her eyes and Christina went sat by her and took her hand. 'Everything is changing now I am of age,' Ari continued. 'I don't think I am ready. I wish we could stay the way we are. Just you and I and Father. We are happy together, why must anything change?'

'Some changes you will likely welcome. I know how much you would like children of your own some day.'

'Oh, yes, I do. But I wish I could have them without a husband.'

'Well, that might be a tad unconventional. Some day you will meet a man you will trust and with whom you will wish to have a family.'

'Don't you wish for that, too? I'm always afraid one of Papa's courtiers will lure you away.'

There was apprehension in her voice and Christina felt a stab of pain somewhere under her heart. One of the King's prisoners had almost lured her away, but she had been too much a coward to risk losing everything she had for a man's temporary whim. No, not a coward. Sensible. She had no reason to regret that. Where would she have been if she had answered that siren's call six years ago? Certainly not at Stanton Hall. He would have left her with sufficient funds to live out her life somewhere as he had no doubt provided for other discarded mistresses. Materially safe and emotionally destitute, far from the people who really loved her, who needed her and gave her meaning after a long and lonely childhood. She had been smarter to reject him than she had ever realised. There was absolutely nothing to regret.

'None of them has ever tempted me and I am too old for folly now, Ari. I shall make do with loving your children.'

'I know it's selfish, but I'm glad. I don't know what I would do if—'

At the sudden knock on the door Christina instinctively clutched the figurine to her chest as if it was to be wrested from her by force. But it was only Lady Albinia who stuck her head around the door.

'Oh, good. You are awake. I was wondering if you would both care to come with me to visit some friends. The men are all busy so we are free to enjoy our own pursuits which is quite a relief. Men can be so wearying.'

Ari choked on her morning chocolate, her eyes brimming over with laughter as they met Christina's.

'We would be delighted, Lady Albinia.' Christina replied.

'Good. I shall meet you downstairs in half an hour.' At the door she stopped and turned. 'That *is* lovely, isn't it?'

For a moment Christina had no idea what Lady Albinia meant, but she followed her eyes to the wood figurine. She turned it over, feeling the long swirls of curved hair slide under the pads of her fingers.

'It is. I apologise for handling it, it is just so…' She had no idea quite how to define it.

'Oh, please do. I think wood wants to be handled.'

'I have seen many others besides these around the Hall,' Christina said a little more confidently. 'That exquisite stag sheltering under the tree, the one in the hallway, and the wooden bowl with the running dogs etched all along the inner rim. And others. I can tell they are all by the same hand; are they part of a set?'

'Oh, no. Not really. If you like I shall show you my favourite; it is a little boy, reading a book. Very clever. But not now. I shall see you in the garden in half an hour, then. Wear something stout as we shall be crossing the field.'

'Stout?' Ari asked as the door closed.

'For the mud. It rained last night.'

Ari sighed. 'It is very strange, this English weather. One moment it is lovely and the next cold and dreadful. I miss Illiakos. At least one knows that in summer there will be not a drop of rain to ruin one's plans.'

Christina glanced outside the window to the scudding clouds.

'I rather miss this changeable weather.'

'How could anyone miss such boring greyness?'

Christina turned at the unaccustomed sharpness in Ari's words and Ari reached out contritely.

'Father said you might be homesick if we came. I know I am being unfair, but I'm so scared you won't want to return with us. I am being a shrew, forgive me, Tina.'

'Oh, my dear, you have nothing to be sorry for. It is true part of me misses England, but the only home I have is with you. Your marriage is much more likely to change our lives than any choice of mine. It is natural that your father will wish you to marry soon.'

Ari snorted.

'Oh, yes. He thinks he is so subtle. I know now he brought me here because he hoped I would charm Lord Stanton and bring him back to Illiakos. Really, sometimes Father is quite medieval.'

Christina tried very hard to keep her voice neutral. 'You don't like Lord Stanton?'

'I like him very well, he has such understanding eyes and he makes me laugh, just as I remembered. But I do not wish to marry him and I certainly don't think he wishes to marry me.

Why should he? He likes his life and what he does and all that would end if he married me. Father thinks being ruler of Illiakos must be the best fate any man could aspire to, but truly, he is a little blind.'

Christina went to sit by her, pulling the younger woman to her.

'You are so wise, Ari. Do please marry as you will.'

Ari turned her face into Christina's shoulder.

'I told you, I don't want to marry for many, many years yet. And I wish you could stay with me always, Tina. I cannot imagine my life without you. You are more my mother than my own ever was.'

'That isn't fair, Ari. She was very ill.'

'As was yours. That is why I am glad we found each other.'

'So am I. Now come, let's put on our stout boots and see what Lady Albinia has in store for us.'

What Lady Albinia had in store was a coven.

At least that was the word that sprang to Christina's mind as she looked around the parlour at Briar Rose Cottage, adorned with hanging bouquets of drying herbs and a row of cast-iron covered pots bubbling on hooks in a fireplace that spanned almost the whole back wall.

There were four women of differing ages, sizes and styles seated on chairs also of all ages, sizes and styles and in various states of repair. The room was infused with a delicious smell of blackcurrants, probably from the large kettle gently steaming on the hob of the enormous fireplace.

'Ladies, I would like to introduce her Royal Highness Princess Ariadne of Illiakos and Miss James.'

There was a rustling as the women rose rather hesitantly and curtsied like a chain of ducklings on a wave. The eldest, an elderly woman dressed in a simple cotton dress and apron, raised an eyeglass attached to a long riband slung around her neck and inspected the newcomers. Christina inspected her in return, surprised by a flickering of memory, though she doubted she had seen this woman before.

'Which is which?' The woman's rough tones were definitely suspicious and Ari edged closer to Christina, but Lady Albinia was unfazed.

'This is Princess Ariadne and this is Miss James. May I introduce Lady Penelope Attwood, and this is Mrs Dunston, Matty Frake and her daughter Mary Frake. Is that your blackcurrant tea brewing, Mary? Marvellous. I brought comfrey, Matty, as you asked. Where is there a chair? Ah, here.'

Christina and Ari allowed themselves to be manoeuvred on to a sofa that had been vacated by Lady Penelope, a pretty young woman with blonde curls who smiled shyly and limped over to sit next to the woman Albinia had called Mrs Dunston, who had the face of a melancholy poet but the bosom of a lusty tavern wench.

'What are they, then? Herbs or flowers?' Matty Frake demanded, clearly disregarding considerations of royalty.

'Princess Ariadne is most definitely a flower, a hibiscus, I think. Miss James is both. Or perhaps neither.'

'Nonsense.' Matty Frake snorted.

Lady Albinia shrugged and held out her cup as Mary dispensed tea, her eyes sparkling through the steam as she filled Christina and Ari's cups, beaming with obvious pleasure at the drama of newcomers and a princess to boot.

Christina sipped slowly, savouring the berry-flavoured tea as she glanced around the room. Her eyes fastened on a little bowl on the table by her side and she gasped.

'Look, Ari, it—' She stopped as everyone turned at her exclamation, her cheeks heating in embarrassment. Lady Albinia followed her gaze to the bowl and nodded.

'It is the twin of the bowl in your parlour at the Hall, but this one is with kittens. Matty is not fond of dogs.'

'Big lummoxy beasts,' Matty growled. 'No manners. You can take a closer look,' she added grudgingly and Christina picked it up. Just like the puppy bowl, a row of kittens were carved into the inside border, caught in lunges and leaps after a ball of yarn. Whoever had carved it had done so with a great deal of love.

'It's exquisite,' Ari said admiringly.

'Made it for me.' Matty beamed, her smile transforming her plump cheeks. 'Ned taught him. My husband. He was a carpenter and a fine hand with wood. Could fix anything, build anything. "Matty", he'd say to me, "you can bring a baby into this world and ease a woman's pain and that's your gift. Mine is to look at a tree and see a table fit for a king".'

'Your husband made these figurines and the bowl?' Christina asked, suddenly realising why Matty looked familiar—she had just seen her, carved into that figurine of a woman with a basket and babe between her knees. 'Is he alive?'

'No and no, girl. He was a carpenter and made chairs and tables and houses. But he taught…'

She pressed her mouth shut and crossed her arms. 'He could have if he wanted to, but he didn't. He was a busy man, my Ned. Not that he didn't always have time for young 'uns.'

'Are you a midwife?' Ari asked with interest.

'Yes, that I am.' Matty replied. 'Like my mother before me and her mother before her. I don't know what happened before that and it's no concern of mine. My daughters are as well, like Mary here. Susan married a foreigner from up north, but she's still birthing, too. I birthed his lordship, I did, since the fool of a doctor was laid up with a broken leg.'

'Lord Stanton?' Christina asked.

'The same. It was a difficult birth and I don't mind saying I was worn to the bone by the end of it, almost as much as poor Lady Wentworth. Young bodies aren't always ready for birth and she was slim as a whippet and scared as a mouse. Wouldn't push, just cried. Finally had to lay down the law with her and out he came.'

'He must have been a beautiful baby,' Ari said dreamily and Matty's greying brows shot up.

'No baby is beautiful when it's pushed into the world, especially not one that was caught midway for longer than it ought. Ugly as a monkey and twice as cross. His father took one look at him and hurried out, pale as a sheet. Men!'

Christina couldn't help smiling and feeling more than a little sorry for the young Lady Wentworth. And her son.

'He were beautiful soon enough,' Matty relented. 'Stubborn as a boulder, though. When he wanted something he didn't scream and yell, he stayed put until he got it, didn't he, Albinia?'

Lady Albinia smiled in assent.

'To be fair he never asked for much, but when he did, or when he thought something was right, it is true he wouldn't budge.'

Matty chuckled. 'Never seen a boy of four stare down a grown man like that. A regular frost would set in with them ice eyes of his and his lordship would buckle like a rich man's belt. But there weren't none gentler with Lady Anne or Lady Olivia. I knew all was well the day Lady Anne was born. Ten years old and a little man already, but he went as soft as a moss pillow as soon as Lady Wentworth told me to put the baby in his arms. You remember that, Albinia. He'll be all right in the end, I said, didn't I? And I was right, wasn't I?'

Lady Albinia's smile was wistful, lost in memory. Christina's mind conjured up an image, too. Wholly fictional but inescapable—a young boy, with hair a shade lighter but already tall, his face cut in serious lines. He was gingerly holding a cloth-swaddled bundle and for a moment she could almost see the softening Matty had described, curving his eyelids, just touching the corners of his mouth. Love.

She leaned forward, placing her cup on the table, sure the thudding of her heart and the burn of tears in her eyes must be obvious to all.

'We never gave credence to those Wild Hunt tales around here, did we, Mary?' Matty continued.

'No, Mother, of course not,' Mary replied with a smile. 'People love a good story, that is all.'

'What tales?' Ari perked up and Matty snorted.

'Nonsense about his lordship and his friends making pacts with the devil simply because any but a blind woman would see they are as handsome as sin and because no one could best them on a horse. Duels and fisticuffs and all manners of nonsense. Wild Hunt indeed. I've seen all too many virtuous women fall prey to men without scruples and I know the difference. I know there was that scandal with that fine foreign lady five years ago, but if you asked me it was more her doing than his, and if it wasn't, he never did the like again after that, did he? Sometimes it takes a scare to get people on course. Straight as an arrow ever since, weren't he? And we certainly never had to worry his lordship would send any business in the direction of the likes of Mary and me.'

'Matty,' Lady Albinia cautioned. 'Perhaps that is not quite the right topic for our company.'

'I don't know about that. If more girls knew the way of the world, there'd be less of the sad side of business for us, isn't that true, Mary?'

Mary sighed. 'It is always hard to see a young woman's life set off its course when a little knowledge might have kept her at its helm. But then I always remind myself that Father wouldn't have been born if not for just such a mistake on the part of Grandmother Frake, Mother, and so we both have reason to be grateful for at least some slips. Good may sometimes come from bad, as the saying goes. Would you care for more tea, Miss James?'

Christina smiled at Mary and nodded, wondering how to coax these women into more indiscretions regarding Alex.

'Mary and Matty birthed all my children,' the melancholy Mrs Dunston said into the silence, a surprisingly childlike smile lightening her features and making her abundant bosom less discordant with her face.

'Mrs Dunston is the vicar's wife,' Lady Albinia explained. 'The vicarage is very low lying, so it benefits from much humidity. Good for watercress.'

'Yes, but my nasturtiums have never taken.' Mrs Dunston shook her head, the poetess-on-a-windy-cliff look returning and Christina groped about for something reassuring to say.

'I love watercress, but we could never grow it on Illiakos. It is very arid.'

'And stony,' Ari added.

'What a shame.' Mrs Dunston brightened. 'Do please come see my garden if you have time. I have quite the largest pumpkins in the valley, you know. Mr Dunston is very proud of them.'

Christina sipped her tea to hide the laughter bubbling up into a smile and met an answering sparkle in Albinia's eyes.

'I would love to visit your garden,' she replied.

'Perhaps when you come to visit the church? I overheard Lord Stanton discussing the possibility with Mr Dunston just this morning. You will come, won't you, Miss James?'

The lady cast a rather frightened look at Ari as if unsure of the protocol for addressing royalty and Christina nodded.

'We would be delighted, Mrs Dunston.'

'Well, that's settled.' Matty patted her knees.

'Now we have some business to attend to, don't we, Lady Penny?'

'Oh, but surely if we have guests…'

Lady Albinia intervened before Matty had a chance to.

'I think her Highness and Miss James would be happy to hear what you have learned, Lady Penelope.'

'If you are quite certain… Well, I received a letter from Mrs Brigham in Teignmouth in response to our query about arrowroot and…'

Christina and Ari listened as Penelope read out the letter discussing the various strains and applications of arrowroot.

Christina absorbed it all, wondering if her life might have been like this if she had remained in England and perhaps eventually met a man and married. Her parents' families were considered respectable country gentry even if they weren't affluent, but her father's choice of profession would have no doubt limited her prospects. Who did doctors' daughters marry? Another doctor? A vicar? Would she have grown watercress and pumpkins like the abundant Mrs Dunston?

It was all too late and far away. She was luckier than so many women—she had found a loving, giving family and even when Ari married she knew she would always have a home at the castle. Not just a home, a family. It was selfish to expect more. She would probably never realise her yearning for someone to cherish and love as she had Ari, a little boy or girl of her own, that warm fuzzy cheek resting on her palm as they sank into sleep. Or the even more unspoken yearning for someone to stand by her over that child. Not just someone…

Ari and King Darius would never forbid her from marrying someone at court, but she knew they preferred she stay as she was, part of their little family in a world where they were allowed few intimate connections in the maze of court life. She was their haven as much as they were hers. It would have to suffice.

'That was lovely!' Christina exclaimed to the fields that stretched out around them on their way back, replete with tea and lemon seed cake.

Ari nodded. 'Is it true? Did Lady Penny's father really divorce her mother?'

Lady Albinia didn't appear at all fazed by the enthusiasm in Ari's question, despite its impropriety.

'We do not often discuss this, but since Lady Penelope herself confided in you, I see no reason not to. Yes, she was only a babe when it happened. Her mama was best friend and cousin to Celia Sinclair who became Lady Wentworth, Alexander's mother, and they were both married rather young and were not happy, to say the least. It was Almeria, Penny's mama, who encouraged poor Celia to follow her heart and run off with that horrid Phillipe Moreau. Unfortunately, not even Celia's death in that snowstorm discouraged Almeria and she ran off with her own lover a couple months later saying she was determined to live her life as Celia could not. At least she waited until spring and her lover was an Englishman who did marry her after the divorce since there never was a crim. con. trial. If there had been and he had been called as party to the divorce, he could not have married her, you see.'

Christina did not see but nodded, too caught up in the tale of Alexander's mother to care much about the luckier Almeria.

'Did you know Lady Wentworth well, Lady Albinia?'

'Quite well. The Sinclairs lived not far from here and though many of the Sinclair men, aside from Oswald, were shockingly scandalous, everyone thought Celia might yet escape the taint. She was so beautiful and so adored, besides being quite an heiress, too, having inherited her mother's fortune. I wasn't among her particular friends, but I met her often once Mama decided she would do for my brother Arthur, Lord Wentworth, that is. Celia's father was ailing and he didn't care to wait until her debut so they settled her marriage before she had even turned sixteen. They were both far too young. Even at the time I knew it was wrong, but what could one do? It was considered the match of the Season, you know. There had just been a dreadful scandal with the eldest Sinclair boy, so the Sinclairs were buying some much-needed respectability and the Stantons a fortune in land. Alexander was born soon after and for a while it seemed she might be happy at least as a mother but then Grandmama sent Alexander to school and that year everything went wrong. That dreadful Moreau came to stay with the Falsteads. An *émigré*, they said. Dispossessed. But it was clear he… Well, never mind. Suffice it to say Mr Moreau thought it was in his interests to secure the favours of the sister of Sir Oswald Sinclair who was already knighted and a rising star in the War Office. I remember Moreau well. He was ten years older than Celia and charming as the devil himself. She was bored and lonely and poor Arthur was no match for him. I love my brother, but he can be a trifle…pedantic.' She sighed.

'How old was Lord Stanton when this happened?' Christina asked.

'Eight. He was home for Christmas, poor boy. It was quite, quite horrid. I was here as well. And Sir Oswald. Alexander found her letter first and took it to Oswald who went after them. For two days we heard nothing. Poor Arthur was distraught and it was even worse when the news came. He was in such a state Mama took him away after that and I went with Oswald to care for Alexander until he returned to school.'

'Oh, the poor boy!' Ari exclaimed, reflecting Christina's emotions, but not her outrage.

'I don't understand. Didn't your brother take Lord Stanton with him? He was only eight, he must have been devastated. How could a parent abandon their child like that? It is unforgivable!'

Lady Albinia met her accusing gaze, her eyes softening.

'Parents are still humans, Miss James. They cannot always be pillars of strength. Oswald and I took good care of Alexander until Arthur recovered his strength. Arthur met the present Lady Wentworth while he was at Harrogate and they were married a couple of years later. Once she was installed at the Hall she insisted on Alexander and I returning, though he continued to spend a portion of his holidays with

Oswald. Eventually he came to care for his new mother very much. She is a good woman and has brought a great deal of warmth and calm to Stanton Hall.'

Christina turned to the ripening field, her eyes stinging. There was nothing apologetic about Lady Albinia's words, nor should there be, but Christina could only think of the boy who had been betrayed and abandoned by both his parents and had only been invited back to his own home by the woman who had taken his mother's place.

'He is very lucky he had you and Sir Oswald,' she murmured, surprised to see a flush rise over Lady Albinia's pale cheeks. The older woman hesitated a moment as they proceeded down the path and for the first time Christina saw something revealing and very human under the placid surface.

'It has not been easy. He was always so bright and handsome, so like his mother, the quintessential Sinclair. Everyone watched and talked behind his back, expecting him to make her mistakes, and he knew it. He kept himself deep inside. It was only with his friends he could be himself. Not even with me and his uncle, though I tried. Sometimes I wonder if that was why—'

She broke off as the ground shivered and

Christina looked up, wondering if this was an earthquake like the minor shivers that sometimes caught Illiakos.

'That's Thunder,' Lady Albinia remarked calmly, bending to pick some dandelions from the verge along the field.

Ari frowned and glanced up at the sky which had cleared during their visit and now sported no more than three stringy clouds drifting lazily above them.

'I don't think it can be thunder.'

'Thunder. Alexander's horse. He has probably been out around the estate with Mr Filbert, the steward.'

The sound was more evident now, just past the copse of trees at the edge of the harvested field. Now Christina could make out the pounding of the horse's hooves over the shiver in the earth.

'You can tell which horse it is just by the sound?' she asked, annoyed at the way her heartbeat rose to match the tattoo of hooves.

'Dear me, yes. No one else would dare ride hell for leather like that through the estate. It used to be the despair of his father.'

'Not any more?'

'Well, riding like a bat out of hell, as Arthur puts it, is marginally preferable to being kidnapped, shot at and generally disappearing for months on end without word. At least if something happens, we know where he is.'

'Papa didn't really kidnap him, you know. It was all a dreadful mistake,' Ari asserted loyally as she scanned the hill behind the copse.

'Oh, I wasn't referring to that incident. We didn't even know about that until much later. The last time he was kidnapped was three years ago while helping the American navy negotiate the release of slaves from the Berber King. Luckily by the time the news reached us, he had escaped and we had only a week to worry.'

It was years ago, but Christina's heart constricted with fear at the thought of Alex in danger. And this had come after he had moved into the safer territory of diplomacy. Despite his protestations of sobriety and duty, she knew there was still a wild side to him that was in conflict with the rest of the dutiful façade and it both frightened and excited her, not least because it sounded an echo deep within her.

Just then the horse and rider appeared over the rise and she stood and watched alongside Ari and Lady Albinia. Even had she not known who it was she would have felt a thrill of excitement at the sight. Thunder was ebony black and he burst from between the trees like a giant raven about to soar into the sky. His hooves hardly scratched the ground, but the rumble reached them through the earth, climbing up Christina's legs to merge with her rising pulse. Alex sat on the horse as if they were made of one element, like the mythical centaurs decorating the walls of the ancient temples on the far side of Illiakos. Then they disappeared behind a line of chestnut trees and slowly the ground settled. Her pulse took longer to calm.

'I wish I knew how to ride.' Ari sighed. 'We only have donkeys on Illiakos, it is too rocky and steep for horses.'

Lady Albinia smiled at her.

'Shall I ask Alexander to teach you?'

'Oh, I couldn't ask that. He is so very busy.'

'Once the discussions are complete there will be a few days before you leave for Southampton. There is nothing to be afraid of, I assure you. Alexander taught both his sisters and Penny as well after she recovered from her fall. She was quite terrified of horses until Alexander took her in hand and now she has a pretty little pony of her own to take her around. I shall ask him.'

Ari's natural modesty was clearly doing battle with her inclination and she finally grinned.

'I should like that. You must come, too, Tina.'

She couldn't help the images, of riding side by

side with Alex, galloping across the fields, her hair torn loose by the wind, laughing with the joy of the speed and power of the horse beneath her. And then another image, his hands rising to grasp her waist, lowering her to the ground beside him, moving towards her…

She bent down to pick some poppies, hoping her flush would pale by comparison.

'There is no need to include me, Ari. I rode often as a child at my uncle's home and I dare say I can still hold my seat. You go.'

'Dear me, it has grown quite hot today.' Lady Albinia fanned herself with her handkerchief and resumed walking. 'Good for my lavender, but the basil will need some extra care. Come along, we shall have some soothing mint tea just as you have shown me.'

Chapter Eight

'Frigates...with an "i". Ships! Not free gates, Stavros! This is impossible.' The King's raised voice heralded his return. Apparently all was not going smoothly downstairs.

'I assure you, your Majesty—' Stavros began to say, but the King's voice cut him off.

'Athena!'

'What now?' Ari murmured.

'We shall soon find out,' Christina replied as the parlour door burst open. 'Yes, your Majesty?'

'Athena, you are coming with me. Stavros here needs a rest from taking notes in English.'

'I beg your pardon?'

'Why do you look so shocked? You take notes for me at the castle when foreign dignitaries come to negotiate, no?'

'Yes, but that is different. This is England.'

'Exactly. This is England, you are English and the notes should be in English, not translated into Greek. It is my foolishness. The Russian and the Austrian sit there with their tame secretaries and I, whose whole future depends on ensuring it is all resolved just as it ought, must dig my way through these mistakes. It is too late to find someone I can trust who can act as secretary. Soon the Russians and Austrians leave and I must decide what will go into this treaty. I need someone I can trust. Now. So tidy your hair. You have half an hour before we continue downstairs.'

The door closed behind him and Ari sighed.

'I wish I could come, too.'

'I wish you could do this instead of me,' Christina muttered, annoyed at her childish anticipation at the thought of seeing Alex.

Alex almost dropped the document he was holding as the King entered with Miss James in tow and guided her towards where the secretaries' desks were set slightly apart from the main table where he sat with the other envoys.

'My secretary has hurt his wrist so Miss James here will continue,' the King said. 'She often takes notes for me in English. You may sit at that desk there, Athena.'

The other secretaries looked even more shocked than the Russian and Austrian envoys. They were men like Stavros or Alex's own secretary, Charles, whose livelihood it was to serve the political interests of their masters. The only one impervious to this unorthodox development was Sir Oswald, who smiled and addressed Miss James.

'If there is anything you need or if you wish us to repeat anything, please do not hesitate to ask. Charles, do please ensure Miss James has whatever writing implements she needs.'

'Thank you, Sir Oswald.' Christina smiled at him, the tension about her mouth lessening.

'You are most welcome, Miss James. Good. Shall we continue, your Excellencies?'

Alex sat, angling his chair so she would not be directly in his line of sight.

If the morning had been uphill work, the afternoon was a slog through knee-deep mud as he actually had to exert willpower to concentrate on the details being assessed. He never depended on Charles for remembering the details of an agreement, but as the afternoon progressed he realised he would have to review Charles's notes to ensure he wasn't missing anything. As they hammered out the particulars of naval rights and trade concessions he could have sworn he could distinguish the particular scrape of her pen on paper and even, under the oppressive smell of Razumov's occasional cheroot and the smells of wine, ink and tension, the scent of wildflowers.

Finally Von Haas sighed and leaned back.

'Mercy, your Majesty. We have made reasonable progress, Lord Stanton, but I believe I need to rest this ageing mind of mine. Perhaps this is a good point to adjourn until tomorrow?'

Alex tried not to show his own relief.

'An excellent idea. It will give everyone an opportunity to review what has been achieved thus far. King Darius, if your secretary is not able to resume his duties, perhaps you would like for me to arrange for someone from the Foreign Office with the requisite skills? We are not far from town and they could be here first thing tomorrow morning.'

Christina stiffened in the act of gathering her papers, but other than the now-familiar tightening of her generous lips she showed no reaction to his suggestion. The King, however, frowned.

'There is no need,' the King stated. 'Miss James is perfectly capable of taking notes and she is completely trustworthy. As you said, we will likely only need one more day.'

'I am sure she is, I am not implying anything

about her skills or trustworthiness, but secretaries are trained to be accurate and to note even the most minute of details. A great deal of damage can be done by the misplacing of a single digit. I believe someone who is experienced in ensuring all the particulars are registered would be more appropriate, for your own interests.'

And mine.

The King's frown disappeared and Alex was surprised to see it replaced by a look of pure mischief.

'You think so? I will wager that Miss James's eye for particulars will surpass that of any of these men.'

That caught the attention of the others. The three secretaries stopped in mid-motion and Razumov's bushy brows arced up towards his balding head.

'A wager? What kind of wager?'

'There is no need to—' Alex began, watching the mix of consternation and anger darken Miss James's blue eyes as she glared at her employer, but the King interrupted.

'I wager that Miss James will remember more numbers on a written list in an allotted time than any of your secretaries. What say you?'

'Your Majesty!'

The King turned at Miss James's protest, his grin wholly unrepentant.

'What? You must uphold the Illiakan pride, now, Athena. Razumov—you will write a list of random digits, let us say fifteen of them, on a sheet of paper, but do not let anyone see until we are ready. Then all of these fine young men, and woman…' he bowed towards Christina '… will each write as much as they can remember. In order. The results are to be reviewed by us.'

'What are we wagering over?' Von Haas enquired, his mournful eyes brightening at the promise of sport. 'Aside from honour and curiosity?'

'I hardly think this is the right setting for wagers, your Excellencies.' Alex tried to intervene, hoping his anger wasn't as obvious as it felt.

'Nonsense,' Razumov dismissed, his eyes also alight. 'Fifteen digits, you say? But there must be a limit in time.'

'Naturally! Let us say a slow count to ten?'

Count Razumov laughed.

'Done. Sit down, my fine fellows, and Miss James, of course,' he ordered the secretaries. They complied, but Miss James was the last to obey, her eyes fixed firmly on her desk.

Alex suppressed a curse. Usually the foibles of the men he dealt with didn't bother him. Men in power were notoriously quixotic and loved to parade, and the King's conceit was an unusually mild one compared to some of the scenes Stanton had had to witness over his years of diplomatic dealings. There was no reason whatsoever to feel so furious.

He directed a glance at his uncle, hoping he would somehow think of a way to stop this nonsense, but Sir Oswald responded with an almost infinitesimal shrug. The message was clear—as his uncle had said, this was as much an emotional as a practical decision for King Darius. If he wanted to play some games to relieve the tension as he readied himself to take the plunge, so be it.

'I know what we should wager.' Razumov announced, inspired. 'A bottle of the finest vodka!'

'*If* you win,' the King concurred. 'If I win, a bottle of ouzo.'

'Cognac for me,' Von Haas said. 'Shall we?'

Alex abandoned the attempt to look away from Miss James. She wore the dress she had worn earlier that day when he had seen her and the Princess through the stateroom windows returning from their walk. It was a pale-yellow gown with darker-yellow flounces and delicate lace-like embroidery all along the bosom and it struck a sapphire light into her eyes. Or perhaps that was the simmer of temper. Right now her gaze was no longer meekly lowered. It skimmed around the table and returned to the King without a word or gesture, but that calm assessment dimmed the jollity slightly and the men straightened in their chairs. This rise to attention didn't calm Alex one bit. It wasn't respect that commanded the response, but a very male fascination with the girl's imperiousness. He felt it himself and would have been very glad if that was all he felt. It was becoming a nuisance, having his body rush into avid attention every time she entered a room. Hell, every time his mind wandered in search of her.

'It is only a bottle of spirits and his Majesty's pride, Miss James,' Von Haas offered reassuringly. 'So you needn't feel the weight of the world on your charming shoulders.'

The King snorted and waved a dismissive hand. 'Come, write down those numbers, Razumov.'

Razumov contemplated Christina, his dark eyes skimming over her before pulling a sheet of paper towards him.

'All four of you, stand up and turn your backs,' he said and there was a scuffling as the secretaries did as they were told.

Alex's hand tightened on his glass as the

room faded away, leaving just the sight of the girl standing with her back to them, her profile half-averted towards the window, swaying slightly as if listening to an internal tune, her lips parted, chin raised. She would stand like that waiting for a kiss, dreamy, expectant, already weaving passion into the air around her. Alex shifted as a shiver of something like fear contracted his muscles.

Razumov concluded his scribbling and raised the page.

'Will you count, Sir Oswald? Good. You can all turn around now.'

The four turned. Stanton counted out the all-too-brief seconds in his mind until Sir Oswald raised his hand and Razumov lowered the page, placing it face down on the table.

'Write down what you remember.'

The King sat back with annoying smugness as Sir Oswald collected the four pages from the secretaries and Alex was caught between the conflicting wishes that she not be humiliated and the need to see the King humbled. He watched as the four sheets were placed face up on the table and Razumov turned over his own.

'Ha! Did I not say so? Ouzo! There is nothing quite like it,' came the King's victorious cry.

Charles had come close, with thirteen out of

the fifteen digits. Sir Oswald reviewed them again, quizzing glass extended as if there might yet prove to be some mistake.

The other men inspected Christina with an even greater intensity while she stared at some point on the wall, her lips still tight. In the silence Alex could feel the same *frisson* as had shook him pass like a wave around the table in the face of the woman on exhibition before them. There was nothing provocative in her stance, but the mere act of performing at their whim and for their pleasure was a flag to these bulls.

More than ever Alex wished he had never agreed to allow the King to come to Stanton Hall.

'May I ask how you did that?' Sir Oswald enquired.

The King waved his hand as if it was obvious.

'Colours. Her father told me about this skill of hers. Very useful.'

'Colours?'

'Explain it to him, Athena.'

She turned towards Sir Oswald and the defiance in her eyes faded a little at the inviting smile in his.

'Numbers and letters have colours when I see them in my mind. It makes memorising easier.'

Her voice was hardly above a murmur, like a child admitting to a misdemeanour. Alex wasn't in the least surprised to see his uncle's usually impassive face light up with interest.

'Fascinating. And very useful. I met a musician once who said he saw musical notes in colour and that playing music was like watching a painting dance. Most fascinating indeed.'

'It is indeed a peculiar talent, young woman,' Razumov mused, his dark eyes roaming over her again. 'Do you understand Russian, Miss James?'

'I am afraid not, your Excellency,' she replied correctly, but without the warmth his uncle had elicited.

'A pity. You put me in mind of a favourite poem of mine. I do not know it in its English version but in Russian it goes thus: *Ona khodit v krasote, kak noch…*'

Alex had never liked Byron's poetry and Russian made it only a little more bearable as Razumov's voice moved between the guttural rasps and the warm liquid sounds of the language. But in Christina's presence it reached its full glory—she became that dark-haired beauty described in the poem, the failing light of the afternoon sun was her starlight, her essence almost liquid, weaving and flowing. Her shoulders sank as she listened, the tension seeping out of her with the music and rhythm of the words, her mouth softening.

A mind at peace with all below,
A heart whose love is innocent...

He gritted his teeth as Razumov finished, but she smiled, her face transforming as her composed mask fell away.

'That sounds beautiful... Is it a Russian poet?'

'No. One of yours. Byron.'

Her eyes lit, completing her transition to beauty. Of course she would like Byron. All women liked Byron.

'Oh! Which poem?'

'It is called "She Walks in Beauty". I thought it appropriate when faced with such a vision.'

Her eyes narrowed, and once again the light utterly faded from their teal depths. She curtsied, her eyes flicking upwards towards him, and Alex felt them like a sting.

'I am glad you did not find my performance contemptible, Count Razumov. Enjoy your bottle of ouzo, your Majesty. Good evening, gentlemen.'

Her swift exit was followed by another moment of silence, then Sir Oswald signalled to the other three secretaries who dutifully filed out in her wake.

Von Haas chuckled as the door closed behind them.

'There is a temper there, without a doubt, despite her demure look.'

The King grinned as well.

'True, but like Vulcano it only rumbles and refuses to erupt. Athena is not merely goddess of wisdom, but also of war, yet Miss James refuses to embrace that side of her nature. Believe me, I have tried often enough to goad her into a reaction, but English phlegm wins every time over her Latin temper.'

'What she needs is some vodka.' Razumov laughed aloud at his sally.

'What she will receive while a guest in my home is respect.' Alex kept his voice calm, barely. He felt a little like a volcano on the simmer himself.

The three other men hastily laughed away their descent into bawdiness and Sir Oswald raised his quizzing glass briefly at Alex, dragging him back from the verge of his temper.

'I think we have achieved enough for today, gentlemen,' Alex continued, more calmly. 'With any luck another day should suffice to cover all our needs and then you may depart to confer with your Ambassadors, Count Razumov and Graf Von Haas, and see if there are any issues which remain outstanding before we finalise the treaty.'

As the other men filed out, each to their room, Alex lingered and was still standing by the table when Watkins entered, hesitating on the threshold.

'Shall I clear the glasses and refill the decanters, my lord?'

'Yes, thank you, Watkins. And air the room please, it is stifling in here.'

'Of course, my lord. Shall I send a maid to assist Miss James? Or perhaps ask Lady Albinia?'

Alex paused by the door at Watkin's strange question.

'What do you mean? Has Miss James not returned upstairs?'

'No, my lord. She did indeed approach the stairs, but she then turned towards the conservatory instead. Perhaps the smoke has rendered her unwell?'

'Perhaps. There is no need for you to send anyone, Watkins, I will ensure she returns to the Princess.'

* * *

Beyond the glass walls of the conservatory the sun had already sunk behind the low bank of clouds at the edge of the forest and the lake sat still and grey, redeemed only by a faint and fading pearly gloss. He had seen this view a hundred times. This was his home and one day it would be his legacy. It made absolutely no sense for him to feel he had entered a foreign land.

At first he did not even see her, she had tucked herself between the urns of flowering plants by the far glass wall and it was only the shimmer of her yellow dress through the dark-green foliage that gave her away. She either did not hear him or did not care because she remained as still as the plant until the last rays of the sun suddenly burst through a rip in the clouds, transforming her skin from ivory to cream and raising a golden sheen on her hair, like sun glinting off obsidian. The lush red-and-peach flowers behind her made the whole tableau resemble a tapestry and she a medieval maiden caught in the moment of yearning for some long-lost knight, wistful and tragic.

He might not like Byron, but right now the poem Razumov had recited was dancing through his unsettled mind—it was not yet night, but those lines might have easily been written for Christina James. Except for the last three lines—this young woman's mind was clearly not at peace and her relationship with the King might be far from innocent.

'Are you unwell, Miss James?'

'If you have come to comment on my performance or deliver more demands, then go away.'

More of the poem crumbled. Serenely sweet she was not. The ice maiden was melting fast into a rock-spewing volcano.

It was her tension, even more than his, that held him there. Whatever she was, she was upset. The least he could do as her host was calm her before he sent her to her room.

'I shouldn't have allowed that,' he offered, aware of the weakness of his apology. Apparently so was she. Her shoulders rose and fell.

'What difference does it make? It all serves your purpose, doesn't it? All this charming male camaraderie just makes King Darius easier to manipulate, doesn't it?'

The truth of that only made it worse. But her concern for the King sank its teeth deeper into his control. He tried to rein in his resentment, but the words came out anyway.

'Does he often do this? Have you jump through hoops? What else do you do at his command, Athena?'

'Don't call me that!'

'Why not? Is that his exclusive domain? Does he own that as well?'

'I am not King Darius's property. I am no one's property!' Her voice was always deep, but her denial came out almost as a growl.

He gathered his scattering control and tried to correct course.

'Miss James…'

'No. You… This is all *your* fault!'

'Mine?'

'Yes, if… Oh, never mind.' She moved past him, but he caught her arm.

'What do you mean it is all my fault?'

'I mean nothing. I. Mean. Nothing.' She tugged at her arm with each punctuation, but he just grasped the other one as well. Her skin was firm and warm under his fingers, he could feel her pulse, hard and fast under his thumb.

'That isn't true.'

'What on earth do you know about it?' The incredulity in her voice was so powerful he almost let her go. 'You were *born* to mean something! Lord Stanton, one day Marquess of Wentworth, with your fingers deep in all these international pies, able to shape and change the way the world is going… I am not one of your diplomatic tasks, don't you *dare* try to pacify me!'

She tugged again, but he wouldn't let her go. He couldn't. His hands were moulding themselves to her arms. Becoming acquainted with the texture of her skin, claiming it. He had wondered what lay behind her veils and here it was—fire, need, demanding. He had been right about her—under her proper façade she was probably like Vera Vidanich, like his mother. Dangerous. But his whole body was humming with the release of a suppressed need to act, to touch, to take…

He had watched many disasters shape and form in politics. Sometimes it was possible to intervene and deflect their progression, sometimes there was nothing to do but stand back and watch and then pick up the pieces. Except that for the first time in five years the disaster in the making was of his own doing.

He should avoid her like the plague. He shouldn't listen to the urge to apologise for what had happened in there, to soothe her and ease that frustrated pain that was already all the warning he needed that this woman was trouble. Could he so easily have forgotten the damage he had inflicted with Vera? How mere chance had prevented him from being to all intents and purposes a murderer?

But even in Vera's case his actions might have

been misguided, but his motivations had at least been altruistic. Here his only intent was to take what he wanted and finally put to rest the niggling frustration that had lingered ever since Illiakos. The most sensible course of action was to put this desire aside. Eventually it would dissipate; these urges always did. He softened his hold and his hands ran down from their clasp on her arms, but snagged on her fisted hands.

Let go.

He breathed in, his mind confounding his good intentions by embellishing her image onto the clearing in the forest where the bluebells were most abundant in spring—a Venus with mahogany hair and lush curves spread on that green carpet, the tiny blue flowers shuddering against her soft flesh, outlining her, buoying her like water.

As he stood there, his mind miles away and utterly with her, it was the most natural thing in the world to touch his lips to the shadow of the veins at her wrist, breaking through the cool scents of lavender and mint to her—to the warm wildflower concoction that had tantalised him six years ago. It was wrong that it should linger so long in his mind and he felt a shudder of fear as it occurred to him he might never be free of that scent.

Let go.

He couldn't do it. As in a dream his mind was shouting orders and his body did as it willed. His lips brushed over the mound just below her thumb, his tongue sweeping gently over that curve as it ached to do elsewhere. Her pulse thudded just below the surface of her skin, each surge asking him for something more.

'Christina.'

It was a mistake to speak her name. She breathed in, twice, her hand relaxing in his. It wasn't surrender, not even an invitation, but it swept over his crumbling defences. 'I'm sorry.'

He had no idea what he was apologising for—failing to protect her, for the obvious privilege of his existence in contrast to hers, for his disdainful thoughts about her, or for what he was about to do. Probably the latter.

She wasn't a child, he rationalised. She could walk out of the conservatory and he wouldn't stop her. She was still standing there, after all, and that in itself was a choice.

As for himself, he was in no danger of losing ultimate control so he shouldn't make more of this than it was. It was merely a kiss, to put to rest a foolish old fantasy. A quick kiss and he would send her upstairs to safety. That was all.

* * *

Christina felt the tension in his hands as he cupped her face, their heat, the shift between the smooth and rough texture of his palms. She knew he was going to kiss her. It was inevitable. Finally.

She stood as still as possible as he brushed a finger down the curve of her cheek, but she couldn't help the way her eyelids sank as his finger stopped at the corner of her mouth, or the shift of her head towards that contact. He met it, his hand rising to spread along her jawline, his thumb pressing on the pucker of her lower lip as if to silence a protest. When she remained silent it shifted, grazing her lips, the sensation lingering, a burning mark. It made no sense that something so simple could be more devastating than she had ever imagined a kiss to be and he had not even begun. She couldn't take her eyes off his mouth, the beautifully carved lines, softening as she watched. Her whole body softened, obeying an unspoken command, tension turning inside even as her skin became pliant, warm, heating the air around them.

She should protest—she didn't want to be appeased or silenced and that was clearly what he was doing. But her pride shrivelled and faded as his head descended towards her and her eyes drifted shut without any conscious thought at all. Her body was gathered as before a blow, her pulse ringing through her like a struck bell. She felt his breath a moment before the feather brush of his lips, a sweep of warmth, soft as the finest silk, but it struck at her like the clash of two flints, a cascade of sparks bursting over her lips and spreading deep inside her.

His hand slid over the curve of her waist, holding her against him as if she might float away, which was close to what she felt as she waited for what was to come. But he just held her there, his lips slanted over hers, wreaking unbearable damage just by the warmth of his breath and the shift of his flesh on hers. She could feel the resolve gathering in him, the tightening of his fingers on the curve of her hips. He was about to pull away, to make this embrace nothing more than an overly familiar apology.

No. For once she was going to take what she wanted and everyone could go to…to the devil! Herself, too, if need be.

She leaned into his hands and breathed. She didn't need to know what to do because her body clearly did. Her lips parted, her lower lip sliding against the gentle parting between his until she felt the moist pucker catch against the smooth, heated surface of his upper lip, that rigidly cut, perfect line. She tasted it, the tip of her tongue tingling at the contact. It tasted like nothing else, a veneer of cognac over a deeper flavour that echoed the scent she had treasured ever since Illiakos, comparing and eliminating all men but him. His presence had lingered with her all those years ago and now it was a thousand times worse. Now she could feel him and taste him as well and it just fed her hunger. She wanted…she *needed* more.

His mouth parted against hers, but she knew it was to voice a denial and she couldn't bear that, not yet. Her hand rose to his nape, anchoring her as she rose on tiptoe, her lips pressing against his to stifle his rejection.

'Please…'

For a moment he remained rigid as a statue against her, even his breathing seemed to stop. But when it came, his surrender to her plea was so absolute it shook her to her core.

'Christina.' Her name melted against her mouth in a rough groan, as with one arm he pulled her waist against him, his other digging deep into her hair, each finger pressing into her scalp as he showed her precisely what a kiss was meant to be. Not a civilised English taste, but a methodical demolishing of her defences, or what was left of them.

She hadn't known this was what she wanted. Her dreams of gentle kisses, mouth against mouth like the brush of a butterfly's wing against a petal, had nothing to do with this. This was animal, deep, demanding and scorching. It was like the half-naked boys plunging off the cliffs on Illiakos, slamming into the water between the jagged rocks, risking everything for the exhilaration, the dare of feeling alive. It was mad, dangerous.

Intoxicating.

'I want…'

His hands moved roughly over her dress, dragging the muslin over her thighs and hips. There was a fury of need there and she felt its mirror in her.

'What do you want, Christina?'

It wasn't a question. He was going to show her. She knew it. One hand was wrapped deep in her hair, his fingers warm and insistent against her scalp as he nipped and suckled and plundered her mouth, the other hand shaping the slope of her hips, her backside, gathering her towards him. She felt the hard slopes of muscle beneath his coat and she was back on Illiakos, her hands on his bare shoulders, pressing him back, but caught in the revelation of their bodies. Oh, God, she wanted to feel him again, her hands ached with it…

And then it stopped. He was a statue again, his hand still warm against her nape but as rigid as a wooden puppet. Her mouth opened in protest, but then she heard the voices coming from the hallway as well.

'Are you certain she went upstairs, Watkins?'

'Quite certain, Lady Albinia.'

'How peculiar. I must have just missed her. Thank you, Watkins.'

'You are welcome, Lady Albinia. Goodnight.'

Her hands fell away as he moved back, coming into contact with the cold glass behind her.

'Bloody hell.' He half-turned away and the curse was so English she almost laughed. 'I never should have… Bloody hell. You must go upstairs or Alby will hunt you down. And probably shoot me if she finds…' He ran his hand through his hair, rumpling it and making her wish she could do the same. She was tipsy with the need to touch him so she closed her eyes, blocking him from view.

'I am sorry, Miss James. That was unpardonable. I never should have…' He ran aground again, but she finally managed to gather herself together. Miss James.

'Neither should I. Goodnight, Lord Stanton.'

She moved past him with as much dignity as she could force into her shaking limbs. The length of the conservatory felt endless, but finally she was in the hall and thankfully met no one during her retreat.

Chapter Nine

There had been many points in his life Alex had faced and overcome adversity and felt he had thoroughly deserved whatever accolades he gathered. In the present case steering and managing the conflicting demands of three empires and one obstinate pawn wasn't easy, but the participants in this particular meeting were all sensible men and understood the need for compromise, so he doubted anyone would consider this his most challenging hour.

But it wasn't the political challenge that was testing his resolve. Not even the scouring of his conscience and common sense at his abject stupidity in the conservatory the previous evening. He had paid the price for that with a night of dreams that alternated between disaster and even more aggravating pleasure. He had woken early, exhausted, painfully aroused and cursing fate. But a cold bath, a long gallop and a pot of coffee had cleared his mind and he had felt moderately prepared to face the challenges of the day, not least of which was the humiliation of facing the author of his discomfort scribbling away at her desk while he tried to conclude the negotiations.

But he had not reckoned on that lock of hair.

No matter how often she tucked it behind her ear, that dark, silky tress escaped. Sliding slowly, first to rest for a while against her cheek, and then, according to some laws of nature as yet unexplored, it suddenly swooped down and settled against the pale skin above the bodice of her rose-muslin dress, curling at the tip like a kitten's tail, until, with a faint sigh, her fingers disciplined it again. He began waiting for that sigh as well, the parting of her lips and then the way she teased her lower lip with her teeth as she secured her hair until its next bolt for freedom.

He kept his mind as firmly as he could on matters of state, thankful they were proceeding so smoothly and were not requiring the best of his skills, because if this was a battle, he was losing. He could no longer prevent the reflexive tensing of his body as the inevitable slide began, the way his eyes followed the curve of her cheek as the hair slipped over it, as if it was his own flesh subject to that caress.

This time she broke the pattern, catching it before it slithered over her breast and contrarily he felt a surge of resentment at the interruption.

He shifted, angry at his absolute loss of sense. It had been bad enough to lose all decorum and kiss her in the conservatory last night, but he at least had the excuse, poor though it was, that she had done nothing to stop him. She wasn't a child and it was only a kiss. Inappropriate, but it was hardly the end of civilisation. In a week the treaty would be signed and they would be gone and that would be the end of it. It was as simple as that.

At least it should be. This inability to focus on his work because of a lock of hair was nothing short of ridiculous. Pathetic.

Von Haas raised his pocket watch, his mouth puckering into a faint popping sound, and Alex snapped out of his descent into folly. He leaned forward, reviewing the list before him and then glanced at his uncle.

'I think we should take an hour to refresh ourselves before we continue, don't you, gentlemen?'

Razumov stretched his arms above his head

and cracked his neck, as if he had been the one scribbling away so industriously.

'A marvellous idea. I think I will take my cheroot out into the garden and stretch my legs. I always think better after a constitutional.'

'Indeed.' Von Haas tapped his own documents together into a neat pile and motioned for his secretary to take them. 'It is always good to establish some distance before taking fateful steps. Too many mistakes in history have attended a lack of distance.'

Alex nodded. That observation was all too true and particularly relevant at the moment.

'Well, then, gentlemen, Miss James. We shall return here on the hour.'

The men filed out and Alex waited by the door, but Miss James did not rise from the desk. She looked up after a moment as if surprised he was still there, the line between her brows pronounced. She was clearly wary of him after last night, which was hardly surprising.

'If you don't mind, Lord Stanton, I would like to remain here a few moments to review what I have written so far.'

She ducked her head over her notes, clearly blocking him from view, and he sighed and left the room.

* * *

When he returned ten minutes later she was still there and she glanced up at his entrance, her hand rising to push back that offending tress. That as much as anything drove him forward. Even if his apology wouldn't be appreciated, at least it might solve his immediate predicament.

'Not done yet?' he asked as he came to stand by her desk, leaning one hand on the desk and the other on the back of her chair, enjoying the marvellous view of her décolletage gained from this angle. With regret he forced his gaze away, focusing on the paper on the desk, and he spoke before he could consider the wisdom of his words. 'No wonder you have to review your notes. Can you actually read what you are writing? Or is it in Greek?'

She tucked her hair firmly behind her ear and frowned at him, but a faint quiver at the corners of her mouth reassured him that he might have hit on the right means of smoothing over the incident of last night quite by mistake.

'It is in English and it is perfectly legible.'

'Barely. If you are an improvement on Stavros, I wonder that he still employs that poor man.'

'Perhaps you should borrow your uncle's eyeglass, my lord. You are exhibiting classic signs of the onset of myopia.'

'What signs? Aesthetic discrimination?'

'I admit my hand was a little fatigued at this point, but a child could read this.'

'Maybe a child could, but I'm struggling. What is this…*limbs*? When did the negotiations enter the bloody phase? I thought we were being admirably pacific.'

'Not limbs! It says *timber*! We were discussing…'

'I know what we were discussing, I was here, remember? Here, give me that.'

He plucked the quill from her hand and crossed her 't', scanning the rest of the page, half-wishing there were many more mistakes for him to linger on. She clasped her hands in her lap like a scolded pupil and her arm was so close to his he thought could feel its warmth through his sleeve. He moved the corrected page aside, exploiting the motion to bridge that inch of space between them for a brief moment. She wavered, as if about to move away, but she didn't and he straightened, slightly ashamed of himself. It was a juvenile act, hardly worthy of an awkward schoolboy, but it still sparked a wave of both satisfied and frustrating pleasure. He was supposed to be lightening the mood, not digging the pit deeper.

'We are close to finishing, aren't we?' she asked and he nodded.

'I would say another couple of hours, perhaps a little more. Unless one of them decides to throw a tantrum at the last moment. Just a little longer and you are done. Your arm must be exhausted. If you need more rest, you have only to say.'

His transition to solicitude did what his teasing taunts had failed to do. She looked down, but he saw the stain of her blush across her cheekbone. It firmed his resolution to follow through on his impulse. He reached into his pocket and extracted the wooden comb.

'Here. This is in lieu of an apology for my… inappropriate behaviour yesterday. My apologies to you don't seem to fare well so I thought a more concrete token would be preferable.'

He placed it on the desk by her hand, resisting, barely, the urge to touch her hair.

'What is this?' she asked, staring at the comb as if it was an exotic insect.

'This is a comb. A common female accessory most often used for—'

'I can see it is a comb, Lord Stanton,' she interrupted but the quiver once again undermined the severe line of her mouth, 'and it is very lovely, but it is not mine.'

'I know that, I borrowed it from my sister's room. Perhaps your penmanship might improve if you don't have to spend so much time battling your hair.'

Making her blush was a mixed pleasure. He enjoyed the initial kick of lust it sparked, but he should really space out his teasing to give the heat time to fade between bouts.

He took the comb from her hand.

'Here. Believe it or not, I've often helped my sisters with their coiffures when disaster strikes.'

It wasn't a lie, but it also was. Sisters had nothing to do with this.

Her hair was warm, as if that dark-wood colour had lain close to a fire, absorbing its heat and life. It was made to be spread out on dark-red velvet. *She* was made to be spread out on red velvet.

She looked up, clearly too shocked to even stop him. With her head tilted up towards him, her eyes wide and her mouth half-parted, his body could be forgiven for jumping to the erroneous conclusion that the natural next step would be to lean down and kiss that controlled but expressive mouth again. He stood there for a moment, poised between two worlds. In the Stanton world he stood back, but in the old Sinclair world his hands dug into that warm mass and sent pins and combs clattering, tipped back her head so he could take advantage of the surprised parting of her lips to taste his fill. He wanted to see if that moment in the conservatory had been an aberration or whether this woman was as passionate as he suspected.

Probably. When her barriers broke she would be like an avalanche. He had seen one once near Innsbruck. One moment all had been as still as if creation itself had stopped, the snowbound mountains carved in shades of white, grey and blue so sharp the trees looked almost black. The next it seemed half the mountain was sinking towards them, sluggish at first, but then faster and faster, with a horrific rumbling and what sounded like pistol shots as massive trees snapped with the ease of twigs under the weight of the careening snow. It had spent itself before reaching them, but it had been a terrifying and exhilarating sight. Two men and a boy had been swallowed up in that avalanche and their bodies had never been found.

And that was precisely why he should step back. He had left the Sinclair world for precisely that reason. Avalanches might be thrilling from a safe distance; up close they destroyed innocent people. He had enough on his conscience.

He slipped the comb into place, his fingers gliding from her temple over the curve of her ear, into the warm recess behind it, just grazing the soft skin of her lobe, coaxing the errant lock of hair into place as he reluctantly slid in the comb. Then he called upon every ounce of his Stanton legacy to beat back the Sinclair heat.

'There. If that doesn't work, you might want to consider borrowing one of Alby's lace caps that look like a soufflé gone hideously wrong. Nothing can escape those.'

She was still flushed, but her shoulders lowered and she laughed, her hand rising to touch the comb.

'Thank you. Or perhaps I should apologise. I didn't even realise I was doing that, let alone that it might bother anyone.' A hint of the mischievous defiance he enjoyed sparked in her eyes. 'I thought Sir Oswald mentioned you are one of the most focused men he knows. You must be dreadfully bored if you are distracted by something so mundane.'

Anything but mundane.

'I have no problem splitting my attention when there is something more enjoyable to observe than politicians debating docking rights and trade tonnage. Then I merely become a little more focused.'

Both her blush and her strict look returned. She clearly didn't take his flirtatious comment seriously, which was probably all for the best.

'I admit I am also finding this a little tedious. The discussions at the Palace that I attended were often much more heated. You are all so… business-like.'

'A good negotiation should be precisely that. Most of the ground work with Razumov and Von Haas was laid before they arrived at the Hall.'

'I can see that. The King might think it is all happening here, but the three of you have drawn most of the lines before we even arrived, didn't you?'

'Does that bother you?'

'Not as long as it isn't at the expense of the King and Princess which so far it does not seem to be. I just find it fascinating—to see how you are weaving that fine balance between all these tugging forces. It seems…fragile. I wish there was some way to set it in stone.'

'There isn't. Once you enter this game it is all about keeping a constant watch on the balances and never tossing anything on to either side until you assess ahead of time how it will affect the other. After all, that is what I am commissioned to do.'

'And your uncle?'

'My uncle is more skilled than I at this game, but then he's been at it longer. He is a master of finesse, but he is also master at knowing when it is right to throw something heavy into the mix. I don't have his touch. The one time I tried such an aggressive manoeuvre people were hurt. So now I stick to what I do best, tweaking the balances of conflicting political powers like a shopkeeper tweaks the weights on the scales, so the world can avoid avalanches.'

She frowned. 'What is an avalanche?'

'That is when there is too much snow on the mountains and for no apparent reason it begins to slide downwards and destroys everything in its path.'

'Can snow do that? There isn't any snow on Illiakos and the only snow I remember from childhood was rather sludgy and grey. I can't imagine it wreaking much damage.'

'Anything can wreak damage when it is gathered in sufficient amount and propelled with sufficient force. Avalanches are everything that can go wrong with this world. So my role, as I see it, is to identify when too much snow is gathering in the wrong place and stop it from becoming an avalanche.'

'And how do you do that?'

'You defuse the building tension in manageable steps and, if need be, you remove elements from the equation. Illiakos is a case in point. Right now it is teetering on a dangerous pile of tension between Russia and Austria, with Bourbon France prodding Russia to march its army across the Continent to help subdue the rebellion in Spain. If that happens… England can't afford another war. Not its government, not its economy, and certainly not its people. I don't want any more men paying the price of the stupidity of a few privileged fools who don't know any better. The cost is too high. So Illiakos may seem like a small piece on the board, but small pieces are the ones that usually tip the scales because we don't watch them closely enough. It is just that one extra flake of snow or an unwary footstep that sets disaster in motion. That is why Illiakos matters and why we are removing it, judiciously, from the board. So you will have to forgive me if I try to avoid unnecessary fireworks if I can manage it. I won't apologise for not providing as much entertainment as King Darius.'

He leaned his hip on the side of her desk,

crossing his arms. He hadn't meant to sound piqued. His annoyance at her comparison picked up a notch as she tried to school her mouth into primness, but her eyes gleamed with laughter.

'There is no need to apologise, Lord Stanton. I would certainly not recommend trying to emulate King Darius's style when matters don't follow his wishes. Unnecessary fireworks is an accurate description. I am merely surprised that in a matter so momentous to the future of Illiakos he is so very…unruffled. It was meant as a compliment. You have a very soothing effect on the players here.'

'For a compliment that leaves a great deal to be desired, Miss James. I don't know whether to be flattered or offended to be told I have a soporific effect. Shall I stir the cauldron a little when they return so we can see some sparks fly?'

The laughter spread to the edges of her mouth and his annoyance ceded some ground to the return of the need to act. The sparks he would like to see fly had nothing to do with diplomacy.

'I said soothing, not soporific. And please don't stir any cauldrons. I have no more wish to witness an avalanche than you, though I am certain you could set one in motion if it served your purpose.'

'You paint a dire picture of my character,

Miss James. I am boring, easily distracted and manipulative. Have I any redeeming features?'

She hesitated for a moment and he waited for another taunt, but she surprised him.

'You are kind.'

Kind. Neither his mind nor body could decide how to react to this comment, annoyance warring with an unfamiliar warmth that tingled along the edges of the old wound in his side.

'Kind.'

'It is nothing to scoff at, my lord. It is a rare quality.'

The warmth was winning, so he pushed back at it.

'I don't think there is anything in these discussions to show evidence of that quality.'

'Perhaps not in these discussions but it is very evident in the way people regard you. It is evident in that Lady Albinia and her friends would do anything for you.'

'Her friends?'

'Her horticultural friends. She took Ari and me to their meeting at Briar Rose Cottage.'

Good lord. He would have to have a word with Alby. He rubbed his forehead.

'That is hardly proof, most of those people depend upon the Stanton estate in one form or another; they have little choice but to be loyal.'

'Perhaps. But I don't think their loyalty is born out of self-interest, they truly seem to care for you. And trust you. I don't think that is possible without some kindness. But I shan't say another word because I am embarrassing you.'

'So now you are adding easily discomfited to your assessment of my character.'

'No, not easily. I find most men are uncomfortable with sincere praise; almost as much as they are with well-grounded criticism.'

'Are you certain you have enough worldly experience to generalise about most men?'

She tilted her head to one side, considering.

'I have seen quite a few men during my years in the court, but they have mostly been on their best behaviour because they fear the King. He himself is a case in point. He is a wonderful man and often quite wise, but he can also be as sulky as a two-year-old when matters don't go his way.'

'What do you mean "also"? I never sulk.'

'Of course not. That would be undignified and unproductive and human.'

Her smile took the sting out of her words and he couldn't resist the challenge.

'I'm very human, Chrissie.'

'Chrissie… No one has ever called me that.' Her voice was breathless and their light exchange darkened, deepened. He had no idea why that name had come to him and even less of an idea why he'd said it aloud.

'No? It suits you.'

'It isn't very...dignified.'

'Do you wish to be?'

'No. Oh, *no*.' There was such emphasis in her answer, even surprise, and it surprised him as much as it did her. It was like a child escaping their tutor, revelling in the wonder of sudden freedom. Or the girl of six years ago, ripping off her veils. For all these years she was still clad in them, not physically but in spirit. He knew what that felt like.

'Well, then Chrissie it is. Chrissie James. That sounds like a little girl picking berries by the stream and eating them on a carpet of bluebells.'

'That is a lovely image, but I never did any such thing so I doubt Chrissie suits me.'

'I think it does. It doesn't matter if you did, merely if you would like to. Would you?'

'Everyone has things they would like to do, but probably never will, don't they? It doesn't change who they are. Those are only dreams. They don't matter, not on any level that counts.'

'Don't they? What does count, then?'

'What you do. The people who need you. Those count.'

'I see. So for you the Princess and the King.'

Her chin rose, but her gaze remained fixed on her desk, like a pupil before the headmaster, overtly obedient but with defiance evident in every line of her stubborn mouth and chin.

'Yes.'

'Yes, I remember you were very clear about that. So—no berries, no bluebells and no Chrissie.'

'Not beyond the borders of my mind at least. I am very grateful for what I have. I have no reason to be discontented.'

It shouldn't annoy him, but it did. Someone like her shouldn't be talking like this. She might believe it, but he didn't. He slid his fingers under the curve of her chin, turning her face towards him. She didn't resist but it wasn't a capitulation.

'Look at me, Chrissie.'

'Miss James.'

'Picking berries won't bring the known world to a crashing end, you know.'

'Is that the current euphemism, Lord Stanton?'

He breathed in, the desire simmering inside him lit by a flash of answering anger.

'Believe it or not, I was referring to berries. Don't lash out at me because you are scared of yourself.'

She surprised him again, her shoulders and lashes dropping like a sail suddenly turned out of the wind.

'You are right, I was being petty again. But it isn't fair of you, either—to make game of my fear of risking what I have. You have no idea…'

Her voice thickened and broke and he stopped himself from pulling her to her feet and proving she was right about him. Oswald had taught him early in life not to mix spirits if he wanted to keep a clear head. Adding compassion and regret to lust was just as detrimental to clear thinking. Yet it wasn't willpower that made him pull his hand away from the warmth of her cheek, but the sound of approaching footsteps. He turned as the King entered.

'Athena, what is this? Still working?'

Christina tidied the stack of papers on her desk.

'I am merely reviewing my notes while the proceedings are fresh in my mind, your Majesty.' Her voice was husky but she spoke with all her usual calm and contrarily Alex wished she would show some sign of the emotions so evident seconds ago.

'I am certain they are accurate enough, Athena. Off you go and rest yourself or your mind will be anything but fresh for the proceedings. Must I think of everything?'

Alex's hackles rose.

'I think Miss James's diligence is to be commended, your Majesty. She has done an exceptional job.'

'I told you she would, did I not?'

Christina stood with a slight laugh.

'Thank you for your defence, Lord Stanton, but as you can see his Majesty has complete appreciation of my secretarial skills and sees no need to waste time on empty niceties like praise and gratitude. I shall return on the hour, your Majesty.'

'See that you do.' The King grinned at her retreating form and turned to Stanton. 'She has quite a tongue, does she not? She looks so prim one hardly notices the sting of the whip. Her father always said he wished she had been a boy, for as a man she could have achieved much.'

'What was he like?'

'Edward? He was a good friend to me and he made my wife's last years bearable, but he was not a warm man and had little use for Athena beyond her help with his patients and herbs. You should have seen her when she arrived with Edward in the castle—all eyes and wariness. I took one look at her and sent her to stay with my

Ari. It did them both a world of good. I could not give my little star a sibling of her blood, but Athena was even better—she became mother and sister and friend combined. Her loyalty is even greater because it is bound by choice, not blood. As long as Ari needs her she will never turn her back on her. She may not look it, but she is a little lioness when it comes to her cub.'

'What of her own life?'

'Athena's? She will never lack for anything on Illiakos. When Ari weds and has children, she will be their family and they will be hers.'

'Most women would prefer a family of their own.'

The King leaned back against the desk.

'So I would have thought, but Athena is different. There are men at court who would be happy to wed her even though she is not Illiakan and not merely because they know it would strengthen their position in court. But she never gives them an iota of encouragement. Some women are like that. Perhaps she has a point; she has greater freedom than many women, whether Illiakan or English. Had she been married she could not have come with us to England, for example. I am happy for it. We both know Ari would be pained to lose her, even to a husband in court. They have no one else but me and I am just a man. Sometimes I think women need each other more than they need us.'

He chuckled a little at his words and moved towards the table. Alex followed, biting down on the instinctive resistance to the King's words. Who was he to decide he knew better? Most of the women he would eventually consider for the position of Lady Stanton were motivated by worldly considerations. At least Chri… Miss James's considerations were those of remaining in the safety of the little world she had created on Illiakos and with the only people she truly cared for. She could live perfectly contentedly, reading all about the great wide world from the safety of a window seat and never risk unleashing those demanding forces inside her she probably hardly even understood. Once he would have had nothing but contempt for such craven choices and would have done everything he could to goad those leashed passions to the surface. He knew better now, though at great cost to others. Freedom and passion were highly overvalued at the expense of stability and safety. She was right. It was unfair to expect anything else of her.

Chapter Ten

Christina entered the portrait gallery a few steps behind the others. The King and the foreign envoys were in a buoyant mood after putting the final flourishes on the negotiations, like children being let loose from the schoolroom. For them the formal signing of the treaty the previous day marked the end of two weeks of tense discussions. For Christina, it marked the end of one of the most bittersweet periods of her life.

Well, not quite the end. The King had announced they would depart on the morrow to visit his old school in Oxford for a few days, accompanied by Lady Albinia, and then return briefly to Stanton on their way to the royal frigate awaiting in Southampton to return them to Illiakos. Still, it wasn't enough. It would never be enough. She didn't know whether to be grateful that Alex had behaved with perfect propriety towards her ever since their discussion in the state room. He treated her as he did Ari—like a favoured cousin to be indulged and amused but put aside when matters of greater import caught his attention. All her years of keeping her thoughts wrapped and sealed helped her respond in kind but with each passing day the effort it took to maintain her façade grew, as did the internal howl of protest. What would happen if she stamped her feet and said she didn't want to leave? Not yet. Not ever.

She forced her attention to the gallery. It was very long, one wall punctuated by a series of tall, arched and mullioned windows leading out to the lawn, the other covered with dozens of paintings in elaborate frames which glowed in the light streaming in from the long windows. There was a conceit to it, but there was still something rather comfortable about the room; perhaps it was the warmth of the wood and the lack of embellishments other than a few delicate chairs placed between the paintings or by the windows.

She followed at the tail of the group as Lady Albinia introduced some of the players on the walls, passing by others without a word. With her vague but humorous touch they took on lives and wove together into a very English tale that held her audience rapt. Amongst the multitude of portraits she did not always choose those with the greatest artistic merit, but when she passed by an exquisitely rendered portrait of a haughty young woman without stopping Christina was so surprised she paused beneath it as the others continued in Lady Albinia's wake.

The painting itself was wonderful. The attention to detail was so superb it was unnoticeable, but the real brilliance was that unlike most of the other paintings Christina could truly feel the person. Not that it was a comfortable feeling. The woman…the girl…was probably younger than Ari and exquisitely beautiful with eyes remarkably like Lord Stanton's. She also seemed to be blazing with feeling though her face was a mask. The painter had captured not only impatience and resentment in the tilt of her chin, but even a sense of fear and despair which Christina felt spill out over her. Her hand rose, but she held it back. There would be no soothing that jumble of emotion. It was clearly too late.

The distinctive scent of Razumov's cheroots signalled he had come to inspect the painting as well, but she didn't turn.

'An interesting resemblance…' he murmured, leaning in.

'To Lord Stanton?' she asked, turning a little so she could put some distance between them.

'That, too. But I meant to Countess Vera Vidanich. It explains a few things.'

There was nothing more annoying than innuendo left hanging. Under the weight of the woman's frozen stare Christina turned to face the Russian statesman.

'Such as?'

His smile told her was enjoying casting his bait and watching her rise to it, just like those ice-bound fish in the Baltic.

'No, no, my dear, it is ancient history. A sad tale and not mine to tell.'

'Well, then never mind,' she said and turned back to the portrait, trying not to grind her teeth.

'The Countess was not quite so beautiful and her eyes were brown, not blue,' the Count continued conversationally behind her. 'But she was very charming and widely adored. The toast of St Petersburg. She could have had anyone, but she was a dutiful daughter so she married her parents' choice, Count Vidanich, a very worthy man, but not the most exciting. It is hardly surprising she was ripe for… This is Reynolds, yes?' He paused again, leaning in to inspect the signature. 'Truly a master. See how he brings life into her hands. Hands are very difficult to paint. Ah, Princess Ariadne. Come, tell me what you think of such a masterly portrait.'

'I think she is quite the loveliest woman I have seen,' Ari replied as she came to stand near Christina. 'Look at that dress…and the tapestry behind her is exquisite. Who is she, Lady Albinia?'

Lady Albinia followed, a little reluctantly, but it was Sir Oswald who answered.

'That was the previous Lady Wentworth, your Royal Highness, my sister and Lord Stanton's mother.'

Even Ari's natural exuberance was dampened by the revelation and Lady Albinia progressed down the row of portraits.

'This next portrait I would like to show you is that of my mother, the Dowager Marchioness. Oh, good. Alexander. How lovely you could join us. Has Count Von Haas departed?'

'Yes. I have just seen him to his carriage. Yours will be ready within the hour, Razumov.'

Christina hadn't even noticed Alex's approach and she took a step back from the painting of his mother as if caught in the act of spying. She cast him a quick glance, not surprised his expression was completely blank, quite as if this had nothing at all to do with him.

'My father, the third Earl of Stanton,' Lady

Albinia continued, 'was granted the title Marquess of Wentworth for services to Old King George. Something rather hushed up, but apparently important and it brought him much to court which was where he met my mother. She was a Davenport and the most courted girl that Season. My father no more saw her than he asked to marry her.'

'Were they happy?' Ari asked.

'Why, certainly, your Majesty!' Lady Albinia said.

'Apparently she made his life a living hell,' Alex said at the same time.

Ari's stifled giggle deteriorated into a cough and Lady Albinia frowned at him.

'Mama was a trifle high handed, but I believe he remained deeply in love with her until his death.' Lady Albinia amended.

'He died quite young,' Alex observed without emphasis.

'Oh, dear, how very sad,' Ari said, her hands clasped before her and Lady Albinia patted her arm consolingly.

'Indeed. He went sailing with a friend and his boat overturned. He was only twenty-five and my brother Arthur was just two years old at the time. Here is a painting of my mother with my brother just before his marriage.'

Christina considered the haughty face of the Dowager Marchioness and the pleasantly boyish face of the current Marquess. She could imagine that in this case the coldness captured by the artist was an accurate portrayal of the woman's soul. There was an echo of that coldness in the beautiful face of the scandalous first Lady Wentworth, but there was much more as well. A vividness that her son kept under firm control and under the cold hauteur so evident in his grandmother's expression. But in Alex's case she sensed it wasn't coldness, just rigidly controlled distance. Not that he had been distant or controlled that evening in the conservatory. Or apparently in his dealings with a certain married countess.

Ari glanced at the painting of Lord Wentworth as a young man and sighed. 'Oh, it must have been hard for your poor papa to lose his own father so young, Lord Stanton. It cannot have been easy for the Marchioness to be widowed so young either.'

Lady Albinia smiled indulgently, but Lord Stanton's expression was anything but sympathetic.

'Hardly. She made the most of her widowhood and ruled Stanton Hall with an iron hand including deciding on my parents' marriage when they were hardly more than children. I'm only glad she lived long enough to see how ill her machinations fared.'

'Alexander.' The note of warning came from Sir Oswald who had returned with the King from inspecting a fine painting of a medieval map.

Alex merely shrugged and turned to examine a painting of a man in court dress with an elaborate wig and a monstrous emerald in prominent display on his white hand. Lady Albinia hurried on, but Christina was no longer listening. There was nothing more revealing than real pain. Lord Stanton's words had been cynical, but once again the lid cracked open, showing another flaw in the perfect clockworks. She didn't want to feel any empathy, but it was there, undercutting her defences like the treacherous currents under the cliffs of Illiakos.

They continued, gathering before a portrait of some unnamed ancestor with his hand splayed on a map of the world, and Christina wandered aside to inspect another portrait, eventually finding herself back in front of the painting of the young Countess. Everything she had heard of this woman was infused into the paint, in the hands gripped together, the lips held tight and the eyes… Christina's hand rose again as if to test the paint, to see if there was any depth to this hallucination.

A hand clasped her elbow and she didn't have to turn to know who it was.

'Has no one taught you it isn't polite to stare at freaks?'

'She isn't a freak!' she protested.

'At lepers, then.' He must have bent down because she felt his breath against her hair and its heat trickled down her side all the way to her toes, pinching her skin as it went. 'Come along, Miss James. This habit of going where you shouldn't is not at all what one expects of a dutiful handmaiden. You are neglecting your fair charge.'

She turned and held his gaze, which wasn't easy with him towering over her, his eyes not merely the colour of clouds on the horizon but in full storm. His anger was peculiarly disorienting after his recent kindness towards her and she wished there was something she could do to reach that core of pain and soothe it.

'The Princess neither wishes nor expects me to trot at her heels like a puppy, Lord Stanton. This might strike you as peculiar, but it isn't duty that binds us.'

'Clearly not, if anything it is rather she who

trots at yours. But I am not one to scoff at duty, believe me. It is a Stanton area of expertise.'

'I imagine it is your motto by the exaggerated importance you accord it.'

'Is it exaggerated? And our motto is Stand Firm, by the way.'

'How apt. Like a mule.'

Some of the tension faded from his eyes, replaced by a reluctant smile.

'Perhaps you prefer the Sinclair motto from my mother's family—*Aspera Virtus*—virtue is hard.'

'Duty and virtue. Did your mother fail on both fronts?'

'Spectacularly.' He leaned past her to straighten a Chippendale chair by the wall and the single word singed her cheek, drifting down her neck, feather light over her bosom. She curled her fingers into her palms, wondering why she wanted to protect the unknown beauty. Certainly someone so lovely wouldn't have even regarded Christina, let alone liked her.

'Perhaps she had good reason.'

'Don't people always have good reasons to do damage? History is nothing but a list of good reasons and counter-reasons and everyone crushed between them. People always have good reasons to betray each other and fail in their duties.'

'So we are back to duty. Is that really your highest value?'

'You are a fine one to scoff, you are duty personified. The ideal handmaiden. At least that is the image you present, both here and back on Illiakos. I always wondered what you looked like under your veils. Until your confession about your fictional marriage I wove a whole tale about a Greek girl on the brink of a life that she had no control over and no real understanding of who and what she was.'

'Like your mother.'

'Transparent, isn't it? I wondered if you, too, would become like her as you realised it wasn't enough, caught and filling with such hate you would destroy what you had. I told myself it was just my own foolish fancy. And it was foolishness, wasn't it? Not merely because you weren't married, but because you are far too level headed to go down that path. You have done very well for yourself. Made yourself indispensable to the King and his daughter, secured their trust and affection. If only my mother had been as sensible and hard-headed as you, she might still be alive.'

The gentleness of his words hid the slide of

the sword as it slashed through her ribs and ripped into her heart. She pulled her hand away, but he caught her wrist, his eyes locking with hers.

'You can be as soft and warm and as inviting as the Mediterranean, but underneath you are also as hard as granite, aren't you? You wouldn't run like she did. You stand firm, like that damn motto. But it's dangerous, all that passion, crushed downwards into diamond sharpness. When it escapes it will slash anything that gets in its way.'

His attack was so sudden and harsh her cheeks stung as if the words had been a slap.

'You have no right to say such things to me. You don't know me!'

'There's that anger you keep so tightly capped. I keep wondering what will set it loose.'

She moved to push past him, but he shifted, creating a barrier between her and the others, shrinking the universe to just them, his hand rising briefly to touch the ridge of her cheek and the intensity faded from his eyes. Now he looked much more annoyed at himself than at her. 'No, don't stalk off, not yet. I apologise. I am being a fool; none of this is your fault. Forget I said anything.'

'Forget?' Her voice squeaked upwards in disbelief.

'That is a bit much to expect. Forgive, then. To err is human and to forgive divine, which would put you on the moral high ground where you obviously belong. Truce?' He smiled and again her anger foundered. She might not understand him any more than he could read her, but she had no defence against real contrition. But when he held out his hand the urge to grasp it and cling was so powerful she stepped back, bumping into the Chippendale chair and sending it rocking. His lips tightened at her withdrawal, but he merely reached past her, steadying it.

'Tina? Is everything all right? Did you trip?' Ari hurried towards her as the rest of the party made their way back.

'The chair is a little uneven,' Alex replied, as if that explained everything.

'Oh, dear.' Lady Albinia said abstractedly. 'Do have a look at it when you can, Alexander. Well, that is enough of these stuffy portraits. Why is looking at paintings so much more wearying than a brisk walk through the fields, I wonder? I for one am quite ready for a rest and I suggest you do the same before we leave for Oxford, your Majesty.'

* * *

Christina glanced over her shoulder. Not that there was anything wrong with what she was doing. Ari was resting and there was still an hour before their departure for Oxford. Christina was free to spend her time as she wished and she wished to see Lady Wentworth again.

It wasn't Reynold's superior skill that drew her. She felt a kinship with the condemned woman though she was nothing like her—neither beautiful nor privileged nor deceitful. Part of her felt a furious contempt towards a woman who could abandon her son, marking him for life, but she could not help feeling a fascinated sympathy. The thought that this woman had been around her age, already a mother of an eight-year-old boy and probably feeling so trapped a devious spy convinced her to risk everything for a love that probably wasn't even real… It was unthinkable but it had happened.

She leaned on the chair by the painting, staring at the undeniably beautiful face with its undercurrents of stubbornness and even a hint of ferocity and she wanted to reach through time and shake that woman and tell her to find another way to bring warmth into her life that wouldn't hurt the people who depended on her and loved her.

'Do you think you will find the clue to her perfidy if you stare long enough?'

She gasped and whirled around, and the much-abused Chippendale chair rocked precariously on its spindly legs before settling back on the wooden floor with a clacking tattoo. Alex stood by one of the recessed windows leading out to the garden, dark against the sunlight streaming in. She felt like the worst of interlopers, every statement he had said about her intrusions confirmed.

'I came… I wanted…'

He approached, his strides long and purposeful, as if he meant to sweep her straight out of the gallery.

'To gawk at the scandalous Lady Wentworth, obviously. Well, you aren't the first. Her tale is quite a curio for guests. Like those agony advertisements you used to read with such relish on Illiakos. Or like people who delight in watching a public hanging.'

'What? You're wrong! That's not…'

'No? Then why did you go straight to her portrait again? And why have you been staring at her for over five minutes? Excuse me for not believing this is a manifestation of your appreciation of Reynolds's artistic skill.'

The confirmation that he had been watching her all along made her blush turn to brushfire.

'I was thinking about her. I felt sorry for her.'

'Sorry for *her*?'

She almost added she felt even sorrier for him, but that would likely bring further thunder and lightning down on her head if not worse.

'Yes. I know it is merely a painting, but she looks like she wants to rise up and shout.'

'Shout what?'

'I don't know. Just shout. "*I am here*", perhaps. "*Look at me*".'

'From what I heard she had enough people looking at her. She was the reigning beauty at the time.'

'That isn't what I meant. You know that.'

He turned his shoulder to the painting.

'Wasn't that what Princess Ariadne said about you? That you are the mistress of the silent shout? Perhaps you are merely applying your own frustrations to your image of my mother.'

'That is nonsensical. I am nothing like your mother. I have neither wealth nor beauty and though I was a burden for my own family, I had the good fortune to be embraced by people who care deeply for me. There are no points of comparison.'

'You make a strong case, yet that silent shout stands. Why is that?'

'Perhaps you are merely applying your *own* frustrations to your image of *me*, Lord Stanton?'

He smiled at the words she tossed back at him.

'The difference between you and me is that I don't deny them, Christina James. I knew full well what I was doing when I turned my back on my hedonistic way of life. Frustration and silent shouts are part and parcel of that deal with the angels. It is called compromise and it is the curse of growing out of boyhood.'

'Was your hedonistic phase so devoid of silent shouts and frustration, then?' She challenged. The man she remembered from six years ago had hardly been the care-for-nobody his words implied.

His hand rose slightly and fell back. It was a strange gesture and her own hand twitched in a mirror response before she subdued it.

'No,' he admitted. 'There were times of rather severe frustration, especially towards the end. At least they helped me realise I was no longer comfortable with a life of indulgence and danger. The Foreign Office suits me. It is a fine balance between Sinclair and Stanton with the Sinclair engaging in the occasional silent howl, but the Stanton having the last word on all matters of importance. It works well. I recommend it.'

'To me? I hardly face the same challenges as you, Lord Stanton.'

'Yes, you do, Christina James.'

The coldness in his eyes faded and his voice sank to a rumbling purr and she took a physical step back, glancing at the painting as she groped for a distraction.

'What is your mother holding? Those are paintbrushes, aren't they?'

His smile turned wry at her diversion, but he answered her question.

'Yes. She loved painting. Watercolours. The house used to be littered with them.'

'I haven't seen any watercolours at all. Were they put away?'

'My father had them destroyed.'

'Oh, no! How could he do that to you?'

'To me?'

'He should have left you something of her. She was your mother, even if she made a selfish mistake. People make mistakes all the time, that is no reason to…to erase them. That is a terrible message to a child—if you disappoint me you will cease to be. I am sorry for your father, but that is just unfair. No, it is cruel.'

'There is a price for betrayal, Miss James. She betrayed not only her husband and family, but was also clearly willing to betray her country. Moreau was a French spy and when she ran away she helped him take some sensitive documents belonging to my uncle. Each act alone would be unforgivable. Together...'

She still felt a desperate need to protect the woman in the portrait.

'If she is such a villain, if he has erased everything else of hers, why keep her portrait?'

'To remind me. Like my grandmother, my father is a firm believer in cautionary tales for the young. He wanted me to always remember to subdue the Sinclair traits I share with her and to focus on whatever Stanton characteristics managed to survive her toxic influence. Judging by my physical appearance he didn't have much hope for me, which is why he often sent me to my uncle when I wasn't in school. Oswald is a master at subduing the wild side of the Sinclair nature. I don't think he has made an impetuous move in his entire life. Brutal, yes, impetuous, no.'

'You cannot be serious. That is...that is sheer and utter poppycock!'

'Is it? He was right, though. I lived up to his worst expectations before returning meekly to the Stanton fold. If it hadn't been for my stepmother and my sisters I wouldn't have set foot in the Hall during those years. It was too depressing watching the portentous gloom on his face as he resigned himself to his only heir's descent into the Sinclair pit of iniquity.'

'Well, if that is the way he acted I am surprised you didn't behave much worse. He certainly deserved worse for sending you away to your uncle when you had just lost your mother and needed the safety of your home…that was unconscionable!'

He shrugged and adjusted the chair with the tip of his boot.

'He wasn't in any shape to care for anyone for quite a while.'

Christina's dislike of Lord Wentworth increased a notch. She was rather glad he wasn't in residence at the moment. She knew she should feel sorry for him as well, but she didn't. She wanted to kick him. And the Dowager. But mostly she didn't want Alex to stop talking.

'When did he remarry?'

'He met Sylvia at Harrogate the following year.'

'Lady Albinia said she is very nice. She looks nice.'

He glanced down the gallery towards the portrait of the plump young woman, the edges of his mouth softening and rising into a kind of smile she had not yet seen except in her imagination. She felt a twinge of jealousy, which was absurd.

'She is. Everyone likes her. I tried to dislike her for a whole year and failed miserably. She is kind and quite clever. When Anne was born she asked Alby to bring me in to see my sister before she even sent for my father.'

His gaze focused back on her, narrowing. This time the heat that coursed through her wasn't embarrassment or outrage or empathy. The spectres of the Stantons and Sinclairs on the wall behind her ceased to exist. Just the man, his outline gilded by the sun streaming in the long windows overlooking the garden.

'If not for my father, I'm at least glad for her and my sisters' sake I changed my life's course. Though to be honest it wasn't out of any concern for them that I did. If I hadn't finally gone too far I probably would still be there, digging away.'

'What happened?'

She didn't really expect him to answer, but she had to ask. She wanted to do more than that. She wanted to take his hand from where it was resting against the back of the chair. No, resting wasn't the right word, it was as stiff as the wood, as if holding back the hordes of hell depended on it.

'I almost killed a woman. Five years ago. It was sheer good luck that she was too small to climb over the parapet of the bridge so she tried to jump from the embankment where the Neva wasn't deep and a soldier happened to see her and pulled her out of the water. That water is ice cold; she never would have survived.'

She knew this particular smile, but she had never seen it so evident—it was hard, defiant and full of self-hate. She felt as cold as if she had been the woman plunged into the freezing river. Five years ago, a year after he had been on Illiakos. She could well imagine an impressionable young woman falling in love with him, she had done so herself and with probably less cause than he had given that woman. It was selfish, idiotic to feel jealousy. All she knew, without the slightest doubt, was that whatever he had done, he had not done out of malice.

Another piece of the puzzle fell into place as Count Razumov's words came back to her and with it another spear of jealousy.

'Vera Vidanich. There was a duel.'

'Gossip travels, doesn't it? Yes, there was a duel. I deserved what happened to me; she didn't. Her husband very rightly wanted to put a bullet through me.'

'Did he?'

'He missed. I deloped. That didn't assuage his honour sufficiently so he broke form and decided to make his point with his fists and I let him beat me so he could at least regain some of his pride.'

'That was probably more satisfying than putting a bullet through you.'

He gave a small laugh.

'I think he still would have preferred the bullet, but perhaps you are right. There is something more satisfying about drawing blood with your fists at close quarters than across twenty paces of snowy ground.'

'Were you in love with her?'

His gaze focused back on her, cynical and harsh.

'No. I can't even claim that in my defence. There wasn't even an affair. Even in my Sinclair heyday I avoided women who weren't completely up to snuff. It was worse than that. Vidanich was being manipulated by some rather unscrupulous French agents and I was in Russia to ensure they didn't extract information from him that was of value to us until certain discussions were completed. Keeping an eye on him was as boring as watching water boil and it gave me too much time to observe his neglect of Vera. Very foolishly I thought I could play the knight gallant and force him to take notice of her. I should have known I hadn't the skills for that. Rakes make very poor Galahads.'

'She fell in love with you?'

He shrugged.

'She fell in love with an idea of herself, not with me. She had no idea who I was in truth and I doubt she would have cared to know. She was sweet, but not very mature, and I was a criminal fool. After the duel I left Russia and my… position and joined the Foreign Office instead. That whole period of my life feels like something out of a Greek play. Complete with washing up wounded on the shores of a Greek island. Every step leading inevitably down the path to destruction. Very Homeric.'

'What happened to her in the end?'

'She now has three children and I am told she and Vidanich appear content which is all anyone entering the blessed state of matrimony has the right to expect.'

'I'm glad for her. Perhaps in a strange way what happened to her was all for the best in the end.'

'Good lord, don't make a virtue of my actions, Chrissie.'

'Not of your actions, of your choices and hers after what happened.'

'Hell, next you'll be patting me on the head.'

She smiled. 'You're too tall.'

'There are other ways you could show your approbation, you know.' His eyes narrowed, his lids dropping as he surveyed her and she felt her skin heat, as if the sun had moved closer in its orbit. He was using charm to disarm and deflect again. She couldn't stop the answering heat unfurling in her, but she could see through it.

'I remember on Illiakos you also used to tease when you were uncomfortable.'

'I am touched you treasure memories of our time together so faithfully.'

'A case in point. But as you have seen, my memory is quite good at retaining all manner of trivial information.'

'So it is. My uncle was very impressed with that trick of yours with the colours and I admit I'm curious as well. How does it work?'

He took her arm as he spoke, moving with her towards the door, but without haste, his fingers shifting the thin fabric of her sleeve against her skin as they walked, lighting up the whole left side of her body. But inside her something was curling into a ball, preparing to be kicked.

'It isn't a trick and I don't know how it works.'

He stopped again and turned her towards him.

'I noticed in the stateroom you were less than happy about the King revealing your talent. Why are you ashamed of it?'

'I am *not* ashamed. I merely don't enjoy being considered an oddity.'

'Why on earth would that classify you as an oddity?'

She shrugged.

'My cousins enjoyed conjecturing why my parents didn't want me to live with them in Edinburgh. They never accepted it was simply because my mother was ill and my father busy. When I was seven they discovered I saw colours where others didn't. They spread the tale that I must be in hiding because I was accused of witchcraft. I became very popular in the village.'

His hands tightened on her arms.

'Didn't anyone, your aunt or uncle, protect you?'

'Why should they? I was a burden they accepted because they were very devout and also afraid of my father. They were relieved when Papa came to take me away after my mother died and he was invited to Illiakos. Apparently he considered leaving me with them, but they refused.'

His hands gentled, his fingers moving softly, almost absently just above her elbows. The warmth that spread out from each stroke pushed back the remembered fear and resentment.

'I'm glad for you they did.'

'So am I. I know you think I am servile to the King…or worse, but I owe him everything. He is more a father to me than my own ever was. He helped teach me Greek himself and when the son of one of his ministers made fun of my accent he said in front of the whole assembly that he had never met anyone who had learned the language so quickly and he gave me his own copy of *The Iliad.* In front of everyone. I was horribly embarrassed and proud all at once. I doubt it was true, but it didn't matter. No one had every stood up for me before in my life. I just remember praying I wouldn't cry. No one made fun of me again. He is a good man.'

His fingers shifted down, gathering her hands in his.

'It seems I owe you another apology, Miss James. This is becoming a habit. I shouldn't have judged you.'

'I didn't tell you that so you would pity me.'

'I don't pity you; I see no reason to. By most accounts you are very lucky.'

'I know I am. Very lucky.'

'Too much gratitude can be dangerous as well. You should want something for yourself, not just for them.'

'Why must you harp on that? As you said, I am very lucky. I see no reason to be greedy.'

'Is that greedy? To want something other than what they can provide? What would happen if you did?'

'I could lose everything that matters.' Her voice was a little ragged and she cleared her throat and tried to laugh. He didn't answer; he looked as forbidding as he had earlier. Her hands hummed in his grasp and her mind rushed back to his room in the castle six years ago when he had asked her to come with him. What would have happened if she had said yes? If she had been greedy? It would have been madness. He would have tired of her, given her the money he promised and continued on his way. There would still have been a Countess Vera and countless others. She would have lost everything and her heart into the bargain. Except she already had lost that.

'I should go. I must prepare for our departure. We leave for Oxford within the hour.' She tried to pull her hands away, but he didn't release them, just stood staring down at them.

'In a moment. You have a little time. You still have to tell me about the colours.'

'There is nothing to tell. I don't know how to explain it, anyway. It is just that letters and numbers and sometimes even languages have a colour so when I look at a number I see it, but also the colour associated with it.'

'Do they ever change?'

'No, never. I don't know why.'

'So, what colour are the letters of your name, for example?'

'Mine? Brown, blue, yellow, pink and red.'

'I'm not surprised you are so colourful. And mine?'

'We have mostly the same colours because L and T are both yellow, but you also have black and two blues—midnight and sky. I only have one.' She tried to be her pedantic best, but the final word caught as her treacherous breath stalled and she had to draw new air into her lungs.

'Midnight and sky. Which letter is which?'

'D is midnight, R is sky.'

'So you take the sky. You mentioned black as well, which is fitting. Which letter is that?'

'X is black.'

She should have been more careful. She realised the impropriety only when she saw his eyes darken. He had thought she was referring to his title, Lord Stanton. Using his given name, even without uttering it, was an intimacy she had no right to, however freely he chose to abuse her name.

'I am glad you don't think of me as Lord Stanton, but I prefer you called me Alex rather than Alexander. You did on the island, remember?'

She shrugged. Of course she remembered, but Alex was even worse than Alexander—sheared of its cool edges, it descended into darkness and flame, dragging her with it.

'Is there a letter the colour of your eyes?' His voice was drawing her in and she tried to find purchase to stop, to think. Be reasonable.

'No. They are the shade of the number two.'

'Two. Is there a language that colour?'

'French. It is a little darker.'

'French. Also fitting. And English?'

'Grey, like your eyes.'

'So, we are back to that—is that what you think me, Chrissie? A dull, grey Englishman?'

She shook her head, unable to navigate an answer as liquid fire poured through her. Why could there never be a moment between them that didn't end with her feeling as though she had been shoved against a wall?

His gaze swept over her and her blood followed its progress, a beating of drums in her veins. What would happen if she stepped forward as she had in the conservatory? It was surely the most natural thing in the world to move towards him, raise her face, touch the tense line of his cheek, feel it soften…

She raised her hand and he took it, turning it upwards, holding it as a gypsy might when searching for revelation.

'I remember your hands…' he murmured. Her hand shook visibly in his and he pressed his other hand on top, either to quiet that shiver or to block it from view. For her it felt like the setting of some fateful seal, a ritual bonding of their fates. In some communities such a moment would be enough to bind them for life. For her it marked something that had already happened. 'I remember how they felt on me, as soft as velvet, but never weak. I told you that you had dangerous hands, do you remember?'

'I remember,' she whispered.

'You had no idea what I meant then, did you? You were little more than a child.'

'I was eighteen. Older than Ari is now.'

'It has nothing to do with age. Now you know

what I mean, I can feel it in you. Right here. Like the ground echoing from a galloping herd of wild horses. Trying to free itself.'

He raised her hand and pressed his mouth very gently to the crest of her palm, his words hot against her skin, pumping fire through her. She wanted to shove everything out of the way, take what he was offering for however long it lasted. Free herself. Lose herself in him even if it meant losing everything. She felt dizzy, the portrait-packed walls leaning in on them, making it hard to breathe. Soon they would collapse on her and she would cease to be.

'I must go. The King and Ari will be waiting.' Her voice was hardly audible, but the transformation was almost instantaneous—he dropped her hand and stood back, both physically and in every other way. The moment was past and Lord Stanton was back.

'Thank you for the reminder of your priorities. All this reminiscing has rather made me forget who and what we are. Run along, Miss James, before I demonstrate I can act in a very un-English manner.'

Chapter Eleven

Alex cursed and put down the gouge, staring at the gash of blood welling on his palm. It had been a long time since he had cut himself like that. Working with wood had become such second nature, he rarely made mistakes. He might often be dissatisfied with his work, but he was too skilled to be sloppy. Usually.

He wasn't even happy about the figurine. The grain was working against him and he wasn't clear how to continue. When he had seen this piece of wood a month or so ago he had had such a clear image of what he wanted, but now it was murky and twisted like an old olive tree.

It was her fault.

No, to be fair, it was his.

It had been difficult enough to maintain objectivity while Chrissie was at the Hall and he had hoped her departure for Oxford would provide some perspective, but she had contaminated Stanton more effectively than ever his father's dour looks had. Absurdly, though he knew it was impossible, her scent was everywhere, elusive but inescapable when he turned a corner or sank into his bath. The surges of lust that followed were like stepping on live coals in the dark—sharp, painful, annoying as hell, and the burn took far too long to calm. Even when it did a tight heat lingered just below his throat, like the beginnings of an illness. It should have been a relief to have the Hall to himself for a few days so he could clear his mind and calm his libido, but it wasn't.

Any pretensions to the contrary were rendered ridiculous by his reactions to Watkins's announcement that his Majesty's carriages had arrived. Alex had stubbornly persisted at his task, refusing to rush to welcome them as he had first been inclined. He would have done better to act the fool rather than continue working while his concentration was completely shattered. The result was blood dripping on his pantaloons.

He cursed again and pulled out his handkerchief, pressing hard on the gash. It wasn't deep, but he should still probably bind it and maybe put something on it so that it didn't turn putrid. Alby always applied that horrible powder when he scuffed his knees or fell out of trees as a boy, or the time Raven had fallen off the gate when they had crept off to the village inn that summer.

He made his way to Alby's rooms, holding the handkerchief to his palm, and stopped short in the entrance to her parlour. She was seated by the table, her back to him, one arm leaning on it and the other outstretched and held between Miss James's hands which appeared to be pulling on it. Meanwhile Susan, the maid, stood clutching a wicker basket full of vegetables, her eyes wide and worried.

'What you did yesterday after I twisted it was marvellous, but it is seizing up again. Oh, heavens, yes, that's the place.'

'You never should have tried to move those pots in the Physic Garden in Oxford yesterday; you could have told the gardeners that the anemones were receiving too much sun. And it certainly wasn't wise to carry up the tubers from the garden yourself just now, Lady Albinia.'

'They weren't heavy,' Lady Albinia protested and then groaned as Miss James moved to press her hand into the older woman's shoulder.

'Yes, they were. You must not pick up heavy objects until your shoulder is quite healed. Perhaps you should even see the doctor just to be quite sure.'

'I shall see a doctor on my deathbed and no sooner, and even then I shall probably send him packing.'

Susan, catching sight of Alex standing in the doorway, squeaked and bobbed a curtsy.

'Alby? What happened to you?' Alex shook himself and strode forward.

'Nothing that time won't mend, Alexander. More to the point, what happened to you?' she exclaimed in sudden concern as her eyes alighted on the bloodied handkerchief.

'I cut myself. Nothing serious, but I wanted some of that powder you used to inflict on us. Are you certain we shouldn't send for Dr Upton?'

She humphed and held out her hand peremptorily, slashing twenty years from his age. The effect was ruined as she groaned and Miss James moved forward.

'Please rest, Lady Albinia. I will see to Lord Stanton's wound myself. Is it basilicum powder? Does Susan know where it is kept?'

Susan bobbed a curtsy and scurried out. Alex tried not to groan aloud himself. He didn't need the cause of his carelessness to tend to its effects.

'There is no need for that, Miss James. Once

Susan brings the powder I shall have my man see to the binding, thank you.'

She ignored him, moving forward to take his hand without waiting for his consent and with the same cool competence he remembered from the island. He should have been grateful, but he wasn't. Still, he didn't pull away when she unwound the handkerchief which clung to the congealing blood and inspected his hand, the dark wings of her brows twitching together, forming a well-furrowed line between them as her lashes dipped and rose. This is what he would have seen had she tended him all those years ago without those foolish veils. She looked serious and impersonal, as if none of the tension between them had ever existed.

Would it have been any better than the anonymity that had forced him to create his own images and injected that false sense of mystery and promise? At the moment he had no idea. All he knew was that he didn't want her to touch him and he didn't want her to stop.

'It isn't as bad as it looks. Most of the blood is from the skin you scraped off here, but the wound itself is not very deep,' she said. 'Still, it must be cleaned and dressed. Thank you, Susan. Could you put that on the table and fetch me a bowl and some hot water? Is there any still hot on the hob over there?'

'I know it is merely a scratch,' he said, but didn't withdraw his hand. Susan bobbed again and hurried to pour water from the kettle heating for Alby's precious afternoon tea. The cut throbbed and stung, but it was more bearable than the firm and gentle pressure of her hand supporting his. He didn't move away when she let go of his hand to dip a linen strip in the water and when she held out her hand he let her take his own again. It was simpler than arguing with her.

He watched her clean the blood, moving towards the gash. After a moment he kept his eyes on the wound itself, a slightly jagged line, broader at one end and bleeding sluggishly. When it was clean she glanced up at him, but then returned to her work, dusting it with basilicum powder and winding the linen strips over it, careful not to press down on the wound itself as she tucked in the loose edge against his wrist. The memory of her fingers working the salve into his skin around the wound in his side came back as fresh as if it were yesterday—the pleasure and the agony, imprinting itself on his body again.

He had missed this. Her touch. Her. It should

be natural to put his arm around her and draw her to him, thank her as he wanted to by kissing her tense mouth into softness.

He held down a groan. This was not what he wanted. More importantly, it wasn't what she wanted.

'There. You should change the dressing tomorrow. It doesn't appear deep, but if it becomes inflamed you should consult the doctor.'

'That's right,' Lady Albinia concurred, nodding with approval at the dressing. 'You don't want it turning putrid, Alexander. Give the woodcutting blades a rest until it's healed.'

'I will if you also do as Miss James suggests and give the garden a rest until your shoulder heals, Alby.'

Lady Albinia waggled a finger at him in an uncharacteristically undignified manner.

'Cheeky boy! Run along now, you two. I can at least be of some use reviewing the household accounts.'

Alex followed Miss James out into the corridor. They didn't speak until they reached the head of the stairs, but then there was no getting around it and he turned to her.

'Thank you for your help and your kindness to Lady Albinia.'

He couldn't help the way his tension made

him sound stiff and priggish. It must have sounded even worse than it did to him because she flushed.

'You needn't thank me.'

'Do you think Alby's… Lady Albinia's condition is serious?'

She looked up with a sudden burst of laughter warming her eyes, reminding him how alive and joyful she was when she let down her guard.

'Overwork?' she answered. 'Exceedingly serious. You should know, from what I hear you suffer from the same malady.'

He was glad the stairwell was dark. It might or might not have been a compliment, but he felt a completely uncharacteristic warmth of pride, as if he were a schoolboy being commended.

'I see. I'm afraid in Alby's case it is incurable. But I probably should have Mrs Bright from the village come in for a few days to help her.'

'That would be a good idea. I don't think your aunt is capable of resting.'

'Probably not. Her work defines her.'

Again her smile encompassed him and though she didn't speak he could hear the teasing words as clearly as if she had.

'No, I don't think the same can be said of me and I certainly know how to delegate more effectively than Alby. If you see her doing anything foolish these next few days, you have my permission to tell me and I shall confine her to her rooms.'

'She will defy you and clamber down the ivy if need be.'

The image of his staid aunt climbing out the window like an eloping damsel threw his discomfort to the winds and he burst out laughing.

'You have a vivid imagination, Chris… Miss James. Is that what you would do if someone dared lock you in?'

'Probably. No one has tried yet.' Her smile dimmed, perhaps because she realised that she was just such a prisoner, however comfortable her cage. He didn't want to think about that, or about his own cage. He wanted her to keep talking to him and smiling, so he grasped at the first thing he could think of.

'Did your father teach you your nursing skills or did you learn by observation?'

'I often helped him on Illiakos. Ari's mother, the Queen, was rather timid and she preferred having me present when my father tended to her. It became a habit for me to help him when he saw patients, especially women. People on the island trust midwives, healers or priests more than doctors. My father was a practical man and he realised that my presence and the use of herbs made his ministrations a little more palatable for them. He might not have been affectionate, but he was always eager to learn and he was very interested in local cures and plants.'

He could imagine her calm, practical presence would soothe women already made timid by tradition and doubly so as they were forced to admit their woes to a foreign male. It was quite a skill, balancing composure and sympathy. An invitation to relieve their burdens and an assurance she would expect nothing in return.

Except that it was a lie. There was a greater need in her than in any woman he had ever met, a subterranean cry she didn't voice, but which hummed around her like a struck bell. Even now he could sense it shimmering just below her surface, whether she was conscious of it or not.

He was. And of the answering reverberations it sparked in him, sometimes as painful and throbbing as the wound on his hand and even more unwelcome.

As she spoke she turned to arrange a row of little wooden birds on a side table facing the stairs. They had been inexpertly painted by his sisters and looked a little like they were suffering from an exotic disease, but she handled them as lovingly as if they were made of spun glass, setting them in a circle, beak to beak.

'What are you doing?' He asked and her hands flew behind her, the picture of guilt.

'Nothing. Arranging them.'

He looked down at the congregation; one was slightly askew, as if hearing something outside the little grouping. Or perhaps watching out for them.

'It is a bad habit of mine. When I'm nervous. Arranging things.' She rubbed the heel of her palm along her cheekbone as if that would erase her blush and began to put them back into a row, but he grasped her hand and plucked the bird from it.

'Do I make you nervous, Chrissie?'

She shook her head, but it didn't appear to be in answer to his taunt. She was staring at the figurines, her eyes wide and full of wonder, like a child seeing a magic trick for the first time.

'You made them,' she murmured.

He stepped away from the table. He should leave now before revealing something he would regret. Again.

'I must go and attend to some business. Thank you for your nursing skills, Miss James. Then and now.'

'I love every one of them, they are so beautiful, but there is one I love in particular.'

Vanity was a strange thing. He wanted to

know and he didn't. His mind was already rushing to defend his other carvings against her favouritism.

'Which one?'

'The girl in the window.'

He should have known she would give the knife a twist.

'Why that one? I made that ages ago. It is utterly graceless.'

'No, it isn't. I can see it doesn't have the same skill as many of the others, but it is so…touching. The way her head is turned to look and her smile. I can't explain.'

'It was a birthday gift for my mother.'

'She must have loved it.'

'Must she? All I remember is that she asked me what the girl was so happy about.'

Her eyes widened and when she spoke her voice was hoarse.

'I'm so sorry.'

'Why? It has nothing to do with you. And not much to do with me any more. It is ancient history.'

'I am sorry for that boy. I hope I would never say such a thing to a child, no matter how much I was in pain. Or if I did, I hope I would at least have the strength of character to apologise. Where do you make them?'

'I have a workshop.'

'Oh. May I see?' Before he could respond she flushed and the shine of curiosity fell back under the veil of her dignity. 'I mean, I think Ari would find it interesting if you have no objection.'

'If you want to see it you can see it now. I have to tidy up the mess I left. But there is nothing interesting about it. Just tools and blocks of wood.'

He didn't wait to see if she followed. He knew he was being surly, again, but he couldn't help it. No one knew about his woodwork but the people closest to him. It was of no interest to anyone else. He didn't want to show her his workshop. He wanted to show her the other rooms in his wing. One room specifically. Which was precisely why he should send her on her way.

Chapter Twelve

She must be mad.

Had she really just asked to go to Alex's rooms? She had. She had blamed him for misunderstanding her position, but within minutes of seeing him again she had jumped on the excuse to touch him and now she was practically begging to be alone with him in a part of the house everyone knew was sacrosanct. His territory.

It was just that three days had never felt so long. When the King had decided to extend their stay in Oxford by a day she had felt like kicking something like a thwarted child and demanding to be taken home.

Home.

It *wasn't* her home. Still, the moment the carriage had passed through the ornate metal gates of Stanton Hall earlier that day she had felt right—even her back had rested more deeply against the carriage squabs, as if she was settling back into her own skin.

So she followed and when he opened the door at the end of the corridor which clearly marked the beginning of his domain and stood aside she walked past him without daring to pause, holding her breath over the threshold as if about to plunge into cold water.

It reached her the moment she dared breathe—scents of the forest, dark brown and green around the silver thread of a stream. Smells of home and mystery all at once. She moved between the long tables bearing blocks of different coloured wood, looked at the tool cases laying open and displaying dozens of different shaped blades. At one end of the room were metal and wood contraptions with large dark steel screws and arms that looked like great birds of prey or perhaps dragons' jaws waiting to sink their teeth into anyone foolish enough to approach too closely.

By the smaller table a chair stood askew on a dusting of wood shavings and on the table was a little wooden boy. It wasn't formed yet, just the beginning outline of a head, the line of a cheek and jaw and the curve of a mouth, but the eyes were there. He was looking up and the lines scored in the blank, still rough wood were full of expectation and wonder and she had no idea how that was possible.

Alex strode forward and straightened the chair and turned the figurine so that it lay face down on the table.

'I told you, there is nothing to see. Just tools.'

She went and turned over the figurine. From here the boy was almost smiling.

This was hers.

Perhaps this was what some people felt when they saw a diamond necklace, or looked across a border to a kingdom they coveted. Looking down at the unformed but absolutely definite face of the boy, she wanted it. Much, much more than it—she wanted Alex, his heart, his children, she wanted to be his home, to make him as safe as she felt right now. She waited for the fierceness of her conviction to wash through her and recede before she spoke.

'I thought it was strange that Alby never answered any of my questions about them. I even had my own story in my mind, but when you told me the truth about your mother I realised I wasn't right.'

He moved to stand on the other side of the table.

'What story?'

She smiled at him, curving her hands around the boy.

'I thought perhaps your mother had had an affair with a carpenter on the estate and that he had made these for her and then it was found out and they tried to run away. That was before I heard about Moreau.'

He shrugged.

'It would have been preferable to the truth. A single betrayal only. But in that case we wouldn't have kept the figurines in the house, would we?'

'No. So I'm glad it wasn't the truth.'

'You prefer the version where she is a traitoress just so you can rescue the figurines?'

'I still feel sorry for her. It's hard for me to think of her as anything other than a sad, frustrated young woman. We can't change the past.'

'I never try. That is why I occupy myself with the future.'

In which she had no role, Christina reminded herself. He would probably try to send her on her way now, but she didn't want to go. She picked up the wooden boy, brushing her thumbs over the rounded cheeks.

'How do you decide what to carve?'

'I don't. I never know what it will be and nothing depends on the outcome. I just sit down, pick up a piece of wood and stop thinking. When

I start thinking I stop carving because then it will go wrong. There are no rules here like there are on the other side of that door. Here I do as I please.'

'I envy you.' She barely breathed the words and hurried on before he could withdraw. 'How did you begin? Do you remember?'

He looked around the workroom, frowning slightly, as if the answer was engraved in one of the wood surfaces. 'I wanted a dog, but my father didn't want any in the house. So one day I was watching the carpenter fixing the panelling and I took a tool from his box and made one from a block of wood lying there. When the carpenter saw it he told me to come to his workshop when I wished. It took me two months to gather the courage to go there.'

'Ned, Matty Frake's husband,' she said, another piece of the puzzle falling into place.

His eyes narrowed, but his mouth softened as he shook his head.

'Do you know that is a very annoying trait of yours?'

'What? Being right? Or am I intruding again?'

'Both.'

'So where is the dog you made? You must still have it.'

'How do you know?'

'I just do.'

He stood for a moment as stiff as the oaks in the woods—the expression in his eyes was both wary and rueful. Then he turned and though he didn't tell her to follow she knew this was the point at which she must choose. No woman expecting respect would walk of her own volition deeper into a man's personal domain. She was already compromising herself by even being in these rooms alone with him. If she did anything other than leave she would be confirming everything he had once accused her of. But he would be right. For now she didn't want to be the upright and proper Miss James or the obedient handmaiden. She was stepping outside of time, just for a moment. All too soon she would have to return.

She breathed in, twice, and followed him to her fate.

Her burning disappointment as she entered the next room was proof of just how far she had fallen. It was not a bedroom, but a study, simply furnished with two comfortable-looking chairs by a wide desk stacked with papers and walls lined with bookshelves where books shared space with more of his wonderful figurines.

'Here. This is Boy.'

'Boy?' She stared down at the lump in his hand.

'I named him after Mr Brickshaw's sheep-dog, he was one of our tenants and he called all his dogs Boy. Here, Boy. Go, Boy. Every time they bred I asked Father if I could have one of Boy's boys and received the expected denial. So I made this.'

She knew that note, light, self-deprecating, dismissive. He was nervous. So she pushed away her disappointment at not being the object of a seduction and focused on Boy, holding out her hand. He hesitated, but placed it on her palm as gently as if it was a soap bubble and she held it just as gently though it was a sturdy little lump. Its legs were just incised lines in the block and his tail was a few scratches, but she could see why the master carpenter had encouraged the young Alexander. Just like the other figurines he had captured an emotion in a few curves of wood. The snub-snouted face was raised to hers, the ears pointing up sharply and the eyes a little slanted. With a hint of a tongue lolling out the puppy looked full of unbridled joy.

'Caught for ever in a moment of love,' she murmured and saw his hands rise slightly as if to take Boy away from her, but he moved towards the desk instead. She kept hold of Boy, tucking him against her chest so she could feel the rough warmth of wood against her skin, drawing strength from the love and need that wasn't only apparent in the carvings but in the fact that Alex treasured them, that his hands, his beautiful strong hands, had shaped them, handled them. She had no idea how to proceed, but she knew it was even more impossible to turn back. For the moment at least, Alex's world was hers.

Alex went to stand behind the desk and watched her walk along the shelves, her hand reaching out to touch the figurines, her other hand still clutching Boy to her breast as if it truly was a living breathing thing and was burrowing into her warmth.

God, he envied that wooden lump; he envied each of the figurines her fingers lingered on.

'They are truly amazing, Al… Lord Stanton.'

He stepped forward, forgetting he was behind the desk, which was a good thing because even that little slip of hers was like a strike of lightning, piercing him. Among the many compulsions he was developing, the need to hear her speak his name outside his dreams was on the front lines.

He leaned his hands on the cool wooden surface and called for calm, but he couldn't think of anything to say and so he just watched her.

'What did your father think of your talent?' she continued and he focused on the bite of bitterness that rose at her question.

'I didn't tell him at the time and then when my mother died it wasn't relevant. He was away at Harrogate with my grandmother most of the year, at least until he married Sylvia. She told him at some point, I think.'

'You told your stepmother before you told your father?'

'He didn't need any added burdens. I was enough of a worry already and woodcutting was not a suitable pastime for the future Marquess of Wentworth.'

'I don't think I would like him.'

'He is not a bad person; he just likes a straightforward world.'

She glanced down at Boy.

'This is anything but straightforward.'

'For me it is. For my father it was another insult to his dignity. Another sign of Sinclair degeneracy.'

'I have no idea about the rest of the Sinclairs. I have only met two, and another one indirectly, but you are nothing like your uncle and I don't think you are like your mother, so I am not quite certain what that name appears to portend.'

'Then you are alone in your ignorance. Ask

anyone in the district, or in London for that matter, and they will answer that it portends self-indulgent sinfulness, not to mention a tendency towards self-destruction.'

'You cannot possibly believe you are limited to being either like your father and uncle or a caricature of a dissolute hell raiser. That is just...childish.' Her disbelief was so potent he felt himself struggling to cling to the distinction that had been so clear to him. 'Your two friends, what are their names? Lord Hunter and Lord Ravenscar—they were also rakes, weren't they? But I would wager you never thought of them in terms of good or bad, even if they did misbehave.'

He couldn't help smiling at the very mild term for some of their younger exploits.

'That is different.'

'Why?'

'They aren't Sinclairs.'

'You do realise how silly that sounds, don't you? Shouldn't a good diplomat try to avoid the pitfall of preconceptions?'

Her smile tugged at him, but he stayed where he was. 'Yes, but a good diplomat should always be aware of his weaknesses and do his best to prevent them from dictating his agenda.'

'Being a Sinclair is not a weakness.'

'I prefer to think of it as a curse.'

She sighed. 'And to think I considered you a relatively intelligent man. How disappointing.'

He couldn't prevent an answering smile. 'You don't believe in curses?'

She picked up a figurine he had made of one of his tutors, a curve of a stick man.

'No, nor in fairy tales either, though I admit that as a child I did daydream I was a foundling and that one day my true family would discover me and tell me I was a lost princess and take me away to my magical kingdom.'

'Perhaps you *should* believe in them, then. That is as close to a daydream realised as I've heard.'

'I know. It is strange, isn't it? When my father and I arrived in Illiakos that realisation terrified me. For years after we moved there I had horrible dreams that I would wake up one day back in Northumberland, with my cousins laughing down at me as usual. I worried that if it was true that I had conjured Illiakos through my daydreams it could be un-conjured. For that first year I went to bed every night resolving to be perfect the next day so I wouldn't do anything to shatter the dream and find myself back in my uncle's house. It was like that story of a thousand-and-one nights—each day I had to earn the next. You deride me for being a tame handmaiden, but I would have done anything, *anything* to stay in the dream. At the beginning I was even too scared to allow myself to care for Ari. I thought—if I start taking anything for myself in this dream, I will eat away at it and wake up. In the end I couldn't help it, though. She is very persistent. She would come into my bed in the middle of the night and curl up like a puppy under the covers.' She caressed Boy absently and laughed. 'In the end I slept better with her kicking and squirming in her dreams next to me than I had in my life, even if I had quite a few bruises.'

'Are you still scared?'

She glanced at him in surprise but the answer was in her eyes. Of course she was scared—that fierce control wasn't manipulative as he had thought, it was the most basic form of self-preservation. He should know.

'Yes. I can't imagine…' She shook her head. 'When my father died I waited for them to send me back. No one said a word, but I knew the axe would fall, because without my father I was of no use to them. What on earth would they need *me* for? I stopped talking because I was afraid if I spoke I would be noticed and remind them they had to be rid of me. They let me be because they thought I was mourning my father. I think it took three months for King Darius to realise how scared I was and to tell me I was not being sent back, that I was to stay with them always. That was the one time in my life I fainted. Right in the middle of the great hall. It was very embarrassing.'

He kept his reactions carefully sheathed. She wouldn't welcome his pity and his need to gather her to him, wrap around her like she had around the little Princess, would likely lead down a very unplatonic path and that would not be right for her, either. Desire and anger did not mix well. He wasn't even clear why the anger was so potent. There were no real villains in her tale—indifference and neglect and pettiness did not justify such boiling, choking fury. But if he could have reached through time to the people who had hurt her he would have wreaked hell on their heads.

She came to the end of the shelves, her finger touching the petals of a rose carved in walnut wood.

'There must be more if you have been making them for over twenty years. Where do you keep them?'

He didn't want her to hide again, but it was

probably safer. For both of them. He crossed his arms and tried to smile.

'You cannot expect me to keep all of them, surely.'

'Oh, no! You couldn't possibly have discarded any, could you? Especially not after what they did to your mother's paintings. Surely not!' Her shock was obvious, her hand holding Boy even more firmly against her, as if he was suggesting destroying it right there and then.

'You are right. My vanity wouldn't allow it.'

'Don't belittle it. It isn't vanity. May I see the others?'

'They aren't here. I gave them away.'

'Oh. I see. Never mind. To whom?'

'Does it matter?'

'I suppose it doesn't, I just… Never mind.'

He relented, trying not to be flattered by her obvious disappointment and failing. 'To a foundation called Hope House. We…they are homes for war veterans and their families. The children seem to like them. Especially figurines of animals.'

'Lady Albinia mentioned you and your friends established homes for war veterans, but I didn't realise there would be children there as well.'

'We have homes for the families of the men who cannot work or care for their families because of their wounds, physical or otherwise. We find it is often better for their recovery to keep families together. Not always. We have schoolrooms and reading rooms for the children. Nell, Lady Hunter, supervises them and she had the idea of creating play rooms as well.' He frowned suddenly, as if just realising what she had said. 'Did you say Alby told you about the Hope House foundation?'

'I'm sorry, shouldn't she have? It was just that one of the gardeners in the Physic Gardens in Oxford lost part of his hand in Waterloo and he was telling us how lucky he is compared to some of his friends and that was when Lady Albinia mentioned he should tell them about Hope House and to contact you if need be and you would arrange for help. I asked her about it when we left and she told me…a little.'

'A little.'

'Please don't be angry with her. She is so proud of you.'

'We prefer to keep our involvement private, so I would appreciate if you do not discuss this with anyone.'

She looked so chastened and worried he moved towards her.

'I am not angry with her, I promise. Hunter and Raven and I established the homes for very personal reasons and we already draw enough notoriety to our names. We did not want that affecting Hope House or the men there. They have enough to contend with. Here, don't hug Boy so hard, you are hurting yourself.'

He reached out to gently take Boy from her, revealing a little red half-moon mark along the tantalising swell above her bodice where Boy's ear had pressed into her. He could feel the pressure of that mark on his own chest, like the tip of a dagger lodged into his skin, and before he could think he reached out, his fingers skimming the border between fabric and flesh. A sunburst of pain-edged pleasure filled his chest, clenching his whole body like a fist around a forbidden act.

He turned away, placing Boy on his desk and trying to anchor himself in the familiar before he did something irrevocable. He didn't want to scare her away or stem her curiosity or her generosity or even her concern. He wanted her, like this, trusting and giving, Chrissie, just a little longer before they had to return to reality. At least his better half did. The Sinclair in him was on the hunt and straining at its shackles. If she knew in what danger she was at the moment she would probably turn and run.

* * *

Christina stood, hardly daring to breathe. She wished he had left her Boy, she needed to cling to something. Did he even realise that these fleeting touches were almost as devastating as the memories of his embrace? Evidently not for him. But there was an unconscious intimacy in them that beckoned her on.

'I'm surprised your mother didn't value your gift if she herself was artistic.'

He hesitated but didn't withdraw as she expected. 'She did in a way. At least enough to mention it in her farewell letter. She said she didn't take the figurine so that it would remind me of her when she was gone. That might count as appreciation.'

'She left you a letter?'

'Us. A communal letter. But I found it.'

'Oh, no!'

'Better I than my father. I took it to my uncle and then when I went to tell my father I remember he sat down and just stared at the wall for a long time. Then my uncle came in to say he had the carriage brought round and was leaving to find them and he said...my father said..."*I can't bear it any longer.*" I think he was crying, I don't know. The next thing I remember was my uncle telling me she was dead and that I was to stand firm. That was two days later. I wasn't allowed to go to the burial. They sent me back to school. I remember it snowed the whole way there and the postilions were worried we would be caught in the drifts and I thought I would end like her, frozen by the side of the road. But we arrived. The school was still almost empty, but at least Hunter was already there and the cook took pity on us and made us hot chocolate and allowed us to sit in the kitchen.'

She couldn't bear the blankness in his voice. Eight years old and thrown into the middle of a storm of betrayal and abandonment and darkness. She took his hand, but though his hand tightened on hers it was an unconscious gesture and she was glad of it; the moment he realised it he would withdraw.

'I remember you spoke of the snow when you were ill. You were so worried about it.'

'Was I? I don't remember. I still don't like it. Foolish, isn't it? It is only frozen water in the end. Russia was the worst. I never should have gone there. For many reasons. I should have turned tail the moment I entered that white-and-grey wasteland. But then it might have taken me longer to come to my senses so perhaps it was unavoidable. Society assures me I am the better man for being reformed, whatever that means.'

He raised her hand, frowning, and she waited for him to drop it. He curved her fingers into her palm, caressing the fist he made. Every inch of space between them was now tangible, an extension of the heat that reached out to her. She searched desperately for something to say that would prolong the pleasure of him opening to her. She didn't want to be sent away yet. Ever.

When he spoke again, he surprised her.

'Wait here. I want to show you something.' He dropped her hand and moved towards the door at the other end of the study, but she didn't wait. She followed.

Like the workshop, the next room was also large and long and with a door probably leading to the corridor and another to a dressing room. The wall facing the garden also had floor-length windows, but these were covered with thick curtains now partly drawn, casting the room into a pleasant gloom. Rays of sunlight filtered through the gaps, one laying a streak of gold along the floor and coming to rest on the bed, picking out shades of red and blue on the brocade cover. It was like an accusing finger—*I know what you are thinking, Christina. You might be untouched, but you certainly don't wish to remain that way.*

She watched her feet cross the threshold, looked up and her heart stuttered and leapt forward. He was standing by the bed, his gaze on her, his hand outstretched. The suspended arrows of light gilded his shoulders and slashed across his chest. Again she realised he wasn't beckoning to her, but holding something. It wasn't a figurine, but a carving on a block of dark wood of a shadowy figure standing by a wall, one hand resting on a windowsill, each finger so distinct she could almost feel their pressure against the sill. The wind was frozen in the billow of long hair and the sweep of fabric against the curve of her hip. She seemed to be just on the verge of turning, perhaps to answer someone's summons, but she was also caught in some dream, something beyond that window.

'Do you like it?'

'Is that me?' She was so shocked she spoke before she could worry about the presumption in her words.

'Yes. I had a dream for a while after Illiakos—just an image of you standing by the window in that room and you would begin turning, but I would wake up before I saw your face. I did this to stop the dream.'

'Did it stop?'

'Time stops pretty much everything, Chrissie. Pain and pleasure both. Eventually. Time, patience and perseverance. You know all about that, don't you?'

She shook her head. It hadn't worked for her. The thought that some part of that episode had haunted him, however briefly and for whatever reason, only made it stronger. She had felt him then, had fallen in love with him as much as a frightened girl of eighteen was capable, and she was in love with him still, only so much more so now.

'It worked quite well until King Darius decided he wanted to interfere in my life again. But time will work its wonder on this, too.'

The sting of his words was brutal. Was she so transparent?

'Time doesn't heal everything.'

'I know that only too well. But you're a survivor, Chrissie. You adapt to the hand life deals you. To your parents' indifference and being shunted off to a family that didn't want you and finally to Illiakos and what the King and the Princess want from you. No, don't shake your head at me. I'm not condemning you. I think you are one of the strongest women I know, you make the most of what life offers you and you deserve the comfort you have earned. I have no right to pass judgement. None. It's not your fault I want to bed you.'

The statement was so bald her body caught its meaning before her mind. She couldn't stop the shudder of excited need that coursed through her and her hand rose towards him. He caught it, bearing it down behind her back as if to hide it from view.

'Don't. Don't test me, Chrissie. I have no incentive to succeed.'

'Alex...'

His name was a whisper, muffled as his lips caught it, his own words a low growl that tingled along her skin.

'Say it again.'

'Alex...'

She had no idea why his name opened the floodgates, but he groaned, his body sinking against hers, his shudder flowing through her.

'They're back,' he said, his words as much a caress against the sensitised flesh of her neck as his lips on hers. 'The dreams. But different. Sometimes you are right here, by my bed, veiled. Remember how you used to put on that salve? No one has every touched me like that, as soft as gossamer, but with a will of steel. Those moments were my worst moments on Illiakos. I was certain you could see what you were doing to me, how much I wanted to pull off those veils and sink into you. I wanted to touch you so that you would tell that cursed husband of yours and he would come and try to thrash me and I would take all this frustration out on the poor fool. When you told me it was all a lie it was worse. It felt like a betrayal and a release, but all I could think of was that I wanted you. You were right to send me packing. Believe me, I felt like a fool for wanting a woman I couldn't even see and for begging you to come with me. I told myself that as soon as I recovered I would be thanking the fates you threw my offer back in my face. I never expected the dreams to linger… No, don't go, not yet. I won't do anything you don't want, I swear. Stay just for a moment. Don't be scared, Chrissie…'

She hadn't been trying to pull away; she just couldn't stop the shudders of need his words conjured, sinking her into an abyss of heat. Right now she wasn't scared of anything but that he might stop. She wanted to enter those dreams and stay. She leaned in to the hands that held her, fitting herself to them with a sigh. This was right. She reached up and slid her hands over his chest, around his neck, the nerves in her fingers alive with pleasure even at the texture of his shirt and the warmth of his skin beneath. They passed the line of his shirt and touched skin, warm, firm over corded muscled, and then they slipped into the silky hair and fire twisted through her, brutal and unfamiliar and terrifying and right. A moan throbbed through her, so powerful it seemed to shake the air around her, echoing in Alex's body as he drew her against him, one hand digging deep into her hair, tilting back her head, and she closed her eyes, her lips parted on a little gasp, between pain and surrender as she waited for him to seal her fate.

With one finger he pulled, very gently, on her lower lip and released it. A stabbing ache of desire burned through her and she slid her hands into the warm hair at his nape, raising her face to his. Finally.

'Alex...'

The faint knock barely registered through the pulse thudding in her ears, but the sudden stiffening of Alex's body did. His hands tightened on her shoulders and he put her behind him, striding towards the door and planting his hand on it.

'What is it?' It was more a snarl than a question and his valet's voice was hesitant as he answered through the door.

'Lady Albinia said to tell you the guests wish

to dine early today after their travels and will be gathering in half an hour. Shall I lay out your clothes for dinner, my lord?'

She didn't wait to hear Alex's answer. She found the latch on the long window opening towards the garden and slipped out, hurrying along the gravel path in the lengthening shadow of the yew hedge. The cool air stung her cheeks.

She knew what would happen now. He would apologise, again, even though this had been utterly, utterly her fault. She had seduced him. Not very expertly, but it had been a seduction none the less. She had not only entered his rooms with him, alone, but she had coaxed him into sharing his pain and past with her in a way that was as much an invitation to take what she offered as if she had undressed in front of him. She had been within a whisper of putting him in an unbearable situation. What would have happened if his valet had entered the room? He might talk as much as he wished of his sinful past, but she knew he would have taken responsibility for their transgression.

His duty.

He might want her, for now, just as he had temporarily wanted the veiled handmaiden six years ago, but she wasn't necessary to him as he was to her. It was as simple as that. He would enjoy her and then she, too, would become a burden and a duty to be shouldered like all the others in his life. He would be kind, but she would know. He didn't need her.

Chapter Thirteen

'Alexander?'

Alex glanced up as his aunt paused in the doorway to the library. He really didn't wish to speak to anyone. He had to call on all his diplomatic skills and reserves of social graces just to navigate dinner while his mind had battered itself uselessly trying to understand how he had so far forgotten sense and every resolution by even inviting Chrissie to his rooms in the first place, luring her across each threshold with his wooden figurines like an ogre casting sweetmeats before a child.

It had been an abuse of his position as her host and a man with much more experience than her with the seductive power of compassion.

It was just that of all times for her to stand firm and follow rather than run, entering his rooms was not what he had expected. Not that it was a decent excuse for his actions.

The worst was that his only regret was his valet's interruption. If he hadn't…

He had been completely lost in the feel of her, his hands burning as they moved over her face, her hair, the delicate lines of her ears and throat. In her scent—those elusive wildflowers and beyond them the forest, faraway and lushly green. A whole landscape. The same way his hands knew how to move over the wood, to bring out its essential shape, they burned to move over the rest of her, ply her, shape her until she released her secrets, until she gave herself to him. Nothing had mattered but the lushness of the curve of her lower lip, the shakiness of her breath telling him she was ready and waiting, the heat warming her eyes to sapphire. He hadn't meant to stop. He had meant to take the passion he knew was in her and force it to its fullest pitch, have it burn through both of their restraints and take all choice away. He hadn't been in any state to consider if it was wise or the greatest folly. It didn't matter.

He should be grateful she had run in the end. Grateful, too, she had avoided him when he had tried to speak with her in the drawing room before dinner. It was madness to try to speak to her anyway while everyone was gathering, though what the devil she thought he would do in full view of everyone he had no idea.

He shouldn't be surprised she had avoided his eyes and clung so firmly to the Princess's side when he tried to talk to her. She was impressively clear-sighted about her priorities. How many times would she have to tell him before he heard her? She might enjoy the undeniable physical attraction between them but it could not compete with what she considered truly important. She had found her haven and she was staying there. Unlike Vera, Chrissie had the good sense to run and hide when someone crossed her lines. Better sense than him because all he wanted was to keep crossing them. He was within an inch of begging, just as he had back on Illiakos. He should take a leaf from her book and accept her rebuff. Not just accept it, but be grateful. It was like his stepmother and strawberries. She knew she came out in hives if she ate them, except that sometimes the temptation to just nibble at one of cook's strawberry tarts was too alluring. Apparently Miss James was his version of strawberries—either avoid her or suffer the consequences. There was no middle ground.

Fool.

'I won't interrupt if you are busy, Alexander. We can talk tomorrow.'

Alex stood, flushing a little at his loss of focus. For a moment he had even forgotten Alby was still standing in the doorway.

'No, come in, Alby. I'm sorry, I'm just a little distracted. Why are you awake so late? Is your shoulder paining you?'

Lady Albinia shifted her shoulder and smiled.

'Not quite so badly as before, thank you, my dear. You know I always find it hard to settle after a trip.'

'I'm sorry. It was kind of you, but there was no need for you to travel with them to Oxford.'

'Nonsense, I had a grand time. It is quite incomprehensible, but I have never been to the Physic Gardens before. I brought back a few interesting samples of sage and tarragon and Mr Dunn, who oversees the gardens, promised he would look in on our own gardens when next he is in Berkshire and see what is to be done about my pennyroyal.'

'I see. That is nice.' The slightest shift of colour in her cheeks made him keep his answer as bland as possible. He would mention to Sylvia that Mr Dunn would be encouraged to stay if he did indeed call at the Hall. 'You should go rest nevertheless. I thought that was the point of having an early dinner.'

'I am about to, but I was considering what we should do for the last day before our guests leave and I have a request.'

Alex turned a chair for her and sat down himself. Alby rarely came with requests. Every so often he wondered if she resented her position at the Hall and wished for a different existence, but the one time he had convinced his father to offer her alternatives they had been met with an uncharacteristically firm rebuff.

'She's not like you, Alex,' the Marquess had told him afterwards. '*I'm* not like you. Well, most people aren't like you. We like a steady, predictable life. That's what she has here. It's a good life and she likes the responsibilities and helping Sylvia with the housekeeping.'

A steady, predictable life. His father hadn't needed to add that his life had been anything but steady and predictable while the first Lady Wentworth had lived and that Alex himself had been anything but steady and predictable at the time. It never needed to be said to be heard.

He wished he was more like the rest of his family at his core so that he would be rid for ever of this drive to go beyond what was comfortable. He kept it on a very short rein, but it was always there, sometimes dormant and sometimes rearing up like an ill-mannered brute of a horse.

Like now.

He shoved that thought away. Again. Eventually it would stay down. He was different now, by choice. It just required reaffirming. Forceful reaffirming.

'What is this request, Alby? You know if there is anything I can do, I will.'

Lady Albinia's vague eyes crinkled in her sweet smile.

'Of course. But you must tell me if this is not convenient. I wanted to ask you to teach the Princess to ride.'

'To ride.'

'A horse.'

'I presumed that. Did she make the request?'

'Oh, no. We saw you riding Thunder on our way back from Matty and she said she had never learned to ride. I thought it would be nice as a last excursion before they must leave.'

'Nice... Alby, I don't know what Uncle Oswald and you think, but if this is some last minute attempt to convince me to offer for the Princess, it will not work. I have no interest in her.'

Albinia snorted.

'Of course not. The girl is a hibiscus.'

'A what? Never mind. And now that you remind me, Miss James mentioned you took her to one of your gatherings at Matty Frake's.'

'Oh, yes. We had a lovely time. The Princess was a little overwhelmed by Matty, but she and Miss James hit it off very nicely with Penny and Mary.'

Alex rubbed his jaw and the stubble scraped against his palm, the sensation grating on his sensitised nerves. Hell, he was tired. He wished everyone would just stay in their place and leave him alone so he could find a stable centre again. It probably wasn't Chrissie's fault that Alby had taken them to Briar Rose Cottage, but it felt like another invasion of his domain. He had spent so many hours in Matty's garish floral parlour as a boy he knew every uneven floorboard and fringed rug and already his mind was inserting Chrissie's image into that space. It was as if she held a map of the Hall and its surroundings and was methodically marking areas that were not meant to be infiltrated by strangers, pushing him further and further into a corner.

'You do know her father might not approve

of your introducing his daughter to an illegitimate midwife and the daughter of a scandalous divorcee?'

'Well, we needn't tell him the particulars. I was merely trying to make their stay more enjoyable. These are friends of ours, Alexander. They were family to you during our worst hours.'

'I am well aware of that, Alby, and I will never forget their kindness.' He winced a little at the use of Chrissie's… *Miss James's* choice of words.

'So will you take them riding?'

'Yes. I will take the Princess out on Marigold.'

'Miss James could ride Charis.'

He leaned back, detaching his gaze from the window seat.

'I agreed to take the Princess out, Alby. Teaching a new rider is tedious business. I am sure Miss James would rather rest or read.'

'Perhaps we should let the Princess decide what suits her?'

'That's no choice. You know full well she follows Miss James about like an adoring puppy. They are inseparable.'

'It is hardly surprising she has a deep affection for the woman who has stood in her mother's stead for many years. I cannot quite understand why you are making such a fuss about something so simple.'

Alex moved towards his desk.

'You are right. It doesn't matter. Do whatever you see fit. Now I have work to do.'

'It is very late, you shouldn't tax yourself so. You no longer need to prove anything, you know.'

He stopped at the edge of the desk and smiled at her.

'I am fine, Alby. Thank you for taking such good care of them.'

'You are welcome and it is no hardship. I like them.'

'I'm glad. Goodnight, Alby.'

She paused at the door.

'I still haven't resolved my conundrum, though.'

'What conundrum?'

'Whether Miss James is an herb or a flower. It is quite vexing.'

'Perhaps she is neither. Goodnight, Alby.'

'Perhaps. Do you have any thought on the matter?'

None that was repeatable.

'None. Just that she isn't fennel.'

'Of course she isn't fennel. That isn't in the least helpful. Well, never mind. Goodnight.'

Alex breathed in the silence as the door closed behind her. Vexing was one way of putting it. Swiftly approaching unbearable would be nearer the mark.

Chapter Fourteen

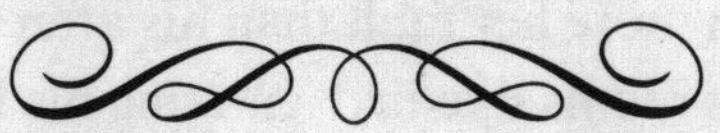

'He is a good teacher, yes?' the King asked as they watched Ari's delight at completing her first canter and Lord Stanton's warm smile as he encouraged his pupil. Despite her initial fears, Ari was proving to be a natural in the saddle and, as much as Christina enjoyed being back in the saddle herself, she wished Ari and the King hadn't insisted on her accompanying them because she was discovering an aspect of herself she had never even suspected existed before meeting Alex—jealousy. Nasty, bitter and green as the greenest pond slime.

For a whole hour she had watched as Lord Stanton encouraged, smiled at and generally charmed Ari while he had barely directed a word at her beyond what propriety demanded of him. As if those moments in his rooms had happened to someone else. She had already seen the regret on his face the moment they had come down to dinner last night. He had become thoroughly Lord Stanton—polite and a little stern and clearly disappointed in his lapse of control. He had tried to speak with her, but she had evaded him, unable to bear another apology. It had been more her fault than his after all, coming to his rooms like that, entering his bedroom, for heaven's sake. If his valet had not come…

She leaned forward to pat the mare's neck, closing her eyes against the stinging, and forced an answer to the King's observation.

'Yes. He is a very good teacher.'

'They look good together, too. Look how he is smiling at her. If only she would not treat him like a brother. He is used to the most beautiful and experienced of women. We are leaving tomorrow, but perhaps there is still some chance they will change their minds. You must tell her to flirt with him.'

'If you want her to flirt with him then *you* tell her.' As soon as the words were out Christina gasped at her own audacity. The King was similarly shocked because he pulled on his reins, gaping at her. Before she could even formulate an apology he burst into laughter.

'I keep forgetting how English you are, Athena.

There is nothing wrong with some games between men and women.'

'Papa, isn't it wonderful? Look!' Ari cried out as she turned her horse and trotted towards them and the King moved towards her, full of praise, while Alex pulled up beside Christina. Astride his enormous black stallion he looked more imposing than usual and Matty's tale of the Wild Hunt Club came back to her. Her hands tingled inside her gloves and she shifted in her saddle, her mare responding immediately and shying away from Thunder. Alex reached out and grasped the bridle, a soft word calming the mare. Embarrassment added to the heat in Christina's cheeks, but he merely caressed the horse's gleaming neck and made no comment. She searched for something, anything to say.

'You are a good teacher, Lord Stanton. The Princess was quite worried at the beginning, but look at her now.'

He didn't. He was watching her and she wished he wouldn't because she could feel the burn of her blush and it wouldn't quiet under his scrutiny.

'I am glad she is enjoying it. She has a natural aptitude for riding. It is a pity there isn't more time for her to explore it.'

The sting of jealousy slipped further under

her skin and she pulled her reins, but he shifted as well, his stallion blocking her mare's path.

'Wait. I have been wishing to… I owe you an apology. Again.'

Oh, she had known this was unavoidable. Still, it hurt.

'Please. There is no need…'

'Yes, there is. I keep crossing lines with you and then blaming you for my weakness. You have every right to be angry at me.'

'I am not angry.'

'Yes, you are. I'm not the King, you don't have to tiptoe around me. I am surrounded by politicians. A little plain dealing is welcome.'

He sounded so exasperated she couldn't help smiling. 'Are you certain?'

'I might regret it later, but for the moment I promise you I am sincere.'

Christina waited out the stabbing ache in her chest at his answering smile, resisting the urge to lean towards him, just touch the hands resting so easily on his horse. She might not dare ask for what she really wanted, but surely she could ask for something little for herself before this idyll was over.

'Do you think it would be acceptable for me to take Charis for a gallop when we are done? This is my last chance to ride before we return to Illiakos. Perhaps a groom could be spared to accompany me?'

His smile gathered back in, the grey in his eyes deepening like the shifting winter skies over the Mediterranean.

'Of course.'

Then he spurred his horse towards Ari.

'No, Miss James won't dismount yet, Henry. Charis here still needs some exercise so I will take them out to Norton's Field. Wait with her in the courtyard while I see our guests to the Hall.'

'Oh, Tina, will you have a lesson, too?' Ari clapped her hands together, clearly still delighted with her success. 'I would come with you, but I am already dreadfully stiff and I'm afraid if I don't get out of the saddle now I shall have to be pried from it like a barnacle from a ship's hull. Oh, Papa, I have done marvellously, haven't I?'

The King considered Christina for a moment and then took his daughter's arm and led her towards the Hall.

'You have, little star. You were born to ride. You must be part English.'

Christina remained in the stable yard, trying to subdue the rumble of anticipation.

'Ready?' Alex asked and again her mare shied at her abrupt movement. She stroked the lovely animal's thick neck, calming herself as well.

'Ready.'

Her nervousness began to fade as they trotted down the lane and then faded utterly when they reached a long flat field cropped clean of its stubble of harvested grain by a flock of sheep now huddled in the shade of a chestnut tree at its centre. She cast a quick glance at Lord Stanton. He was watching her, his mouth just curved up at one corner, his eyes hooded.

'Ready?' he asked again and this time she didn't bother answering.

By the time the mare slackened from her gallop at the other end of the field Christina was laughing and close to tears. She had forgotten what it was like to feel so alive and free. Just being, the way children were—without barriers between her and the sensations of her body and the utter joy of riding. But there were still barriers and they held her back from doing what she wanted most: to throw her arms around the difficult man who pulled his horse to a halt by hers. The impulse was so strong and felt so real and possible she slid off her mare, leaning against her neck.

'Are you all right?'

She smiled up at him, she couldn't help it.

With the mare between them she was at least safe from her own folly.

'Better than that. Oh, thank you so much. That was sheer heaven. I had forgotten what it felt like.'

He swung off Thunder, gathering Charis's reins from her as well and leading them towards the shade of the trees where he tethered them to a branch. She bent to pick a spindly stemmed poppy, amazed at the impossibly vivid red petals. Everything felt alive, expanded, yet comforting.

'You must have ridden often as a child.' He turned to run his hand down his stallion's gleaming neck.

'I did. That was the best part of my childhood. My uncle bred horses and exercising them was part of our duties. Whenever Ari asked me to tell her tales about my childhood I would tell her about the horses until she quite expected England to be full of them. I think that was one reason she was so excited about learning how to ride.'

'She was very lucky to have you with her growing up. Sometimes I wonder what my life would have been like if I had had a brother or sister closer to my age. I used to envy my cousins Lucas and Chase, they were only two years apart and very close.'

'But you had good friends.'

'Yes, thank God. Hunter and Raven were the best thing that happened to me. I would do anything for them.'

Just like she would for Ari and the King. That thought dimmed her pleasure, staining it with a sense of betrayal, though she had no idea why. She had done nothing wrong, just taken something little for herself.

He turned at her silence, his brows drawing together.

'What have I said to send you scurrying up your tree?'

'Nothing. We should return. Thank you for the ride, Lord Stanton.'

He didn't answer. Just stood there with his hand on her reins and suddenly Matty's description of the two-year-old Lord Stanton came back to her.

Stubborn as a boulder... When he wanted something he didn't scream and yell, he stayed put until he got it...

Then the moment passed, but instead of helping her back on to her mare he pulled the horses towards a tree.

'Come, whatever I did to ruin your pleasure, I didn't mean it. To atone I want to show you something you might like.'

Alex showing her things she liked had led her into trouble before. But when the path through the trees became uneven and he held out his hand to help her over a tangle of roots, it was the most natural thing in the world to place her hand in his. There was nothing unusual about a gentleman offering a woman assistance over rocky ground, but in her mind at least this was no perfunctory hand clasp.

'The forest marks the end of the valley,' he explained. 'They left the trees here because of these hills and how rocky the ground is. And for other reasons.'

'I smell spring water,' she said and he smiled at her. There was something almost boyish about him, as if they had been propelled back in time merely by crossing from the civilised field into the forest. She felt it as well—they might as well be children, off on an adventure in the woods. The oaks rose around them like petrified giants and the air was cool and sweet. Sound muted as they went, the birds were higher up and the buzz of insects was left behind in the fields. The scent of cool clear water became stronger and then the sound, like a breeze, carried to them.

'Oh.' She stopped just as they came around an outcropping of rock. It was like walking into a story. The clearing was wide and green, bounded on one side by a stream that sloped downwards in a series of tiny waterfalls and on the other by a tumble of stones that had possibly once been a dwelling, but now looked like a giant's sofa, even more so because in front of it was a great stump of a tree, like a table waiting for the giant's repast. Her exclamation startled two rabbits out of the tall grass and they vanished like fleeing fairies between the trees.

'Your spring water,' Alex said.

'It's beautiful,' she whispered and he nodded.

'We used to come here as children. We were convinced this was the remains of a great fortress and that it was up to us to hold it against the French.'

'We?'

He glanced at her, the smile she liked so much turning wry.

'My Sinclair cousins and I. The Sinclairs' land is on the other side of the hill, and two of my cousins were wild even then and they would sometimes ride over to escape their family and their tutors.'

'You were friends?'

He nudged one of the stones with his boot.

'I suppose one could say that. At least until my mother died. By the time I returned to the Hall, Lucas and Chase had moved away with their parents because of some scandal. I frankly can't remember the details, there have been so many scandals among the Sinclairs.'

'Haven't you seen them since?'

'Rarely. I try to avoid all forms of trouble and I really don't need any reminders of the Sinclair taint.'

She looked around the clearing, imagining the three boys lost in their imaginary world of bravery and valiant deeds. She found it hard to believe that anyone with a fervent imagination could be truly bad.

'I wonder if they would have had a better chance had they been named Stanton.'

'You don't believe in inherited evil, then, Miss James?'

'I don't know. I do find it hard to believe that a whole family is tainted as you said. You certainly aren't.'

'How do you know?'

'I just do.'

'And you are an authority.'

'I do think I am more objective than you on the topic.'

He laughed and glanced up at the trees.

'I know why I brought you here. You can be as stubborn as these trees. In fact…' His voice trailed off and the smile faded again. 'Alby was right. You aren't really a flower or herb, you're a sprite.'

'A what?'

He moved away from her before turning, as if putting space between him and some new and unclassified species that might yet prove dangerous.

'A wood sprite. The locals believe there are beings who guard these woods and live in the trees. They are benevolent and guard over travellers passing through, unless someone fells a tree.'

'And then?' she prompted.

'Then they own you, or your soul. You trade your soul for the soul of the tree you have taken.'

'It doesn't sound very benevolent. I don't think I care for the comparison.'

He didn't answer and even though it was cool there, she felt a prickle of perspiration form on her nape. She moved away from the force of his gaze and stopped by the tree stump and another exclamation escaped her. It must have been felled many decades ago, because its edges were softened with age and moss, but the dance of shapes and swirling patterns carved on to the surface of the stump looked more recent, though still softened by time. She traced her fingers over the dips and whorls.

'This is yours as well,' she said. 'It is lovely. Do these shapes mean anything?'

'Not really, just idle carvings. I spent a great deal of time here.' He shrugged and took her hand, drawing her towards the stream. He pulled off his gloves and cupped his hands to drink. She knelt as well and copied him.

'Wait,' he said, stopping her before her hands touched the silvery surface. 'You have to make a wish.'

'A wish?'

'The woods are a superstitious place. You are supposed to make a wish before you first drink from the spring.'

She looked down at the sparks of light dancing along the current. A wish wouldn't make it true.

'Chrissie! You're crying. Why?'

She hadn't realised and she hadn't even seen him shift towards her. His fingers were warm and firm against her jaw and cheek as he raised her face and through the film of tears she saw concern in his eyes. His finger brushed over her cheekbone and she felt the friction of dampness there.

'Tell me, Chrissie.'

'It was a happy thought.' It was only half a lie, but enough to make his mouth curve up slightly.

'You're a contrary young woman, Chrissie; you sparkle when you're angry and cry when you're happy. Tell me what the happy thought was.'

His voice was hoarse and the unconscious intimacy of her name coursed through her, like a warm breeze filling her sails. It wasn't fair. She wasn't strong enough.

'You will think it foolish.'

'Probably not, but even if I do, that is my problem. Tell me.'

'I would like to have a place of my own. Like Mary and Matty have Briar Rose Cottage. With window seats and books. And friends who would visit.' One friend in particular.

'A cottage. Wouldn't you miss the excitement of living at a centre of activity?'

'Perhaps. Since this is a fantasy I could have both, couldn't I?'

'Since this is fantasy you could have anything you want.'

His words were muffled as he turned away from her, dipping his hands into the water. Then he took her hands, cupped them as if she was a child and dipped them into the stream. The water was icy, it pinched at her skin and then eased as she kept them under the surface, the water shimmering as it rushed over them. She watched his hands raise hers, large and strong.

'Drink.'

It was so cold it burned her lips and stung her throat. This time she actively held her breath, afraid to release the pure, sweet sensation of being filled, possessed.

Water. Always changeable, but never losing its essence, immeasurably powerful and both threatening and soothing. Necessary.

'Water.' The word burst from her, a little too loudly.

'True. What about it?' He laughed; the tension that had gripped him before faded and he looked joyful again.

'I just realised why Lady Albinia cannot find a plant for you. I might be a wood sprite, but you are water.'

She shouldn't have spoken and now she couldn't, her breath all but disappeared at the flash of animal heat in his eyes before he lowered them.

When they stood it was just as natural for him to take her hand again, but it was different now. Without gloves, both their hands chilled from the water but warming fast, it was just different. His tale of wood sprites felt real. Perhaps merely by touching that carving on the stump she had unleased their power, she could feel her soul seeping out of her, into him.

He raised her hand, turning it, and the drops of water ran down, seeping into the fabric of her sleeve. His thumb smoothed the moisture along the base of her wrist, but the chill of the breeze on her damp skin only made the heat of the pulse beneath inescapable. She touched her tongue to her lips, remembering the taste of the water, the taste of his lips.

His hand tightened on hers.

'Don't do that.'

'Do what?' It was only a breath because she knew precisely what she was doing. No, precisely what she wanted. What she had wished for.

Alex.

He looked away. 'We should return. However magical this corner seems, this is still the real world. The King and Princess will wonder what I have done with their handmaiden.'

'The King might employ me, but I belong to no one. If I chose, I could leave at any moment.'

'You could, but you won't,' he said dismissively; his voice icier than the water.

She turned from him, knowing he was probably right. She stood on the edge of the clearing where the sunlight glistened on the grass like scattered coins. She breathed it in; trying to capture it so she could take it with her, but it wasn't enough. She wanted more. She walked around the edge of the clearing, where the ferns rose high in the shade of the tree trunks, around behind the tumbled boulders and past the stream back to where she began, but she didn't stop.

'What are you doing? Have you lost something?' His voice had lost its ice and he sounded curious and a little amused. She shook her head.

'No, I am making a magic circle.'

'A what?'

'Like in the fairy tales. A magic circle.'

'What does it do?'

'It doesn't do anything, or rather one does things in it.'

'Such as?'

'Whatever one wants. Because what happens inside a magic circle stays in the magic circle. For example, you can discover the future, but once you step outside, you forget.'

She continued her circuit and he moved into the centre of the clearing by the tree stump and stood with his hands on his hips, watching her, the sun striking gold on his hair and silver in his eyes.

'Convenient. What would you do in your magic circle, Chrissie?' He lingered on her name and she took a step towards him, and another. His hands fisted as if she was an approaching threat, but there was such heat in his narrowed eyes she couldn't stop. Two steps from him he reached for her, but she raised her hand and ran the tips of her fingers down his cheek.

'Tomorrow I return to Illiakos with Ari. What I would do in this magic circle is ask you to show me what it is I know can…happen, so I can take that with me. I want to feel it. That is what I would do.'

She hadn't thought it through so she was not prepared when he caught her hand against his cheek, holding it there against the warmth of his skin and the prickle of stubble while his other hand grasped her nape, pulling her towards him with a groan that ended shuddering against her lips. She was too shaken to find her balance and she just sagged against him, her hands instinctively grasping his shoulders, her breath a startled gasp against his mouth a second before it closed on hers.

Their kisses in the conservatory and in his bedroom hadn't prepared her for this. His lips were burning hers, his tongue sending shivers of need through her, shooting arrows of agony through her breasts and gathering like a fever at a point between her legs that had only been a suspicion until then and now she knew was waiting only for him. Her fingers slid deep under his coat and around his back, fisting in the warm fabric of his shirt as she dragged it up, and the contact with the hard planes and muscles of his back was like a benediction. As she feathered her fingers over the ridges of his muscles she realised with wonder that just as she had remembered her hands, she remembered the texture of his skin from all those years ago. It had never left her.

He stiffened at her exploration, drawing her against him with a groan. She wanted to feel that almost animal growl again but without the artificial barriers of all the clothes separating them. She wanted them bared, flesh to flesh. He wanted it, too, she could feel it in the way his body surged against her with each caress of her hands along the borders set by his buckskins, in the way his hand was tangling in the limits of her skirt, dragging it up her thigh until he reached the bare flesh above her stocking, his finger splaying on her heated skin, his thumb sliding against the softness of her inner thigh, brushing upwards and sending a sharp flame right through her centre, burning through sense and logic and leaving just need.

She twisted against him with a yearning

mewl and his answer to her cry of need was to ease her down to the grass, his mouth plundering hers as his hands sought and found points of pleasure that made her squirm. Her hands roved over his body in unconscious imitation of the torture he was inflicting, the tension in his limbs contrasting with the gentle touch of his hands. She arched against him as he half-lay on her, bracing his weight on the ground, but anchoring her with his leg as if she might float away like the sprite he had accused her of being.

'Alex.' She called his name to the forest and the sky. It was right that her fate should be decided here, in the forest clearing. The ferns rose around them like a feathered nest, shivering just as she was, their tips straining towards the faint sunlight spearing through the treetops.

She wanted more, she wanted to bare him as she was bared, feel every inch of him. Her hands shifted to his abdomen, confined by his shirt. He was as smooth and hard as marble, but as warm as melting wax. She was shaping him or he was shaping her, they were both just coming into being right here, like Adam and Eve, primeval, needing nothing but themselves…

He groaned against her mouth, his body shuddering against her.

'This is madness.'

She shook her head. She didn't care if it was mad. It was as necessary as breathing. She wouldn't let him become Lord Stanton again. Not yet. She touched his lips, raising herself on her elbow to follow their trail with her lips.

'Don't think, please, Alex…'

Madness.

Oh, God, he wanted her. One didn't die from lust, but it felt like he might. It felt as though he was dying with this need to make her part of him and if she didn't do something, give him something… She was unleashing a rabid beast of need he had no idea how he would drive back into its cage. He could feel every inch of his body as her destructive hands explored him—the expanse of his back, the resistance of his spine and the taut strain of muscles as he held himself from wreaking havoc, the whole physical order of battle raised to combat his need to plunder what he wanted.

He traced her lips with his fingers. He had watched them so often, so intently, it was like coming home. Her breath, warm and unsteady, moved over his skin, softening his touch, drawing him on to trace the shadow between her lips. It was like trying to caress a living flame, but he was incapable of stopping. He needed more.

Her lips shivered, parted, breathed him in and he bent to touch his mouth to hers. He had never felt so acutely before—it was just a brush of flesh on flesh, but he could feel it possess his whole body, like sliding naked over satin sheets.

'Chrissie…' He groaned and sank his head against the fragrant curve of her neck.

Her hand tangled in his hair, but he caught it, anchoring it in his to prevent her from doing any more damage. This had to stop. This was the real world. There were no spells, or sprites.

'We have to stop.'

Her gaze lost its dreamy heat at his words, focusing and filling with the determination he had always felt in her and he didn't know whether to be terrified or triumphant.

'No.' She shook her head, her voice fierce. 'No. I don't want to stop. I want this. For myself. You owe me! You brought me here. To this place. You shouldn't have brought me here if you meant to stop!'

She was right. He couldn't even blame her for intruding into one of his most private places on Stanton land because he had brought her here with one purpose. He had dreamed of her in the forest, lying in the clearing, though there were no bluebells now and she wasn't naked, but that snug-fitting riding habit and the dappled gleam of sunlight on her dark hair and lush lower lip was as erotic as any display of bare flesh.

She was right—he owed her, not just his life but atonement for every cowardly attempt to create distance between himself and this need. He might hate that she didn't want anything more from him than physical pleasure and release, but he owed her. He would just give her pleasure; a woman like her deserved to know what she was capable of, on her own terms. She wasn't like Vera.

Her whimper of pure pleasure the moment he touched his mouth to hers was a seal on his choice. He had no defence he wanted to marshal against her eagerness, her hands sliding through his hair and the warmth of her body pressing towards his, promising everything. His body surged ahead, enveloping her, raging with the foreign need she unleashed in him, going beyond his control before he even knew he was lost.

It might be madness, but nothing had ever felt so right. There was no one else in the world right now. Nothing hung in the scales. There was only Chrissie. She was where she belonged.

He didn't say the words that were pounding through his body: *Right here, right now, you are mine. I am yours. There is nothing else.*

He would strip her, body and soul, as he had wanted to strip away those veils six years ago. He wanted her bared of everything that was between them—clothing, rules, convention—leaving her like Venus rising from the green waves in nothing but her mahogany hair tangling over her shoulders, rising and falling against her generous curves. He would anchor his hands in it, hold her there until she opened to him. The image was so powerful, he could feel her hair in his hands as if he had already unwound it.

His fingers found and slipped away the fastenings of her dress, the laces of her stays, easing away her bodice to reveal the rosy nipples that were already puckered with need, waiting for his touch. He pulled away her chemise to uncover her to the kiss of sunlight filtering through the trees. Bared, she was as magnificent as he had suspected and he traced her curves, pulling back on the need to plunder so he could explore, imprint these moments on her memory so she would never forget his touch just as he had never forgotten hers. The dark-rose tips of her breasts gathered under his fingers as she shuddered, her body rising towards his, her lips parted as she watched him. His gaze locked on hers as he bent to touch his mouth to one hardened peak, brushing it gently, hardly more than a breeze. She moaned, her hands shifting and clutching at his hair, whether to pull him away or pull him close didn't matter because he tugged the tip gently into his mouth, soothing and teasing as she shuddered under him.

'Tell me. Is this what you want, Chrissie?' His voice was rough, almost an accusation, but she just nodded, her teeth sinking into her lower lip, her leg rising against his, and he obliged her, slipping his hand under her skirts, finding the warm skin above her garter, spreading over it as it burned against his hand and he stopped, battling a wave of lust that surged to his erection, demanding instant action. He had been waiting for this for so long, so long. It was dangerous. *She* was dangerous.

But his fear was a distant second to the lust that was raging through him and the need he felt vibrating through her like thunder through the air—inescapable, inevitable. There was no point in doing anything but embracing it.

'Chrissie… Oh, God, I want to see you, all of you. you're so beautiful.'

She raised her hands as if to push him away, her withdrawal palpable.

'No, no, I'm not.'

He caught her hands, pinning them back so

that she arched towards him and he bent to taste her offering, his lips tracing gently around the hardened crests of her breasts.

'Yes, you are,' he murmured against her warm flesh as he approached his goal. 'Beautiful. I can't stop looking at you. It's driving me insane and making me useless. All I want to do is this…'

Her disbelieving laugh transformed into a gasp as he took her nipple back into his mouth, into a shuddering moan as his tongue and teeth joined the teasing. She might not believe his words, but his erection was evidence she couldn't deny. Not that she understood what he was telling her yet, but she soon would. He didn't want to hurry, he wanted to take all the time in the world, but he knew their time was limited.

'Chrissie, touch me. I need you to touch me.'

As if she had been waiting for his hoarse demand, her fingers dragged up his shirt, spread under it and pressed into the muscles of his back, then slid forward to spread out over his abdomen and upwards. With a little muted cry she drew back suddenly and for a panicked moment he thought she was stopping, but she reached out, just grazing the pale skin of his scar. His pulse was slamming through his body, but outwardly he froze, as if a deer had stumbled into the clearing and mustn't be frightened.

'Alex…' It was just a whisper, full of wonder and worry, and it cleaved through him. When she pressed her palm against that ragged remnant of his wound as gently as a breeze, a wave of heat seared through him, driving into his arousal with all the force of a spear splitting an iron shield. She must have felt that surge against her thigh because she shifted, her hips rising, accommodating him.

'Chrissie.' His voice was a rumble of fury and need. For days he had struggled not to say her name, but it was like an undeniable itch. It rushed through him, sultry, subterranean, tearing him from his moorings as it went.

'Christina…' That was almost worse. He couldn't deal with either of them at the moment. 'Oh, hell, Chrissie. We either stop now or not at all.'

His hand was saying something completely different, shaping the swell of her thigh, sliding under the soft muslin undergarments. He drew it back, but it rebelled, sliding up the curve of her waist and pausing just below her lush breasts. He might still have managed to draw back if she hadn't made that sound again, the little gasp and moan, shifting towards him so that his hand was somehow shaping itself to her breast. She caught it, pressing it to her.

'Then not at all,' she gasped. 'You owe me. I saved your life and you owe me this. I know you will be careful, but this I take with me.'

She shuddered, the fingers of her other hand breaching the waist of his buckskins, digging into the rise of his buttocks as she drew her hips against his, the pressure a welcome agony against his arousal. He abandoned the fiction of control and stripped them both of what remained of their clothing until she was as bare as his dream of the unveiled Venus, but far lovelier, her skin a warm pearl sheen against the tapestry of rumpled clothes beneath them and her hair a dark mass of tousled brown catching the warmth of the sinking sun.

This you will take with you.

He would pleasure her until her screams of joy could be heard above the treetops.

He eased her back, mapping out her defeat, dismantling her defences and control inch by delicious inch, using every skill at his disposal. His mouth and hands and body found every place of pleasure, the satiny slimness of her ankles, the beautiful roundness of her backside, the twin dimples above it, all the way up to the sweet warmth of her neck. He explored and plundered until she was writhing beneath him, her nails biting into his back as her hips ground against his, her eyes a deep blue, begging. Then he slid his fingers through the dark curls to the damp heat of her arousal, finding its core and teasing and taunting until he knew he held her at the very edge of annihilation.

'Chrissie. Tell me you want this. Now.'

He could barely talk, his whole body poised as before a blow, but he had to be certain.

'Alex. I want you. I need you.' She arched back, moving against his fingers, her own fingers digging deep and painful into his back as she moaned, driving him wild.

He didn't wait for more. Already he could feel the waves of her pleasure begin to break and he wanted them to break over him. He wanted to go slowly, but he couldn't, he pushed in, greedy to feel her heat and ride the crash of pleasure with her. She gave a cry of pain and he froze, panting for breath and control, but then her whole body released on a very different cry, shuddering and rising against him and he abandoned thought and conscience and anything but the sensation of being inside her, part of her, barely clinging to the knowledge that he had promised to keep her safe. As he drove into her, through the receding waves of her orgasm, he almost gave in and broke his word, but even as the agony of holding back plummeted towards pleasure he managed to pull out, shattering even at the friction of that withdrawal. Everything but the pliant body beneath him and the knowledge that he had branded her ceased to exist.

He had no idea how much time had passed, but when he opened his eyes he could tell by the fall of the shadows it was late afternoon. Soon their absence would be noted and someone would come looking for them, but he didn't want to move. To move would mean to dislodge the soft, warm weight of her body, half-stretched out on him and half-burrowed against his side. To move would be to face reality. He closed his eyes and breathed, gathering his resolve. His body was still humming with fierce satisfaction which just proved how frail men were, to allow such a disconnect between rationality and the raw hunger of physical needs.

He knew she was awake but he could think of nothing sensible to say, or of anything sensible at all. Everything had happened so fast, but it also felt they had been gone a lifetime. Everything had changed from the moment they had entered the forest and it was his fault. He should have known never to bring Chrissie here.

He *had* known. Another sign of precisely how dangerous she was to him that she could make him act against all reason and good sense and not even realise what he was doing. He had brought her to a place he knew they would never be interrupted. What had he expected to happen? He had walked into a trap of his own making and he didn't know whether he was furious at himself or relieved that the choice had been taken away from him.

'You understand what this means, don't you, Chrissie?' he said at last, brushing his hand down the indentation of her spine. 'When we return to the Hall I will speak with King Darius and make arrangements for a special licence. I doubt he and the Princess will be able to delay their departure to wait for the ceremony, but perhaps once my duties at the Congress of Verona are over we can visit them on Illiakos for—'

'What on earth are you talking about?' she interrupted, pushing away from him and dragging her chemise to her. Her eyes had widened into dark-blue discs of sea turning to storm. 'We said… I told you I expected nothing from you…'

He sat up as well, taking the chemise from

her fumbling hands and helping her dress before he reached for his clothes.

'Words are one thing, actions are another, Christina. I took your virginity…'

'You didn't take anything. I *gave* it to you!'

'So you did, no strings attached. I believe you really mean it, but that is merely proof of how naïve you are. Aside from everything else what do you think will happen if King Darius were to hear of this? Do you honestly think he will still consider you a suitable companion for his daughter?'

'There is no reason for him to hear. Unless you tell him.'

His jaw clenched.

'So that is it? You have had your fun and now it is back to your duties?'

Hurt and anger chased away the remnants of languor and confusion in her eyes, but before they could spill over he reached out and placed his hands on her shoulders, anchoring them both to the new physical reality between them.

'This is all immaterial. You are going to marry me. It is as simple as that.'

'Simple.' She laughed and brushed her hand over her eyes as she stepped back from his hands. 'You should have stopped me if that is what you thought.'

I didn't think anything but that I wanted you and I couldn't have stopped if the whole forest had been on fire. That's how far I've fallen.

He didn't say the words. She looked calm now, which made no sense. Surely a young woman who had just been deflowered on the forest floor… On the forest floor, for heaven's sake. He hadn't even had the self-control or decency to offer her a bed.

She had told him what she wanted—just like the English brought back a statue or a painting from Italy or Greece. This was to be her *souvenir*, something to add to her reading about exotic travels and those agony advertisements while she sank back into her life. Nothing that was worth risking her safety for. She was worse than Vera—at least Vera had expected something from him, everything. Everything he was offering Chrissie. No, Christina. Chrissie was a fiction of his own making.

'Come, we need to return before they come looking for us. We will discuss this later.'

She opened her mouth to speak, but he took her hand and pulled her along the path down towards the fields and the waiting horses. He didn't want to hear more sensible reasoning right now. He just wanted quiet so all the crashing and conflicting voices in his head could settle back into their respective corners and he could think.

Not that there was anything to think about. The deed was done.

Christina settled into the saddle and arranged her skirts before turning her horse towards the Hall. Her body was still shaking, half in remembered pleasure and half in shock that it had happened, that she had instigated the most amazing thing that had ever happened to her. She wished they could have stayed there, lingered in those amazing sensations of pleasure and being close and cared for by someone who listened to her body and her needs and answered them, someone who at least for those moments showed her just how much he wanted her.

She wasn't ready for the reckoning; for the cold purposeful man who was telling her he was willing to pay the price for their mistake. How had it never occurred to her he would feel duty bound to offer her marriage? She had just presumed the difference in their situations was so extreme that it wasn't even a consideration. He had called her naïve and she hoped it was just naïveté that had brought this blindness—perhaps deep inside her she had planned to tie him to her?

She glanced at the man riding beside her. This was Lord Alexander Stanton, the diplomat she had watched conduct the negotiations with the ease of a master driver, hardly even needing the whip and never tangling his reins. She searched his profile for some sign that she was allowed to be weak and take something for herself, but there was no hint of hidden clockworks, no pain and certainly no need.

He must hate her now, but himself even more. She knew what he was thinking—that he had allowed the Sinclair to win again and the Stanton would pay the price and marry her in penance just as he had paid penance over Vera by changing his whole life to pursue duty over inclination. She would be just like his mother's portrait on the wall. Another reminder of his weakness. Virtue might be hard, but the alternative came at a price. He was not a man who carried debts.

She tightened her hands on the reins to stop the shaking. She wanted it so much, to stay with him, that it surely must be wrong, this need to turn her back on Ari and stay with the man she loved even though she knew it was wrong for him. She wanted it so much she felt ill with it, her body losing the pleasant hazy sensation that had followed their lovemaking and filling with a roiling queasy heat heightened by the afternoon sun pinching at her nape as they crossed the fields. He had been right about her, there was a volcano or an avalanche or another natural disaster barely suppressed inside her.

She was glad he wasn't speaking. If he said anything now she didn't know what might come out of her. Nothing good. Something that would damage them even more than she had already…

I know what I did was terribly wrong, that you must think I have ruined your life. That you have allowed a mixture of gratitude and lust to force you down a path you have tried so hard to renounce and now you will be forced to marry a woman past her first youth with no looks and no prospects and no family, who does nothing but get in your way all the time and has now thoroughly tripped you.

I am thoroughly, utterly selfish and I can't help it, all I wish is to be with you. I want you to pick holes in my dignity and remind me I'm alive for myself as well, I want you to show me things that open the world to me. I want you to make me stretch my mind and body to their fullest extent. I want the way you make me feel safe when my world is shaking, even the way you shake my very foundations and drag me into unknown territories. I want you to touch me the way you did and shatter me from the inside out and never stop.

But it isn't all selfish. It isn't. I want to make you happy and ease that anger and need and make you see how beautiful you are and how right. That there isn't any need for your battles because what you call Sinclair and Stanton are just parts of the same amazing man. They don't matter, but you do. I want to make you smile and hold your hand. I want to be your home.

I love you, Alex.

I never meant to cause harm.

The words danced through her, a whole universe of wants, trying to force their way out, but she remained as silent as he. There was nothing that could be said to make this right. He had been correct to say that words are one thing, actions are another. Now she must think how she was going to fix this before she hurt someone. Someone other than herself. There was really only one action she could take and that was to stand as firm as any model of Stanton rectitude. She refused to ruin his life any more than she already had.

Chapter Fifteen

'Everything is ready, my lord. The carriages are loaded and waiting on the drive. Lady Albinia took the King and Princess and Miss James earlier to say goodbye to the vicar and Mrs Dunston, but they should return soon if they are to reach Southampton in time for the evening tide.'

Alex rose from his desk, moving towards the window and back.

In an hour the Hall would finally be empty of guests. Everything that had happened in the last couple of weeks would be part of the past—another chapter in his life and definitely not one of the best.

It wasn't quite done yet, he reminded himself. By pleading a headache to avoid coming down to dinner the previous night it was clear Christina was signalling that what occurred in the forest would remain between them. He had no reason to feel surprise or resentment. He should be applauding the way she embraced his advice to take what she wanted. She would probably prefer to avoid any confrontation at all, but he wouldn't let her take that cowardly path. If she wanted to send him to the devil, she would have to tell him to his face.

'Have Thunder brought round, please, Watkins.'

He spotted the Stanton landaulet outside the church gates before he reached the vicarage.

'Where are they, Henry?' he asked the groom who nodded towards the church.

'Inside with Mr Dunston, my lord.'

'Here, keep an eye on Thunder.' He tossed the reins to the groom and marched towards the church. Perhaps in the cool sanctity of the structure he had known since infancy it would finally be clear he had merely been suffering from temporary instability of the mind. Perhaps seeing her there, in the church where he would one day put the seal on the next phase of the Stanton legacy, would break the spell that was clouding his judgement and convince him he should be grateful for the reprieve she was offering.

He opened the door, the screech of hinges finding an echo in the grind of pain in his chest and sending a flock of sparrows fluttering upwards on to the beams above the nave, their wings filtering the light and making shadows dance on the stone floor.

'Oh, how lovely. Look at the birds!' Ariadne exclaimed and Mr Dunston, the vicar, smiled apologetically.

'There have been sparrows here for as long as I can remember, I'm afraid.'

For as long as Alex could remember as well. His father had been convinced it was Alex's fault, which it might very well be. Every Sunday he smuggled crumbs in his pockets, scattering them surreptitiously and waiting for the sparrows to appear and then at least he had something to watch during the interminable sermons. There had been a logic to the way the fragile birds approached and fought over the crumbs, a pecking order he found fascinating. When his father finally caught him in the act of sprinkling the dry bread up the aisle and he tried to explain his fascination, he had earned himself a lecture on proper occupations for the present Lord Stanton and the next Marquess of Wentworth.

Then as now.

Currently the proper occupation was to wait with as much grace as he could muster until Mr Dunston finished his lecture on the history of the chapel, its architecture and the rich history it shared with the noble Stanton family that had come to the valley some four hundred years ago. Alex was only too aware of that history, good and bad. He had certainly done his best to atone for the Sinclair contribution. He glanced about the church as the King and Princess obediently followed the sweep of the vicar's arm as he indicated the Gothic masonry above the apse.

'Where is Miss James?'

Mr Dunston stopped mid-sentence and everyone turned to him. Hell, he was losing his finesse. Thankfully the Princess answered matter of factly.

'She and Mrs Dunston were discussing herbs and I believe they went to inspect some plant named after a saint.'

Mr Dunston's lines face crinkled in a smile.

'Mrs Dunston is very fond of her garden. I'm afraid if she has found a kindred spirit, your Miss James will be a while. Shall I fetch her?'

'No, not yet. When you are done here.'

'Very well. As I was saying, after Cromwell…'

Alex crossed his arms and ignored the urge to head out to the vicarage. Finally it was over and everyone filed out towards the landaulet.

'Shall I rescue that young woman from my

wife's toils, Lady Albinia?' Mr Dunston suggested.

'We shall drive by and collect her ourselves, Mr Dunston. The carriages are no doubt awaiting us,' the King replied and the vehicle pulled out of the churchyard, the rasp and creak of wheels and clatter of hoofs fading away. Now it was quiet, just the music of a late English summer, insects buzzing above the wisp of breeze and below the chirping of the birds. Alex approached Thunder, but stopped at the familiar rush of flapping sparrows and turned back towards the church porch.

Christina was standing at the end of the nave, looking up with her head tilted slightly to the side, mirroring a sparrow which had settled on the eaves and was looking down at her. The light from the simple stained-glass windows in the chancel haloed her like a supplicant gazing heavenwards, raising amber lights in her dark hair and striking her lower lip with gold, as if an angel had just kissed her and she was watching its ascent.

She had a way of looking utterly alive without any outward show of expression, as she had while playing the pianoforte for the Princess or working away at her herbs or riding Charis. Or in the forest clearing, her face raised as it was now, gathering the sun that filtered through the oaks. And then in her moment of climax—so deep inside some rich inner world it pushed everything else out of the way. It was almost tangible, to the point he felt if he moved forward he would be absorbed into it, like stepping through a runic arch into a faerie world.

Just look at her. Smiling at that sparrow as though it was a visitation at the very least. It was just a sparrow and few rays of sunlight, for heaven's sake. There was no reason to look like she was a bride about to meet her groom…

The thought was unavoidable. He might not want to marry anyone else, but at some point in the future he would have to. Would he then remember this moment as he entered the church? See instead of his own bride the young woman standing there, looking up just where he would be, smiling…

He leaned his leg against the pew, letting the wood press into his flesh through his buckskins, as if that point of pain could quell the surge of queasiness. He was so used to this little church, there was no reason to feel it was suddenly a foreign place, the solid Norman structure too low and oppressive. It had stood for hundreds of years and would continue standing for probably as long. The thought should have comforted him, but it didn't. He dragged his gaze to the aisle floor. He knew every crack in the worn and shiny flagstones, every rise and fall of the uneven surface. He shifted and the wooden bench creaked like an outraged crow, sending the sparrows fluttering again.

Her smile disappeared as she turned and saw him. Her hands were gloveless and she was holding a sprig of some plant, probably from the Dunstons' garden. He could imagine her, her hands moving through the herbs with the vicar's wife, touching the leaves and flowers, absorbing them with all her senses, taking possession of them as she did everything else in his world, just as she had from the day he had come across her in the library—his books, his gardens, his woodcuttings, his tenants, his life. Isn't that what ivy did? Encroach, possess, choke…

'Where is everyone? Outside?' she asked, her voice a low thrum in the silence.

'Gone.'

'What do you mean, gone?' She looked stunned, the colour draining from her cheeks. It was a cruel jab and he deserved the despair that welled through him at her shocked response. What had he expected? Relief that she might be forced to remain with him? He knew her loyalty and love for the Princess and King were above all else in her universe. She had told him so with absolute clarity back on Illiakos when he made his foolish proposal that she come with him and nothing had changed since. If anything the bond between her and her adopted family was stronger. She had never hidden that truth, or the fact she was using him. He should be grateful for this little reminder of their respective priorities.

It shouldn't hurt. Not like this.

'Don't panic, they have just gone to find you at the vicarage. Your King and Princess would no more contemplate leaving you behind than surrendering their kingdom to pirates. But as much as you seem determined to avoid facing it, you and I have our own business to resolve. Don't shake your head. You cannot honestly expect me to just let this go in silence. What happened yesterday…' Heat spread outwards from some deep cave inside him, not just heat but a possessive yearning that demanded he wrap around her, claim her. 'You gave me your innocence, Chrissie.'

'That was my choice. It was never meant to be a burden for you.'

'It isn't a burden, it is a gift. You can't just walk away from that as if we had done nothing more than shared a country dance.'

Her eyes finally rose to his and it hurt because he saw sadness and regret there. He almost raised his hands to stop her answer, as if that could stave off the inevitable. When she spoke her voice was hoarse.

'You don't need me. Not in any way that matters.'

He turned towards the chancel. *Not in any way that matters.* Not to her obviously.

'Is it a contest between who needs you most, the King and Princess or I, then? This has nothing to do with need, only with what is right. We both made a choice yesterday in the forest. I might be a rake, but I accept the consequences of my actions. This is the only course of action that is acceptable.'

The stone walls brought back his voice, hollow and a little sullen. At least he didn't sound terrified. She looked terrified, though, as if this were one of those tales of the wild hunt and he was bearing down on her, intent on stealing her soul. Perhaps he was. But more than anything he wanted to risk his, if only she could risk hers. Why couldn't she just take that risk? She would for Ari. For Ari she would brave anything: pain, rejection, frustration, snowstorms. Even as the words played out in his mind he knew they were childish. But true. He didn't merit that kind of sacrifice. Or love. He never had. It hadn't mattered before, now it did.

His lungs felt full of fog, thick and resistant. He pressed his hand to the scar on his side. He remembered this feeling. Six years ago in the castle, her backing away from him as he stumbled over the need to keep her, not lose that essence he had barely even understood, not even certain why it was so important.

'That isn't fair, Alex. You kept telling me again and again to take what I wanted. It was never my intention to extract such a price. I just wanted...'

She remained standing, staring straight ahead though there was nothing to see but the dull surface of the great wooden door. He touched his fingers to the line of her jaw, turning her face towards him. There wasn't much light at this end of the church, only two narrow windows forced into the thick stone walls on either side of the door, and her face was a study of shadows and sombre illumination, an oil painting in a room descending into dusk. Before she had looked like a supplicant painted on to the shimmering glass, now she looked the image of a young martyr. The tears hadn't fallen yet, but they were gathering. Any moment now that tear balanced there would reach a critical weight and escape, skim down the soft sweep of her cheek, perhaps catch on the edge of the parting between her lips… He was vengeful enough to want to see them fall. He wanted to hate her, find the force to crush the link binding him to her. He wanted it crumbling to dust and careening into a chasm. He wanted her never to have existed.

As he watched the tear spill and slide downwards he knew all his brave protestations were as useful as a teaspoon against a mountain. He didn't want to hurt her; he wanted something very different from her. It wasn't her fault she didn't want to give it.

'Chrissie, I'm sorry. You are right—about everything. I have no right to punish you for my mistakes.'

'Please let me go. I can't bear this.'

She sounded as defeated as he felt. He should never have started down this path with her. That she was as poisonous to him as he had been to Vera. It was time to do as she asked and end this.

Another tear slid down and he grasped her wrist as her hand rose to brush it away. When it reached her mouth it curved over her upper lip, settling like a pearl at the corner of her mouth, and he touched his thumb to it just as her lips parted. The bead of moisture burst and spread, warm on his skin. He could almost taste its salty heat, he could already taste her. He kept his thumb just there, where her breath shivered on the now-damp pad of his thumb, and pressed his palm to her cheek, his fingers slipping over the ridges of her ear, into the warmth of her hair. She closed her eyes and two more tears coursed down, one catching on the valley between his finger and thumb. He was within a whisper of breaking, of completely losing his footing.

This was how avalanches began, with a shudder and whisper. And then destruction followed. If she had to leave, it should be now.

'Oh, God.'

The irony of those words, spoken while standing in the Stanton church, dragged him back to sanity.

He pulled away. 'It is time for you to leave. You have made your choice.'

The squeal of the iron doorknob as it opened was so loud, or his senses were at such a pitch of sensitivity, the sound hurt.

'I must do something about those hinges,' Mr Dunston said as he entered, his ridged forehead puckered. 'Ah, good, there you are, Miss James, we must have just missed you at the vicarage. The landaulet is waiting outside, my dear, and you had best hurry; his Majesty does not wish to miss the tides.'

'Thank you, Mr Dunston,' Alex replied, surprised how steady and commonplace his voice sounded.

'Yes,' Christina murmured as her fingers secured the ribbons of her bonnet. 'Pray thank your wife again for me, Mr Dunston. Goodbye. Goodbye, Lord Stanton. Farewell.'

She didn't look up as they stepped outside and he helped her into the landaulet, the rim of her straw bonnet obscuring her face. The King was talking and he forced himself to turn to the man.

'You needn't see us back, Stanton. I never liked elaborate farewells and no doubt Stavros is already champing at the bit in the carriages for us to be off to make the tide. Suffice it to say that I will never forget what we have achieved here and I hope you will come one day soon to Illiakos so we can return your gracious hospitality...'

There was more, but though Alex said everything that was proper to the King and Princess it all faded away from him. He didn't look again at Christina and when the landaulet disappeared down the lane he turned and walked slowly back into the church. It was empty again and he sat down in his old seat, watching the sparrows pecking at the floor.

One day his child might sit there and scatter crumbs for them. His children. And there would be a dog. Boy. Or whatever they wanted to call it. By that time all this would be a distant memory. Everything would be in equilibrium again and he would look back and commend himself on refraining from succumbing to the need to lay himself open to a woman whom he would never be able to control and who didn't need him.

Eventually it was Thunder's whinny outside that recalled him to his surroundings and he stood up, feeling as stiff as an old man.

The driveway before the Hall was empty of carriages and the building stood mute and solemn under gathering clouds. This was his home. This was where he would eventually bring his family, his wife, raise his children.

He stared at the blank windows, hardly noticing when the door opened and Alby stepped outside.

'They left, Alexander.'

I know they left.

'I wish they could have stayed just a little longer. We needed more time.' She added.

He quieted Thunder. He could think of nothing to say. His chest and shoulders ached as if after an illness. The thought of getting off his horse, going inside, something so mundane he never gave it a thought, appeared impossible, beyond him. What would happen if he just sat there?

Predictably the skies began to leak and Thunder shook his mane, but Alex still didn't move.

More time. What difference would it have made? He would still be the same person and so would she.

But she would be there.

'Go inside, Alby. You will get wet.'

She clasped her hands together, hesitating, and then went back up the stairs.

'More time for what?' he asked and she paused.

'For you.'

He didn't stop her again. The rain was pearling on Thunder's mane, gathering into rivulets snaking down the short black hair of his neck.

More time.

What had he expected from her? For her to throw herself at his feet and beg to stay? Tell him he mattered more than her family? More than anything. To take a risk he was too afraid to take himself? He hadn't even risked telling her how much he needed her. How impossible it was to imagine his life emptied of her again. No, not emptied—gouged. Her not being with him wasn't an absence, it was a gaping, throbbing wound.

He hadn't even risked telling her he loved her.

She might be a coward, but so was he. They deserved one another.

'Sorry for this, Thunder. It can't be helped. I have to do it.'

Thunder stamped his hoof, but gave no protest as Alex set him at a gallop down the drive.

Chapter Sixteen

'The captain says the storm is moving inland and that the Channel is quite calm. We will embark in an hour so come into the parlour and eat something before we must leave.'

Christina didn't turn from her contemplation of the darkening port and it was Ari who answered.

'In a moment, Papa. I need to tidy up.'

'What is there to tidy? Never mind, join me when you are done.'

'Tina?' Ari asked as the door to the private parlour of the inn closed behind him.

'You go, Ari,' Christina answered. 'I'm not hungry.'

'I didn't want to say anything in the carriage, Tina, but please talk to me. What is wrong?'

Christina pressed her fingertips to her eyes.

'Please, Ari. I need a moment alone. Please.'

She held herself for a moment longer as Ari's arms came around her, but it was too much. She was tired and miserable and she ached and ached and ached. When the sobs and words came they were a child's, but she didn't know how to stop them.

'I can't bear it. I don't know how I will do this. I keep telling myself it will go away, but I don't believe it and I don't want it to. I want to be with him even if it is wrong for him and that makes me a horrible person, but I don't care, I can't bear the thought that I won't see him again. I can't.'

When it finally stopped it was because she was exhausted, not because the pain had washed away. It sat inside her, a great ugly lump, mashed together with anger at herself, at him, at Ari and the King, but mostly at herself for being too scared to demand something for herself. She groped in her reticule for a handkerchief and wiped her eyes and blew her nose and tried to dislodge Ari's arms, but Ari didn't move and so she just sat there.

'It isn't like you to run away, Tina,' Ari said after a while. 'You never run from Papa though everyone else does. You've never turned your back on me and goodness knows I have sometimes given you reason. If he wants you, you should have stayed.'

'It isn't that simple. Besides, I couldn't leave you, you are my family.'

Ari's arms tightened.

'But you could never lose me, Tina. I want your happiness as much as you want mine. Don't hide behind me.'

'Oh, Ari, you are so dear to me, thank you for that. But it isn't just you. I am all wrong for him.'

'How could you be? You are the most wonderful woman I know—he won't find another like you, that is certain.'

Christina laughed.

'He doesn't want someone like me. He wants someone like his stepmother, solid and undemanding and reliable. He told me so himself. What happened between us was a mistake. For him I am a mistake, from the very beginning, except that this time it was all my fault.'

'Well, I don't know what happened between you and I probably shouldn't ask, though I am dreadfully curious, but do you know, you are painting a rather different picture of Lord Stanton than the one I have in mind. None of this sounds like him at all. None of this sounds like either of you. Love is a very strange thing. What shall you do?'

What *could* she do?

He hadn't told her he loved her, not even that

he needed her. He had just stood there, his hand pressed to her cheek while she fought to keep her heart from spilling on to the church flagstones along with her tears.

She pressed the palms of her hands to her eyes, trying to think. But all she could see was Alex standing in front of her in the church, trying to do what he thought was right. Intense. Demanding. Cynical.

Hurt…

She couldn't bear it. She needed to see him, to speak with him. Tell him the truth, everything that was burning inside her even if it was a mistake. Even if she lost everything in the end.

'Ari, I need your help.'

'Anything. You know that. Tell me what I must do.'

Chapter Seventeen

Alex knew the depth of King Richard's desperation when he had offered his kingdom for a horse. He stared through the sheets of rain at the rolling fields, his hand on Thunder's streaming black coat, and cursed the fates. But if they were trying to tell him something, he wasn't listening—it would take more than a thrown horseshoe for him to turn tail. At least the fates were kind enough for it to happen within sight of a farmhouse.

'It's not your fault, Thunder. This is just a temporary setback. I might be a blind, obstinate, cowardly fool, but it will take more than a storm to stop me. Come, don't take it ill, but I might have to leave you to rusticate for a while. I just hope they have a mount I can buy.'

'Two hours ago, sir. They were already delayed, but she had to leave before the tide turned.'

The harbour master wiped away the rain from his gingery beard and stared longingly at the lights of the Green Dragon, but he waited as Alex stared into the darkness at the ships rising and falling on the frothing swells.

'I need a ship.'

'A ship, sir?'

'Something fast. I need to catch them.'

'Lord help you, sir, you can't catch them. First, there's not a captain alive who will take his ship out with the tide against them in this storm. Second, that was a Boston frigate, built by Edmund Hartt himself. You won't see the tail end of it this side of Gibraltar. If they stop to restock there, you might be lucky, but maybe not. You come into the Dragon and get dry and tomorrow we will see…'

'I'm not going to wait until tomorrow. There has to be someone willing. I don't care how much it costs.'

The harbour master shrugged, tugging his hat lower and letting loose a cascade of rain from its curling brim.

'There's always a fool to take another fool's gold. You want names? I want a hot toddy.' He inspected Alex's clothes and then raised his chin in the direction of a large well-lit hostelry across the way. 'The Green Dragon's the best hostelry nearby. So you can follow me into the

Dragon or go and find another madman by yourself. Sir.'

The harbour master lowered his head and hurried towards the hostelry and Alex resisted the urge to curse him, the weather, the world. He knew the man was right and he needed his knowledge of the ships currently available for charter. Besides, the simple fact remained he didn't have enough funds on his person to commandeer a ship to convey him to Illiakos. He had missed this particular boat, literally, and he would just have to plan his next step with less histrionics. It was time to stop acting like Don Quixote tilting at windmills and start acting sensibly. That meant he should rack up at the Dragon, find a suitable vessel for such a long voyage, send for a representative of his bank so they could prepare the funds he would need for the voyage. Not to mention send word to the Hall and to London that he would be disappearing for several weeks, possibly longer if Chrissie proved stubborn.

The fact that he wanted to howl with frustrated impatience and force the world to bend to his will was immaterial. If he had to follow her to the Antipodes, he would. It was as simple as that. Chrissie was his. He would take as long as necessary to make it as clear to her as it was to him. She didn't trust anyone, least of all herself, and that meant it would be an uphill slog to make her trust him. But if it took a lifetime he would do it. He knew how hard it was to trust. As hard as it was to need someone. To love them.

God, he knew. But once you did… Whatever it took, he would do it.

He turned for one last look at the roiling sea just as thunder went from a grumble to a roar and the blackness turned for a moment into an etching of rabid waves attacking yellow sails and spiky masts. His heart constricted in fear and desperation—was she out there, being tossed about, afraid? Hell. If he could have made a deal with the powers that be to transport him across the distance between them he would probably offer everything he had to be with her that very second. Not even to have her for himself, just be certain she was safe.

He clenched his jaw and wiped the stinging rain from his face. Big oaths were worth less than the breath they wasted. The devil was in the details and it was time to go and see to them.

'Alex?'

His heart stopped, lost its place, gave two painful thumps and began to race. He turned, preparing himself for the joke his mind was playing on itself. He wasn't prepared for the cloaked figure standing three yards away. The hood and darkness completely obscured her face, but he didn't need to see it. He had a very vivid memory of her veiled figure.

He strode forward, pushed back her hood, his heart contracting and expanding at the sight of her. However it had happened, she was here.

'Chrissie.'

He didn't hear the thunder and the lightning was just a flash of light that struck her eyes into sudden sapphire brilliance, but the torrent of rain was harder to ignore. He took her hand and pulled her towards the Green Dragon, but she halted just outside the door.

'I came out through the courtyard, the side door…' Her voice was swallowed by another crack of thunder, closer this time. He didn't question her, but followed towards the arched entrance to the hostelry's entrance. The rain had created a small lake at its centre, cobblestones dimpling through the rushing water. He swept her up and strode through it towards a sliver of light from a door slightly ajar and felt a shudder, of resistance or of laughter, course through her. Inside he nudged the door closed behind them and the rumble and rush of the storm muted.

'Which way?' he asked, but just then a maid holding a coal scuttle entered from the other end of the corridor and stopped, gaping at them. Christina squirmed out of his grasp, but he kept hold of her waist as he raised a finger to his lips, addressing the maid.

'Shh… We're trying to elope. Once the rain stops.'

This time the silent shaking of the body next to his was definitely of laughter and it warmed him from within. Whatever happened, this was right.

'Elope? In Southampton, sir?' the maid asked, her eyes wide with incredulity and excitement.

'Everyone has to start somewhere, don't you agree?'

She grinned, showing two missing teeth. He fished a coin from his pocket and she took it and continued on her way, humming a ballad about lovers coming to a sour end.

'You need anything, you ask for Sue,' she called over her shoulder and disappeared.

'I don't think so,' Alex murmured and grasped Christina's hand, turning her to him. 'How did you know about the side door? Have you a room here? I thought the King's ship sailed. Are they still here because of the storm?'

He was babbling and she was staring up at him as if he had dropped from the moon, or as if she had just woken from sleep. Except her eyes were red, or perhaps that was just the cold. He wanted to pull her to him, wrap himself around her. Never let go.

She shook herself suddenly like a dog.

'Upstairs. On the right.'

Questions would wait. Nothing mattered at the moment. The harbour master must have been wrong about the King's sailing, thank God. He had no idea what Christina had been doing out in the docks alone, but not even that mattered right now. All that mattered was that she was here, her hand in his. *His.* He would explain to the King and the Princess, and to Christina as well, that she was staying. If she insisted on going, then they would have to make room for another passenger. It was a simple as that. He wouldn't mind a long cruise with Chrissie in close quarters. They might have to make do without him at the Congress in Verona, but the world would survive without him.

'Here. This room.'

He followed her into a large parlour with a generous fireplace. The table was set for one, with a napkin draped over a loaf of bread and a jug. The curtains were fluttering a little in the wind and a line of moisture marked the floor where the rain had blown in. She hurried over and closed the latch on the window, touched the mullioned frame lightly and turned to face him.

The fire turned the rain to a sparkle of diamonds on her hair and face and cloak. He had never seen anything more beautiful in his life.

He smiled and her hand fisted on the fabric of her cloak at her throat.

'I saw you.' Her voice was hurried, almost apologetic. 'I was looking out the window. I was certain I was seeing things, but then the other man left and you were still there and I had to be certain. It didn't make any sense, but…' She spread her hands wide, a gesture of helplessness that reached through him. He still had so much to learn about her, but most important was to stop and listen instead of jumping behind his guns whenever the pain struck. He would have to make a note of that. Write it down and put it somewhere prominent. She deserved his patience and more courage than he had shown thus far.

'Chrissie.'

'You must be cold. Has something happened? With the treaty? Is that why you came to Southampton? Would you like some wine? I think there is some in that jug. They are very nice here.'

'Chrissie.' He said again. He didn't seem capable of saying much more. He grasped for something sensible. 'Where are King Darius and the Princess? Did you not sail because of the storm?'

'They did sail. A couple of hours before the storm broke. The Captain said the storm was heading north-east so they should be clear of it and I hope he is right. I'm so worried. What if something happens to them and I wasn't there? I'm horrible and selfish and they must be hating me…'

He grasped her hands and her agonised monologue stumbled to an end.

'Chrissie, I don't quite understand what happened, but I am certain of one thing—they don't hate you. They might be angry with you, but they are incapable of hating you. They love you. Look, your hands are frozen. Come here. Sit.'

'Your hands are frozen, too.' She sniffed, but did as she was told and after he untied her cloak she sat on the chair he drew up by the fire. He turned the key in the lock and poured her some wine. She took the cup, her eyes moving from his face with a peculiar look of weariness and pain to the locked door.

'I'll open it if you wish, but I prefer we are not interrupted for the moment. We have some matters to discuss, you and I.'

She wrapped her hands about her cup and sipped. And stared.

He pulled over another chair and sat and did some staring himself. He didn't want to talk yet. He wanted to pull her out of that chair and towards the very nice bed he could see through the half-open door behind her, but that would wait. Right now all that mattered was that she was here, with him. And that was precisely where she would stay. She was his.

He smiled.

Christina's nails pressed into the cold surface of the cup. There was nothing she could do against that smile. He had smiled more on Illiakos, she realised, and restrained the urge to reach out and touch the curve of his beautiful mouth. She wanted him always smiling and laughing as she knew he could. He was too serious. She could do something about that. She would. That conviction flowed through her. Whatever happened now she didn't regret staying. Certainly not now that by some miracle he was here in Southampton.

After the King and Ari sailed she had remained by the window, staring out into the darkening docks and willing the hours to pass until morning when the post chaise would take her back to Stanton Hall. When she noticed the two men stopping at the edge of the dock she had been certain she was hallucinating, or at least misled by the distance, the dark and the rain. But when they didn't fade into the fog she had grabbed her cloak and run for the stairs.

Thank goodness she had. Even with him standing right in front of her she found it hard to believe that he was here in Southampton. With her. In her room. In her locked room.

Smiling.

She smiled back.

'I don't know why you are here, Alex, but I am so happy you are.'

By some miracle most of the wine stayed in the cup as he took it from her and pulled her out of her chair and into his arms. His coat was damp and a button was pressing into her chin and his arms were crushing her and it was wonderful. She burrowed against him, listening to the racing thud of his heart.

'Alex. Will you take me with you?'

He stilled and she curled one hand hard into the fabric of his coat and let the words come.

'Do you know how often I regretted not being

brave enough to go with you when you asked me six years ago? It would have been wrong, I know that. I was too young and probably so were you. But that didn't change the fact that I was in love with you. And scared. I'm not very brave, Alex. I want to be, but I'm not; I'm terrified of stepping off my safe little stone in the river. The bravest thing I ever did was seduce you in the forest. No, that's not right. The bravest thing I did was tell you I wouldn't stay with you. Because I never wanted anything more in my life. I don't know if what I have done now is brave or the most cowardly act ever, but I don't care. All I know is that I can't bear the thought of not seeing you again and that is why I told Ari and King Darius I had to stay and see, if there was even a chance… When I'm not being utterly terrified I know you are as scared as I am about trusting anyone and I wish I knew how to make you feel safe with me. Please, *please* say something…'

'Look at me, Chrissie.'

She looked up and caught on the flames reflecting in his eyes.

'Do you know how much I love you?'

She shook her head.

'Well, we will have to work on that. I'm obviously not much of a gallant knight because

I'm rather grateful you saved me the bother of chasing you across the Mediterranean, no matter how grand a gesture that would have been. I prefer showing you what I feel in a rather more direct manner. But first tell me again, my brave love.'

'I'm not brave.'

'Yes, you are, but I meant the other part. Say it.'

'I love you, Alex.'

'Every day. I'll need you to tell me every day, do you understand?'

'You'll soon grow bored of that.' Her voice was hoarse and his lips curved into a smile as he brushed his thumbs over her cheeks, tracing the line of her jaw and settling just below her mouth, his eyes darkening as they following his fingers' progress.

'I doubt it.' He bent and kissed her once, gently, and then gathered her against him, stroking her back with long soft strokes. 'You're shaking. Don't worry so, Chrissie. This isn't a Greek tale and I am not a siren luring you to your doom the moment you step away from safety. You won't lose Ari or the King. They will always love you and you them, but there can be more. I want us to build a life together, better than we can apart. I know it's possible. You are so much stronger than you realise. I am offering you my love and I want yours.'

'You have it, you always have. I'm not shaking because I'm scared. I'm just so happy you're here. Even if it rather ruins my grand gesture of appearing unannounced at the Hall. I was hoping to take you by surprise.'

'I think sneaking up on me at night in a thunderstorm when I was just imagining you out in the middle of the Channel qualifies as taking me by surprise. I'm glad you did. I was about to go and charter a vessel so I could hare off in pursuit of the King's ship.'

'Oh, no, and I would have been on my way to Stanton. That would have been horrid.'

'That is a colossal understatement, Chrissie. I would have found you in the end, but by then my list would have been as long as a Homeric saga,' he murmured against her hair, the warm whisper of his breath sending a tingling shower over her scalp and down her back. She shuddered and tightened her hold and his grip loosened, his hands sliding lower.

'Your list? What list?' she asked but her mind was following his hands' descent. When they reached the rise of her bottom her body arched against him involuntarily. He shifted, spreading his legs a little and arranging her more securely against him, and a sharp stab of need shot through her at the unmistakable pressure of his arousal against her. She tried to move against him, but his hands held her still, his voice soothing her with the same deep murmur as his lips moved on her hair, her temples, downwards…

'Thirty miles out of Stanton Thunder threw a shoe. In the pouring rain. The sensible thing would have been to find a way back to Stanton and bring my curricle, but I didn't. I bought a horse and cart from a farmer, left Thunder with him, and continued south. I kept hoping the storm would delay your departure because my not-so-noble steed was more donkey than horse. The whole damnably slow way down I made a list.'

He had reached her neck and she arced to give him better access, shivering as his lips scudded down and found a spot so unbearably sensitive her body lit from within, like a paper lantern. He paused, tasting that spot, his leg moving between hers and raising her so that she could feel the burning heat at her core.

'Are you listening, Chrissie?' he prompted.

To what? A list...

'A list of what?'

'Of all the places where I will show you how

much I love you. My bedroom. No, our bedroom. Every night. The library…'

'The library?' she mumbled, trying not to sway against him as the rough silk of his voice worked deeper and deeper into her.

'The library,' he answered. 'The window seat. Then you can arrange those damn pillows and we can do it again. The stateroom. On the desk where you were scribbling so diligently. I'll cross your Ts for you again and other things.'

'Alex…' She didn't know what to do against the onslaught of the images and the drugging heat of his mouth and hands so she anchored her hands in the damp fabric of his coat as his hands slid deep into her hair, twisting and gathering it between his fingers, drawing back her head. His mouth hovered over hers as she drew breath. She felt again the cool satin slide of water just under her skin, as if he was entering her, and her legs shuddered against the pressure of his in a surge of need. His lips brushed hers, slowly, testing every line of hers, every breath of his drawing some fear from her, coaxing and softening.

'The forest,' he continued, his mouth nipping at hers, teasing and suckling her lips into throbbing awareness that echoed in every inch of her body. 'As often as we can before winter sets in. But especially when the bluebells come. I'm going to make that particular fantasy a reality—you, naked, on a bed of bluebells. And in every place you will have to tell me you love me. That you need me. I give you fair warning I'm going to be a nuisance about that.'

'The herb garden,' she gasped. 'Your workshop.'

He laughed against her lips.

'That's *too* brave, love. I draw the line at risking splinters in your lush behind. Not the portrait gallery, either. Too many disapproving eyes. The conservatory, yes. We have a score to settle there. Then, back to the bedroom. Then…'

'Alex, you needn't marry me, I am perfectly wil—'

The kiss that silenced her was hard, deep, possessing her in a way none of his kisses had before. She lost all track of her fears and rationalisations. She was just Christina with the man she wanted, loved, needed. When he finally raised his head she didn't need the burn of emotion in his eyes to tell her he loved her. For the first time she just knew.

Alex loved her.

'I think you do need to marry me after all.' She touched his cheek, once, lightly and laid her own against his chest. She could hear his heart, feel it.

She was home.

Epilogue

Illiakos—1823

'Scared?'

'Terrified. You're mad! The only way we make it down is in pieces on those rocks.'

'Trust me.'

Christina's eyes were a shade darker than the sea stretched out beneath them, narrowed in the smile that was the delight of his life. Of course he trusted her. With more than his sorry hide. He put his hand in hers and followed. The basket lurched and so did his stomach, but she tucked her hand into his arm and leaned her head on his shoulder for a moment before turning to the others standing on the wooden platform that led to the suspended basket.

'If you prefer you can take the cliff path. Yannis will show you, but this is faster if you want to wait for the basket to come back up.'

'There's a path?' Alex asked hopefully, taking in the old rope and the creaking of the pulleys. But it was too late. Chrissie gave the command to Yannis, wrapped her arms around Alex's neck, rising to press her lips to his and took utter possession of his mouth as the world fell out from under them. Vaguely he heard his friends' laughter snatched away by the wind above them and the roar of the surf below. Everything else was the sensation of falling, of the demanding passion of her embrace, her body the only firm point in a collapsing universe. It was only seconds but it felt immense, a whole existence. Then weight returned and the creaking of the rope and she pulled away a little, her eyes warm with pleasure. They were slowing, the shore coming towards them in a dazzle of brown, honey and blue. By the time they reached the platform constructed on a shelf of rocks above the line of the sand his breathing was settling, if not his pulse.

'Well?' she murmured.

'You are right, that was amazing. You are amazing.'

She laughed and unhitched the gate on the side of the basket.

'I didn't want to warn you because the first time is always the most nerve-racking. The King had this constructed for Queen Sabina so she could bathe in the sea for her health.'

Alex took her hand to help her out and looked up as the basket was hauled back up towards the top to the cliff. Even from here it looked dizzyingly high. He wanted to do it again.

'That ride has a very uplifting effect. It's a pity we can't operate it ourselves. I rather like the idea of trying that again and then spending a few hours down here alone.'

He slid his hands over her hips and bottom, pulling her against him, to show her precisely how uplifting. She tucked her hands under his shirt, scraping her nails down his back for a moment before pulling away with an embarrassed laugh.

'Your friends can see everything from up there.'

He sighed and turned to watch as Raven and Lily took the plunge. It was wonderful to have Raven and Hunter and their wives join them in Venice after the Verona Congress ended and come with them to visit the King and Princess Ari. He wasn't in the least surprised Chrissie, Nell and Lily had become such fast friends despite Chrissie's initial fears. But just at the moment he wished his friends elsewhere. He wanted Chrissie to himself. They were still owed a proper honeymoon since they had hardly any time to themselves before having to travel to Verona ahead of the Congress. Perhaps they should adopt Lily and Raven's idea of retreating to an island for a month. Just them, some books, the sea…

'Plotting something?' Chrissie asked, not raising her head from where it rested on his shoulder.

'Why do you think I am plotting something?'

'I can feel it.'

'Am I so sadly transparent?'

'Not sadly. Don't complain, you know you love it when I read your mind.'

'Of course I do. It saves so much time.'

She laughed, her breath warm through the linen of his shirt, her fingers sneaking under the material again.

'So, what *are* you plotting?'

'Your downfall, my love. Again.'

She smiled, rising on tiptoe to kiss him before hurrying to help Raven and Lily exit the basket as it reached the rocks. Lily jumped out with all her customary energy, her tawny eyes glistening with excitement, her hand twined with Raven's.

'May we do that again?'

'*You* can, you madcap.' Raven laughed as they watched the basket begin another journey up to where Hunter and Nell waited. 'I'll watch from *terra firma*. Has that thing ever broken?'

'Not yet. It is modelled after a contraption the King saw when he was visiting the monasteries of Meteora in Greece. What do you think, Nell?' she asked as Nell and Hunter stepped out of the basket.

'Now I know what it must feel like to fly. I was certain we would crash. It was marvellous! May we try again?'

Hunter groaned.

'Next we'll be spending the rest of our stay here plunging to our doom, serially. I was hoping for some restful hours of sea bathing. Or perhaps not that restful.' The descent and the wind had undone Nell's fine flaxen hair and she twisted it into a knot, but Hunter pulled away her hands, anchoring them in his. 'No, leave your hair down, seeing you windblown gives me ideas. How private is this beach, Christina?'

Alex tucked Chrissie back against his side.

'As the newest to the state of matrimony I claim precedence over the use of the beach. You two go find your own corners. Is the water still cold this time of year, Chrissie?'

'It is still chilly. By the end of the summer it as warm as a bath, though.'

'Chilly is good. Trust me, I'll warm you.'

Her eyes widened.

'Alex, you're not serious, are you?'

'You can swim, can't you?'

He hauled her up, holding her firm against him as she squirmed, caught by the feel of her in his arms, bringing with it the ache which was so familiar it was becoming almost normal.

'Alex! At least take off your boots and coat. You might be cold later,' she said and he burst out laughing and hugged her to him as he strode towards the water.

'I love it when you worry about me.'

'I know you do. Now, if you'll just be sensible and… Alex!'

* * * * *

COMING SOON!

We really hope you enjoyed reading this book. If you're looking for more romance, be sure to head to the shops when new books are available on

Thursday 28th June

To see which titles are coming soon, please visit **millsandboon.co.uk**

MILLS & BOON

MILLS & BOON

Coming next month

ONE WEEK TO WED
Laurie Benson

Charlotte's gaze dropped to Andrew's lips just as a giant boom reverberated through the hills. They both turned towards the house to see more colourful lights shoot into the sky and crackle apart.

'I'm thinking about kissing you.' He said it in such a matter-of-fact way, as if the idea would not set her body aflame—as if the idea of kissing this practical stranger would be a common occurrence.

Charlotte had only kissed one man in her life. She never thought she would want to kiss another—until now. Now she wanted to know what his lips felt like against hers. She wanted him to wrap her in his arms where she would feel desirable and cherished. And she wanted to know if his kiss could be enough to end the desire running through her body.

He placed his gloved finger under her chin and gently guided her face so she was looking at him. The scent of leather filled her nose. There was no amusement in his expression. No cavalier bravado. Just an intensity that made her believe if he didn't kiss her right then, they both would burn up like a piece of char cloth.

It was becoming hard to breath and if he did in fact kiss her there was a good chance she would lose consciousness from lack of air. But if he didn't kiss her…

She licked her lips to appease the need of feeling his lips on hers.

He swallowed hard. Almost hesitantly, he untied her bonnet and put it aside. Gently, he wrapped his fingers around the back of her neck, pulling her closer, and he lowered his head. She closed her eyes and his lips faintly brushed hers. They were soft, yet firm, and she wanted more.

Continue reading
ONE WEEK TO WED
Laurie Benson

Available next month
www.millsandboon.co.uk

Copyright © 2018 Laurie Benson

LET'S TALK *Romance*

For exclusive extracts, competitions and special offers, find us online:

facebook.com/millsandboon

@millsandboonuk

@millsandboon

Or get in touch on 0844 844 1351*

For all the latest titles coming soon, visit millsandboon.co.uk/nextmonth

*Calls cost 7p per minute plus your phone company's price per minute access charge

Want even more ROMANCE?

Join our bookclub today!

'Mills & Boon books, the perfect way to escape for an hour or so.'

Miss W. Dyer

'Excellent service, promptly delivered and very good subscription choices.'

Miss A. Pearson

'You get fantastic special offers and the chance to get books before they hit the shops'

Mrs V. Hall

Visit millsandbook.co.uk/Bookclub

and save on brand new books.

MILLS & BOON